# The Extraordinary Ordinary

By Natalie Rodriguez

Based on the Award-Winning Feature Film

Published by Natalie Rodriguez
Los Angeles, CA



Cover Design by Shari Ryan
Edited by Katherine Walsh
Additional Edits by Ben Parris
Layout Design by Wendy C. Garfinkle
Special Thanks to Sarah Fader

# Table of Contents

# Erica

*Wake up/*
*Grab a brush and put a little (makeup)/*
*Grab a brush and put a little/*
*Hide the scars to fade away the (shakeup)/*

Serj Tankian screams through my ears. Not literally. It's my new headphones from the Love is Louder campaign. The sort of headphones that catch my attention because they include all the elements of a recorded song, including the bass line—the *ba da ba da*— of the guitar, drum pickups and slowdowns.

I've never seen System of a Down in concert. I became obsessed with them as soon as the song "B.Y.O.B." came out in middle school. I've always wanted to go to one of their shows. But mom…she's always been overprotective since…well, since the…

A cold sensation takes over my hands. I wipe their clammy surfaces onto my Levi's, but that does not help. I sit up straighter, but my shoulders only heighten and touch the bottom of my ears. My foot begins to *tap tap tap* onto the tile floor, as my left knee bounces up and down, down, and up.

Shit, now there goes my right knee in unison.

*Just breathe, Erica, I told myself.*

It is like an endless cycle of girl gossip and their high school bullshit drama…

High school…

Shit, there it goes again. My chest rocks my shoulders—that tight compression like someone is squeezing my air passages together—

*Breathe, Erica. Just breathe…*

But my eyes refuse to open. It would probably help though, to open them, to get some daylight. Because right now the smell of old man spice cologne mixed with that shitty cleaning supplement, you know the sort where you walk into the public bathroom right after the janitor cleans it, and your nose makes your stomach churn.

Tightening and tightening. Oh, fuck…up it comes—

*Swimming through the void/*
*We hear the word/*
*We lose ourselves/*
*But we find it all?*

Serj's voice slowly fades out, as my heart skips a beat and suddenly picks up and grows louder and louder—

*Ouch.*

A small gasp slips through my parted lips. Fuck, that hurts…like A LOT. Too much.

And then my eyes shoot wide open, all bold and "blue" and wild. My eyes are not blue, but I remind myself as soon as I glance over at the nearby window, where the sun seeps in like a mother's fingers running through her baby's hair that my eyes might as well be like the sky, as in nature.

For the glowing of the full sun is serene and even peaceful. The rays leave kisses all over my pale skin, reminding me that, perhaps, it will be okay.

I've done this before.

A voice.

"Erica Mantes?"

I jerk to the opposite side as I slowly remove my headphones. The nurse lingers in the doorway with a clipboard—my charts and records. She is no more than thirty feet from where I sit. Alone, in the middle of two empty chairs. "Erica, the doctor is ready," she says to me.

I gradually stand until my backpack grabs onto my knees, and I nearly eat shit. Forgot it was there between my legs. Then I notice it around the grip on my backpack: sweat stains from my fingers.

*Tick. Tick. Tick.*

I swear I'm going to punch that clock in the face, especially sitting here on my bare ass. I go to wipe my hands on my knees, forgetting. This dress-napkin-looking thing doesn't come with anything but the front side. Ugh, really!

Fuck, it is cold.

I shiver and cross my arms and then cross them the other way. Yeah, none of this is helping. Especially when the doctor finally reenters with the clipboard, a.k.a. my records and charts.

"Hi, Erica."

"Hi," I say and immediately my fingers find their way to my mouth. Chewing. Chewing. It does not taste good.

"All right, lie back, honey."

I obey and lie back all the way on the cold and god-awful stiff napkin on the table. Well, it's not a napkin, but I can already feel my back sweat bleeding through. Fuck…

I take a deep breath, as Dr. Mansell has advised me. But… my heart picks up speed. I don't know why. I've done this before—the exam.

My eyes refuse to open as I hear clinks and clanks and then the cart and chair rolling closer. Both objects stop a few inches from me. Here it goes…

I hear my doctor sit down. I can tell because she mutters something to herself and her breath hisses onto my knees as she says politely, "Please scoot down, honey."

Honey…Jesus, if she calls me that one more time. But I listen and wiggle down until my ass cheeks are practically falling off the edge. My legs straighten further into the stirrups. I hear her reach for the first object—

My heartbeat shoots throughout my entire body like electroshock—more like an aftershock—starting with my head, where that tight compression goes all the way around like a hot sweatband, ending at my feet. Fuck…I breathe and breathe.

"You might feel some discomfort," she advises me calmly, like the last water drops from the kitchen sink, "but no pain. I promise."

Yeah, let's hope.

*Breathe, Erica…*

And I do. But suddenly…it hurts as the device slides into me—

"Ah!"

"I'm sorry!"

"That's *really* uncomfortable."

Oh, God, I feel bad because she looks like shit. I refuse to lean onto my elbows and to see more.

"I'm just going to adjust it if that's okay."

It was a question because silence stands between us, as well as the humming of the AC.

"Yeah. That's fine," I finally manage to spit out.

My face crunches together as I can feel the cold metal gently pull out of me.

"Better?"

"...Kind of," I lie, without looking at her face.

*Breathe...*

And then it hits me! Something that Dr. Mansell, had once told me that helps her other clients—

"Can I have my iPod?"

She nods. I go to sit up until she tells me she can get it. I point to my backpack on the chair, but she is already passing it over to me. Shoot, she could've just lugged the thing at me since it weighs no more than a bag full of feathers.

I know where they are, but my fingers shake as I dig and dig and seem to miss them. Found them! As I go to pull them out from the front pocket, I feel her hands cover over mine...because my breathing is harsh...like at the last exam...seven years ago—

"It's okay, honey," she consoles me. "We can always reschedule if we need to."

That would be easier, but…I'm already here. I told Mansell that there was no turning back, and I meant it. Now is the time. "No," I finally say. "I'll be okay."

Without hesitation, I lie back down and put on my headphones. They almost slip off as soon as the back hits the small, rigid pillow. But somehow it still works.

*Sometimes I feel so happy/*
*Sometimes I feel so sad/*

Ah, Lou Reed. One of my personal favorites; it definitely fits today's mood. My eyes immediately find the fluorescent light hanging above me, concreted into the ceiling. Just stuck there for life, unless of course, they decide to tear down the hospital and put in something else. It is perfect lighting, and I can sense its halo forming around my face and my neck; no other part of my body, just those two parts. Sort of like a calling from above…but for what, exactly?

"Just relax, honey."

And I do, taking in a deep breath as my belly poofs out, exhaling while my belly goes back to its normal size. I'm pretty skinny, I guess…I don't know. I try to avoid mirrors at all costs sometimes, something that Mansell is helping me work through ever since…well, since the…

I bite my tongue as my eyes grow warm, stifling back tears.

"Everything looks fine. You're doing great, sweetie…"

Her voice drains away, as Lou's picks up—not louder, but it is as if his smooth, charming voice is serenading my ear. Just one ear, not the left. I don't know if that makes sense, but it does to me. Only to me, like always.

I think of a stream zooming down the kitchen sink as the lady doctor's voice is finally on mute.

*Sometimes I feel so happy/*
*But mostly you just make me mad/*
*Baby, you just make me mad/*

As I stare above into the fluorescent light that casts down upon me, I feel the same effect rolling down my cheek...

Tears.

# Bianca

*Alabama, Arkansas/*
*I do love my ma and pa/*
*Not that way that I do love you/*

I just fuckin' love Edward Sharpe and the Magnetic Zeros! Seriously, whoever hates them can kiss my fat ass!

Okay, so my ass isn't big, nowhere close to it. I'm far from being one of those rappers' B.B.W. chick. Or Amber Rose. Either one, really. But low key, I'm jealous of those hip-hop video chicks who have the nice bookshelf asses—not circus freak kind of thing **cough cough** the Kardashians.

Or, as I like to refer to them, the TRASHians.

Alex likes that one. He won't necessarily laugh at it, but he just shakes his head at me, and I spy with my little eyes that crooked smirk that spreads across the left side of his face. I know him too well. He knows me too well—

Oh, my GAWD! Here comes the best part!

*Ah, home, let me go home/*
*Home is wherever I'm with you/*
*Ah, home, let me go home/*
*Home is wherever I'm with you/*

*KNOCK. KNOCK.*

"Alexander!" I scream at the top of my lungs, beating out Mr. Sharpe's vocals.

"If I wasn't mistaken,"—and in pops Alex—"I'd say you were pulling a Tom Cruise moment."

And he's right. I'm close to it with one of my legs stretched out to the side, like I'm holding a heavy metal band's guitar, mid *Risky Business* pose. Tom Cruise…his younger days…fine ass… ugh the *Outsiders*—

Only, I have clothes on.

*"Because I jizzed in my pants,"* I quote the Lonely Island and wiggle out my non-fat-ass butt. That makes Alex grimace, and he peers away.

"Gross, man."

I catch the left side of his face crunch into a 'u' shape because of that crooked smile. Girls often go crazy whenever they see him do that. Not that any of them have the lady balls to tell him that. Or the damn cojones (like I speak Española or "Mexican" as I'd referred to it once as a kid to Alex). I'm the whitest Hispanic you'll ever meet! I usually tell the ladies to pimp Alex out, which he hates. But he just needs to shut the fuck up sometimes. Like last night at Legend Café, I'd noticed this cute, petite blonde (with big titties) stealing glances at my Alexander. So, I'd stopped on our way out and said, "He has a nice ass, right?"

Alex had only grabbed my arm, "Bianca," and pulled me away like a parent who was about to put a can of whoop-ass on their brat child. I laughed. He didn't. Man…the so-called cat had the blonde's tongue.

I circle my room, using the vacuum cord as my dance partner because Alex just shakes his head and leans against the door frame when I try grabbing him to boogie.

"Hey, Alex!"

"Yes…?"

"How do you get a tissue to dance?"

He nearly slaps his hand against his forehead because he's already heard this one.

"You put a little boogie in it!"

*La, la, la, la, take me home/*
*Daddy, I'm coming home/*

Even with my headphones tightly secure on my ears, I can still hear him sigh from what I guess is his favorite spot in my bedroom—the doorway. "Bianca, we're going to be late."

He looks calmer than his tone.

"Got it! I'll be down in a few!" I think I'm screaming louder than expected since he glimpses over his shoulder and waves down the hallway. Then he takes a step forward and shuts the door, but it's still ajar. Then, he presses his finger against his lips.

*Shhizznets…*

Forgot Mr. Perez had a long night shift.

"Man," I mutter and sadly, and unfortunately, scroll the volume to the left…all the way…on my iPod. "It was getting to the best part of the song."

# Alex

Bianca and I are in the bedroom, listening to music. We are trying to be quiet. But it's the moment of the song that she and I would've shouted like a pack of wolves at karaoke. But no…my dad…

*"Alexander,"* she whispers her verse anyhow. Her eyes are dilated…oh no…because she is begging me to sing. Otherwise, it will take another hour to get her out of the bedroom and then out of the house.

I've been dressed for the past two hours.

*"Jade, do you remember that day you fell outta my window?"*

She's a weirdo. And I shake my head to tell her that. It only brightens up her smile, an eagle spreading its wings across the crystal blue sky.

*"I sure do. You came jumping out after me."* And now, she shimmies her way over, still using the vacuum cord. This time as a microphone, far better than an air guitar.

*"Well, you fell on the concrete, nearly broke your ass, and you were bleeding all over the place, and I rushed you out to the hospital, you remember that?"* I have to clear my throat since this random cough comes up. For some reason, it makes my shoulder tighten up, edging closer and closer to my earlobes—

Bianca grabs my wrists and swings them back and forth like a child playing in that song game, Here we go, Zudio.

*"Yes, I do,"* she says in her best *Harry Potter* accent; because to her, everyone who is British is secretly—in her words, 'low key'—mocking *Harry Potter*. Sometimes, I wonder if Bianca is fuckin' around or not on that one. Who knows. She starts tilting—

Mercy!

Jesus, I catch her in time for the song dip, which messes up my verse. The near death fall pushes off her headphones. "Momma, I'm comin' home!" she heavy metal sings it, tossing her arms up, like Ozzy.

And before I know it, the song is soon over, followed by a knock on the wall adjacent to her bedroom door.

"Hey!" my dad orders. "Keep it down!"

"Sorry, Mr. Perez!" And she looks back at me. For some reason we both laugh as she bounces up onto her colored-toe socks. "Alright, let's go."

She grabs her Carlos Santana bag that has those small fringe things or whatever on them. I jokingly call them lint. Bianca calls them "sex whips"...

Yeah, she goes there often with her remarks. It doesn't bother me; it never has. But, sometimes, it DOES bug those around her. Especially girls. Yeah...girls the most.

I watch her as she shuffles around and tries to find her missing black Doc Martens. *"OH...where is my shoe,"* she sings softly. *"OH...where is my shoe..."*

No luck. Shit...

"Where the fuck is it," she repeats a few times before finding it under her pillow. What the heck—

"Too much late-night coffee again," I say and indicate to the five empty coffee cups on her nightstand.

"Always. You know, I'm always on them deadlines." And she bobs her head towards the door, slipping on her missing boot, and heads on out. "Come on, Alexander!"

"Bianca..."

And I have to keep "shushing" her on her way out, down the hallway, down the stairs, down the family/living room, and down the last hallway before we make it out the front door.

"TAXI!" she screams as soon as we both step out into the blazing August summer sun.

# Erica

My knees bounce up and down without my approval—

I shift around in the flimsy gray chair, hoping for some comfort. But my foot falls asleep. Fuck!

My headphones fall off as I reach down to grab my foot. Eric Clapton's voice is cut short—

*Cocaine —*

"Erica."

Mid-shake with my dead foot, I peek over at the doorway, where Dr. Mansell awaits, giving me a hopeful smile.

I force one back and, slowly, rise.

---

Dr. Mansell sits patiently across from her client (a.k.a., I am the client).

Now in my daily attire of a T-shirt, jeans, and a small amount of makeup…I dab at the four corners of my face to wipe off the makeup. The skinny jeans are tighter than expected, making me shift to my left…and then right when I fail to get comfort.

*Breathe, Erica…*

"…First time Pap Smear is uncomfortable for *many* women," Dr. Mansell carries on with her lecture. Shit…I must have tuned her out for the first half. *Fuck.*

"Some associate it with having no control over their body."

*Yeah, I know.*

"Well,"—I set my palms down onto the black leather of the couch and straighten out my posture—"Coming here has helped. A lot."

My eyes drift away, not on purpose or anything…It has just become a habit whenever we head down the route. The subject. That…night…

My fingers find their way to my mouth. Before I start gnawing, Mansell's sigh, the one she gives before changing subjects, yanks my eyes back up.

"So, tomorrow's the big day. You all packed?"

I nod and find myself staring back down at the floor. The carpet is this odd polka dot color, like someone threw up and the janitors refused to clean it.

*That. Night.*

"Erica," I hear Mansell's soft tone warp its way into my black abyss as soon as I close my eyes and breathe…and breathe… "Remember what I said, it's common for a lot of students to have anxiety. Especially transfers. You have the tools."

"Yeah. I know."

The carpet is soft because my feet are dragging themselves back and forth as if it were warm sand on a sunny summer day…

And suddenly, I open my eyes and immediately meet Mansell's concerned gaze. This time, she does not smile or attempt one of those empathetic looks. She only watches me until her eyes level a few inches down…

Then, I look down. I forgot. I am biting my nails until my teeth meet blood.

---

*Here she comes, you better watch your step/*
*She's going to break your heart in two, it's true/*

The Velvet Underground & Nico just knows how to set this quiet end of summer's mood. I crank up the volume and sit upon my bed, which is the only item that has not been, well, torn down or packed up.

My walls are the only areas in my bedroom that catch my attention. It feels like the room is spinning as my eyes scan all the artwork that is nailed or cheaply taped on the walls. Not my artwork, but those from whom I have always admired from the time I was a young girl.

Andy Warhol
Keith Haring
Vincent Van Gogh
Gregory Crewdson
Kara Walker

I had to pack away my old college papers from my sophomore year (well, technically from these past two semesters) into one of many boxes that sit around on my floor. Shit, I need to finish labeling a few of them. After dinner for sure…

My stomach rumbles as I get a whiff of Mom's barbeque roast and macaroni side dish.

*'Cause everybody knows/*
*(She's a femme fatale)/*
*The things she does to please/*
*(She's a femme fatale)/*

I had aced my final term paper for my Art History course, discussing the background of Andy Warhol. It was how I had then discovered my favorite band, The Velvet Underground. There was just something so pure and nostalgic about the first time I listened to them. Well, those feelings are still there whenever I listen to the band—*period*:

*The things she does to please/*
*(She's a femme fatale)/*
*She's just a little tease/*
*(She's a femme fatale)/*
*See the way she walks/*
*Hear the way she talks/*

A packed suitcase and my carry-on bag sit by the door, ready for tomorrow's destination. New York City...Which reminds me—I turn around and grab the two folders on my nightstand, adjacent to my alarm clock. Shoot, I should have packed that with miscellaneous items. Tomorrow for sure. For now, the item goes with the two folders in my hands: NYU, Tisch School of Arts, undergraduate - Photography & Imaging and Campus Life.

And then I see it peeking out from the interior of the Photography & Imaging folder. I open it and out spills something that I have kept…after that night even…

*Winners receive up to $4,000 and publication!*

At the bottom of the postcard advertisement:

*BOTTOM - Deadline: January 13th!*

Four years...

Has it really been that long? Oh, how time flies. It sure does fly by. Too much. Too fast—

*Breathe, Erica. Just breathe.*

*I don't know just where I'm going/*
*But I'm gonna try for the kingdom, if I can/*

Oh, Lou…You're triggered too, huh?

*'Cause it makes me feel like I'm a man/*
*When I put a spike into my vein/*

My palms shake as I crumble up the postcard. Shit—

Too late.

The advertisement is ruined by the sweat that clams up my palms. The letters on the postcard are starting to smudge off like running mascara.

"Erica! Dinner!"

My mother…

I shut my eyes and take a deep breath—belly out, breathe in/belly out, breathe out. I repeat and repeat, but my eyes start to itch and burn…I start crying.

"Erica?" Then I hear footsteps ascend the stairs, her tone filled with worry.

I only look at the spot that I should continue to ignore. But it is too late as my eyes settle upon it: the taped-up shoebox that sits underneath the wooden desk that had once belonged to my dad, all by itself…There…The only box…

"Erica?!"

And I yank off my headphones, cutting Lou short again, and toss them down onto the bed—

*You can't help me now, you guys/*
*And all you sweet girls with all your sweet talk/*

I don't have to even peer at the doorway to know that my mother is already there, lingering and watching me as I dab at my wet eyes with my sleeve and ascend to my feet. Forgot I was barefoot because the coldness of the wooden floor shoots chills up my spine. Plus, my nostrils twitch from the Chanel perfume that my mother consistently reapplies throughout the day, even if we are just at home like any other ordinary day. Like today.

I can still hear Lou singing as I head towards the door:

*You can all go take a walk/*
*And I guess I just don't know/*
*And I guess that I just don't know/*

Inches from the door, I come to a stop and look up at my mother. She, too, has tears in her eyes. Only, they have not fallen…yet. "I'll see you downstairs," is all she says before turning on her heels and walking away. Forever out of my sight unless I decide to follow her lead.

And I do.

# Bianca

"Taxi!"

Our driver breaks to a screeching halt, which is normal in the city of New York. I once heard that Californians get all high maintenance and shit and prissy from the traffic and overpopulation. But again…

They do have the Kardashians a.k.a., the KarTRASHIANS in my book.

"Keep the change," Alex says before my hand even reaches for my bag. He sees that I am making my 'face,' forcing him to shake his head. "Don't."

"Huh? What? I didn't say anything." And I hop out of our taxi, my feet hitting the sidewalk of 42nd Street.

Ah!

Nothing like the smell of body odor and gutter water, burnt like coffee…

But I can't hold still. My feet push themselves up onto their tippy-toes as I watch the flashing neon sign call our name. Chromatics come to my mind—

*"Everybody's got a secret to hide/Everyone is slipping backwards!"*

# Alex

And now Bianca is hauling my ass across the sidewalk, all the way down 42nd Street. We must look like a couple of kids running towards the Empire State Building, which is another popular tourist attraction. Most of the tourists go INSANE at the landmark whenever B′ and I decide to head over there to chill out.

God, it smells here.

I don't care how long I've lived here in the city—we've relocated to the Lower East Side—but still the steam coming out of the vents gets to me and isn't any better than the west side.

I scrunched my nostrils, yearning for the burning sensation to escape. I feel claws wrapping around my windbreaker sleeve and there go Bianca's fingernails, as she grips on tighter to me.

I can already smell the scene before Bianca skirts to a stop. Right in front of a building that attracted tourists from all over the world. It stands out with its sharp, neon pink and purple brick design; not to mention the lime green neon sign with an arrow pointing to the door, "Karaoke HERE!"

Surprisingly, the line is longer than usual, regardless of how early it is.

"RICKY!" And now Bianca tows us to the door, where the bouncer steps aside, letting us slide right into the corridor of the place. The music is bumping throughout the building—it's music for my ears to bleed to and I LOVE it.

"Hola, chica!" Ricardo, a.k.a. Ricky, greets Bianca back with a kiss on the cheek. Before I can even sneak down the dark, red lit hallway Ricky grabs my arm and twirls me around, directly into his arm like he is an eagle.

"Hola, chico!"

And there goes his red-painted, and extremely wet lips, compressing down onto my cheek. I can sense Bianca smiling, stifling back her laugh. I don't need to be told. My cheek is already beaming from the big lipstick marking on me.

"Let me guess…"

Ricky taps his acrylic finger against his cheek, which has glitter glinting back at Bianca and I. "…Chromatics on this lovely afternoon."

"You know it." Bianca bumps her hip back with Ricky, sending a spiral of fear throughout my system because Bianca is, let's just say, A LOT smaller than Ricky's football player stature. Not that he was a football player. Bianca and I were assured by Ricardo-the-gay-bartender, that he was too busy watching the football players on the bench.

He once said with his hand on his hip, "Honey, I'd rather be eating, not feeding."

Whatever the hell that meant.

"ALEX!"
"Come on, slowpoke!" And as she slips backward, behind the curtains on center stage, "*Alexander*!" Even though I am well aware that we are not singing Edward Sharpe & the Magnetic Zeros…at least, not yet…I don't think—
Jesus! When the hell did she get over there?

"Well, giddy up, chico," Ricky says before I feel a pinch, followed by a soft pat on my ass before he spins over to the bar to pick up an empty tray.

"Oh, my God," a nearby pixie blonde man fake-whispers to his red-haired friend. "It must be Mexican music, happy hour!"

Wow…

I climb on stage, joining Bianca in her purple dress and fake fur coat. She looks pretty cool; I guess. Like a young Janis Joplin, but prettier.

Much prettier.

I stand there in my awkward red collar shirt and black slacks a.k.a. my work uniform, as Bianca hands me the second microphone. "Ready?"

"Always," And I smile back before my attention goes to the small crowd. I squint from the overly bright spotlight as Ricky adjusts it.

# Erica

I can only hear the clinking and clanking of our forks and knives hitting our plates. Bone China plates—to be precise. The good stuff.

"…and can you just believe it," my mother's high pitch tone drags me back into reality. It becomes a habit of hers when her voice drains in and out like television static every so often.

She'd expected joint custody after what she had DONE. Ha!"

*Really? Ha? Please, stop talking.*

"Typical," my mother snorts and cuts deep down into her steak. "Just sad how mothers act like that with their own children."

*Oh…the irony.*

"Erica?"

*Fuck.*

I don't even have to turn my head to the side to know that she has been watching me. Besides, the clanking of her steak knife and fork is a giveaway that it's her. God…I can feel her eyes burning a ring of fire on me, conquering the barbeque sauce that was so spicy it was bristling in my nostrils.

"I'm eating," is all I say, and exchange a glance with my mother. Then, I finally take my first bite of steak before I decide to twirl it round and round in the glob of tartar sauce on the corner of my plate.

Dad just sits there, his eyes leveled down at his half-eaten plate of food.

Typical.

Dad puts the last suitcase into the back of our Tahoe. "Well, that's everything." He gives me a smile; one of his many kind ones.

And then I hear the high heels approaching closer and closer, until: "And what on Earth is that?"

My mother stands nearby, overdressed in her cream-colored sweater and white skirt, and high heels. Okay, so her outfit isn't what you would call overdressed *per se,* but today is important. She made it a bigger deal as this particular day got closer.

She shakes her head in disapproval, as my fingers tighten around the shoebox that I have been holding for the past hour, ever since waking up this morning. Its texture keeps me warm.

Shoot, it keeps me stable…standing…even with the itch to drop everything and run upstairs and jump back underneath the covers.

"Pictures," I say without meeting her burning red eyes. Instead, my eyes find their way to my father's, who only takes in the cold air. His breath escapes into tiny white air clouds, matching the color of his hair before he peers away. Down at the ground…

*Typical.*

"Right…From the camera that broke."

That makes me look at her immediately. That pain creases her upper lip before she bites it down and straightens herself up. If it weren't for her sunglasses…I'd say the tears are already there. But knowing my mother, she does a terrific job at constricting any sign of emotion.

Backward. Timing…That night—

"Well," Dad interjects in the stillness that circles our circle, "Erica, we should really get going—"

"Are you sure about this?"

And standstill.

*Great.*

"Cathy."

"I just want to make sure because it's going to be difficult if you need something."

God, she looks worried, with zero attention towards my poor dad who turns, breaking our circle trio. He appears distant, probably soaking up his inner thoughts.

I feel bad for him. Mom never listens to him or—

"Erica?"

"Yes! I'm sure."

My tone was louder than expected, but I can't help it. This raging ring of fire of my own builds its way higher and higher. I can see how scared shitless it makes my mother. Her mouth is ajar, just enough for the air to suck right through her teeth.

I'll be honest…I feel my upper lip twitch, the temptation to smile.

But she beats me to it.

"Alright." As soon as her spine uncurls from its already straight as a pencil posture, she runs her hands over her thighs. "Well, I have some work to do—

"Cathy—"

"Have a safe flight."

"—I thought you were coming with us!"

But she heads back into the house, not even glancing over her shoulder."

---

Loud. If anyone were to ask me what I think about airports…the answer is loud. Too loud.

Dad hands over my suitcase. He takes a moment to process, allowing the silence to sit between us. But with the hustle-bustle of goers and arrivals, I get a whiff and taste of the countless body odors and overly scented perfumes—

I cough, making Dad think that was on purpose.

"I feel bad," just blurts out of him.

"Dad, don't. I sort of had a feeling that she wasn't going to come."

It still bothers him. She is like that heavy weight that droops his shoulders further and further, just like his eyes and mouth.

"Well, hopefully, this is the perfect timing."

The roar of an airplane taking off stalls time, while Dad retrieves to the trunk. It only takes a second before I see it—a gift bag.

"Happy going away gift," he says and passes it over.

*Dad...*

I can't take it, but his action of tilting the bag side to side doesn't help either. "Come on."

*Fine…*

I obey and receive the bag—it is heavy and squared. I open it right away—

Oh, my God…He didn't.

A Polaroid camera.

*The vintage kind and everything…*

"I know you wanted to save up for your own," Dad speaks up, forcing me to meet his gaze, "but you've worked hard these past two years."

*Vintage one and everything…*

"Did Mom pitch in?"

His silence is enough to make me certain that my disappointment is visible. When he glimpses away, so do I.

"I'll pay you back—"

"*I* wanted to buy you a *new* one. Save your money for the film and whatever else is needed. Just don't pay me back. *Please*."

Shit, there's the look again in his eyes; the kind that a lost puppy gives when they crave food. Or shelter. A home.

I nod, suddenly dabbing at my eyes. He reaches for me. I'm the one to hug first.

"You're an extraordinary person, Erica. Really, you have no idea."

*How though?*

I try to let those last words digest, my head resting against Dad's arm. My mind drifts. My gaze prolongs on the sun that parts its way through the cotton candy texture clouds…

Dad's arms tighten around me, and he kisses the top of my head.

My eyes start to burn from the tears.

# Erica

*Spent my days with a woman unkind*
*Smoked my stuff and drank all my wine.*

Ah, Robert Plant, too…

I've always had a big ass crush on these singers from back in the day. Not that the seventies and eighties are "old." More like the sixties, a.k.a. Jim Morrison…

Ding. Ding.

The buckle your seatbelt thing goes on. A stewardess pops on out, parting through the curtains like she is about to break out into high notes ala Adele. I only spy her lips moving, because my ears are all for Mr. Plant at the moment:

*Took my chances on a big jet plane/*
*Never let them tell you that they're all the same/*

All passengers are settled in. I don't know why I'm surprised…I mean we are about to take off—

*Just breathe, Erica.*

One hand starts to tremble, while the other grips firmly onto the handle of the gift from Dad…not from Mom.

*Erica…*

I close my eyes, entering my black abyss of thoughts. Breathing. Belly in—exhale. Belly out—inhale.

I find my non-shaking hand tightening around the cord of my headphones, mocking the tightness that compacts my breasts and possibly my heart.

I reach for my carry-on bag, on the empty seat next to me, but remember that my headphones are already on. Not to mention…the song has yet to finish:

*I think I might be sinking/*
*Throw me a line if I reach it in time/*

*Open your eyes, Erica.*

And finally, I do. Taking a deep breath. My eyes are already fixated on the window…as serene as the clouds drift on by in the sunny blue sky…

And then I see it all below…New York City.

*Standing on a hill in my mountain of dreams/*
*Telling myself it's not as hard, hard, hard as it seems/*

---

A one-eighty. Fast-paced. Energetic. People are just...*everywhere.*

My hair blows back as I poke my head out the window of my taxi, as I whiff in the sweat and grease of the city. My stomach growls at the sight of cooked hot dogs. My eyes scroll up and all I see are skyscrapers. Then my eyes narrow back down. Lights. Cameras dangling on cords toted by tourists, who have mistaken New York for Disney World. Phones flash as teenagers bounce and stomp around, convinced that they are taking over this world. Well, maybe they are. To be young…er and to feel that everything is a moment of serendipity…

I used to feel that—nostalgic or whatever; but not so much anymore. In fact, not…ever, if I must be honest.

"And here we are," my taxi driver says, tailgating the vehicle in front of us. "NYU."

The cab jerks to a halt, seconds after my driver nearly kills us when he decides to not keep a lookout for pedestrians and almost slams into this chick with big curly hair—

*THUMP.*

She slams her fist onto the hood of the cab, not *once* or *twice,* but *three times.* "Watch it! ASSHOLE!" And she storms off, flipping him off and strutting away…her middle finger remains up the entire time. She even has on this fake purple fur coat, cropped off midway like a crop top. Shit, she must be Janis Joplin in this modern-day world.

Oh, man, is she pissed—returning to spit on the windshield.

# Bianca

Okay, so the spitting was too much, but this fuckin' prick had almost killed me!

"Hey!" he shouts out the window, poking his head out like a dog. "Fuck you!"

I flip him off again. "Suck my DICK!" I grab my twat and give a quick dry hump in the air, catching more attention from the fellas on the street. But whatever. I'm too exhausted for this shit and being coffee-less is not helping either!

Abdul the cab driver flags his hand and makes an "ahhh" sound before he escapes back into his side of the cab. The poor girl in the backseat...she just eyes me and then her driver, her eyes wide and hopeless—probably debating if she should tip the guy or not.

# Erica

Wow.

She has no shame, but I cannot help but find myself smiling. *Gotta love New York.*

He clears his throat as my side of the door opens. "Miss." He gestures out his arm. "Welcome to your new home."

I step on out, soaking in the rays of the afternoon sun. NYU dormitories. Buildings that just stretch on up and up and up…

I catch my balance and have to look away. Forgot how vertigo-inducing it can get here sometimes. My cab driver rings around my luggage. He says something to me, but like Ms. Joplin earlier...I can't understand what he is saying and only hear her Indian mocking tone while she threw him shade.

---

An overwhelming load of unpacked movers' boxes and other missing items from home (clothes, artwork, etc.) sit around. At least my bed is made…

I close the sheer lavender curtains, shutting out the moonlight, and return to the floor. I'm tired…bummed even as I just sit there, cross-legged, staring at the multiple tabs and Word documents opened on my laptop—resumes and cover letters. The Metropolitan Museum of Art website is what keeps my laptop awake until it decides to take a power nap and the screen fades to black.

*Shit.*

It is a quarter past eleven and I should be in bed by now, but it is too quiet here. I look around my room…new bedroom for the potential next two years and spy nothing but boxes and other crap and bare walls. Well, except for one…

*"Remember, if you ever need a helping hand, it's at the end of your arm, as you get older, remember you have another hand: The first is to help yourself, the second is to help others."*

The Audrey Hepburn portrait sits directly above my bed. My shoulders rise to my ears and that tightness returns in my chest, making my hands clam up. I lean my head against the bed, so I no longer have to look at it, but my sight immediately goes to it…the Projects box underneath the desk, all taped up. Thank God the box is not see-through plastic. Otherwise, my deepest, darkest secrets would be seen. I don't want that. I hope to GOD that never happens.

The cold air makes me shiver. I retreat to the window and slide it downward, closing out the small gap. I stare momentarily out at the sheer expanse and the world is just one lavender mystery. Drawing back the curtain, I shut my eyes and breathe and *breathe*. My fingers lock into fists. My nostrils burn from the lump that clogs up my throat.

# Alex

It enters loudly from the speakers right above...and even outside of the store too:

*If you're horny let's do it, ride it, my pony/*
*My saddle's waiting, come and jump on it/*
*Let's do it, jump on it/*

"Hector..." I say, failing to hide my smile.

Hector, my co-worker (or as Bianca puts it—the crazy "beaner"; her choices of words), dances around the counter, leaving us stranded at the registers. There are only two because there aren't too many fans of the old-school way of listening to music with a CD or a vinyl record.

Basically, I work at a cheap knockdown—rip-off—of that one popular music shop on Sunset in Hollywood, Amoeba. Or, Imodium, as Bianca calls it because she can never get the name right...

I do miss her, regardless of the fact that she threw me under the bus earlier while I was ringing up these two girls, who must've been in their thirties. I picked up their signals—the usual—where they keep making intense eye contact from across the room as they ask a bunch of questions, even though I answer them; or not asking anything at all, leaving that awkward air roaming between us as they took turns approaching me at the shelves earlier, ruining my workflow—

Wow..."workflow," like I'm one of those rappers for the Generation X crowd. No wonder Bianca laughs, like turning red laughs, whenever I drop "lit/bruh/breh" and so on. She'll usually just tell me, "*Shat up*, ALEXIS!"

Alexis, being my drunk alter ego. Bianca's is Paige from *Degrassi*.

*If you're horny, let's do it, ride it, my pony/*
*My saddle's waiting, come and jump on it/*

Jesus, Hector.

He sways over to the opposite side of the counter, giving a few dry hump thrusts. I just shake my head, knowing that he is in deep shit as soon as—

"Alex!"

Too late.

We both look up from the registers—well, the counter for me, because I had my forearms resting on top of the cold glass. Not that I was slacking off or anything; today's just been a slow day. Plus, Bianca has been blowing up my phone every ten to fifteen minutes, wanting me to join her and Ricardo at the karaoke spot—

*My little prince! My little prince!*

Ah man…it's one thing when Ricardo calls me that, but when he actually steals Bianca's phone to text me that—He had called once/twice; hard to remember since I was drunk—low-key, it freaks me out.

"*Alexander*!" Janet, my boss, shouts at the top of her lungs like Edward from Edward Sharpe and the Magnetic Zeros—I'm assuming that's the dude's name. Bianca knows everything about that band from head to toe. She's the one person I'll listen to that song for a million times.

Only, Janet is nowhere close to being upbeat like Mr. Sharpe—more annoyed as she approaches us, while Hector continues to sway, less sexually, and gradually makes his way back around the counter; the closer our boss gets to us.

"Hey, Janet…"

She doesn't even need to say it because her eyes are already wide in alert, cueing Hector to change the station—Ah, Lou Reed…classic Hector move to kiss her ass; it never works though.

"Hector," she then says and tosses a folder onto the counter. That thing must weigh at least five pounds with all the crammed paperwork, pages bent and sticking out from the corners. Janet is an intelligent lady, but a slob. The Al Bundy of all Bundy's and biggest hoarder to date; her office…the worst.

"Ah, come on, Janet," Hector retorts more than he should. "Was just having fun because it's Sunday Funday!"

Oh, no…not the 'Shimmy Jimmy,' as he calls out—puffing out his chest and shaking forward and backward…

Jesus…Come on, dude.

"Yeah. I get that," she obliges. "But, the boss, a.k.a. ME, and my manager, a.k.a. Alex, got a *whole lotta love* to do with these apps."

Led Zeppelin reference—I'm not surprised if Janet was a hippie around our age. She did brag about that "one time" when she had smoked out with singer Eric Burdon…

And I was low-key jealous of that, or as Bianca would put it, "Low key. High key. Al keys!"

"Skedaddle." She shoos Hector away and I swear he is out the door, finishing up the lyrics to—

*"Jump on it, let's do it!"*

HA! Janet watches in horror as Hector saddles on out, backing up and somehow managing to open the door…butt to glass. There is a group of girls passing by and they giggle as he keeps going…and going until he is out of sight. Well, our sight, at least.

"Anyway…" Janet finally finds her voice again. "Never let him touch the stereo ever again. He has horrible taste in music."

"Oh, come on. 'Pony' isn't so bad—"

"Alex, please," she cuts me off with the hand. "Now, let's pretend you never said that, and let's get going with these new potential applicants."

She leans against one of the nearby stacked crates that hold nothing but cracked CDs and cassette tapes; most of the customers break them throughout the day just by picking them up.

Two fingers snapping in front of me, coming into full sight of my blurred vision because of my wandering daze, forces me to look back up at Janet. "Focus, kiddo! We got some resumes to look through." And as she opens the folder, she adds on, "Giddy up, Ponyboy."

OKAYYY…I get her point.

"Pony" isn't that great because of the one too many disturbing dance moves from Hector and now, with my boss saying it today…

It cues my realization that my shift ends in five minutes. I lock up the register, overhearing Janet shuffling through a few filled-out job apps already. "Too vague…Too wordy…Liar." She snorts at that last one and just as I'm about to ask what, she hands over the bottom half of the stack to me, "All yours."

Janet takes her stack of apps and slides a few ways down—mainly to back her control on the music coming from the stereo—still Reed. Like me, she has to find the right tune to go along with her workflow...

I arch forward, down onto my forearms, staring back at the bold name on the first resume of my pile of job apps: **Erica Mantes**.

# Erica

The sun is already streaking its rays through the thin crack of my curtains. My hands clam up and my fingers find their way downward, squeezing aggressively onto the bedsheets. I take one deep breath, inhaling the cold morning air…

All for nothing—here it goes.

I roll over and toss the blankets off of me.

---

*Sometimes I feel so happy/*
*Sometimes I feel so sad/*

The class is already crowded by the time I got here. But it had worked out perfectly—there was an open seat in the back. Well, technically two since my bag is sitting next to me in the empty chair.

I assume that people are talking or even snoring off because it is only a quarter until the big hand hits the twelve, making it seven o'clock…

Jesus.

Why the hell did I decide to take this class so EARLY?

I turn up Lou's words, twisting my earbuds back into place because for some reason the room ambiance seemed to get louder and, well, I just don't know anyone. As weird as that sounds because, well, nobody really knows each other…

And then the ambiance grows louder—

"Alright everyone!" the great and powerful shouts. "I'll explain the confusion in a minute!"

Finally, I look up, lowering the music from my phone. Because anyone who can power over the next song on the playlist, "Bleed It Out," has my undivided attention. Really, they do.

She does.

My first professor of the day, Mrs. Newman, approaches the podium. She is so tiny, making me fear she is not tall enough to speak directly into the microphone. Instead, she reaches it all too well and her voice fills the room like an opera house.

"I'm Mrs. Newman," she carries on. "And for most of you, your first college professor ever. For those of you who haven't taken a seat: you're in the right class. There were some last-minute schedule changes."

A few students linger by the door, confused...They are *definitely* freshmen. Most of them look like me, although I'm not new to this. They are smaller and shorter than the rest, or at least compared to the five dudes in the front row. One of them had pumped his fist into the air like Judd Nelson in *The Breakfast Club*, announcing, "FUCK YAY! ONLY EASY 'A' CLASSES THIS SEMESTER!"

Well, hallelujah bro…! I pump my fist, too, in solidarity.

Ugh, I hate when I do that. Whenever I bypass a group of guys it happens. A knee-jerk reaction. Yeah, what girl DOESN'T feel uncomfortable whenever she is cat-called? You have to do *something*. Yes…it has been an ongoing process in therapy; well, it HAD BEEN an ongoing process. To…relearn and understand that boys are boys and men are men, just like how girls are girls and women are women—human.

*Shit*.

I tuck my head down as soon as one of them looks my way. I can still see them from the corner of my eye as I grab my pencil and pretend to write something down. My van Gogh's "A Starry Night" pictures capture my attention from the cover of my binder. Like capturing a sign of life through the lens of a camera. A Polaroid camera.

The projection screen wakes to life with an ad similar to the one that I was looking at—before leaving California. I feel my hands reaching for the edge of my binder, tightening around the slipperiness of the plastic cover, diagonal from Mr. van Gogh's work.

"Welcome to the Introduction of Pictures and Words." She said, motioning with her hands like a magician.

Then, I notice what she is gesturing at exactly. My pupils dilate by the second as I glance from my class schedule, where **Photography 101 – Introduction to Photography** is written in bold, to the advertisement that is displayed. There is definitely hard work put into it. But, Pictures and Words? No…

**NYU'S FIRST EVER PHOTOGRAPHY AND WRITING SHOWCASE**
**OPEN TO ALL NYU PHOTOGRAPHY & IMAGING AND ENGLISH MAJORS**
**HONORARY AWARD ANNOUNCED AT SHOWCASE – DECEMBER 20TH**

"Now, you may all take a seat."

Those who remain standing obey her, and sit.

"This semester will solely focus on collaboration..."

And I can't hear the rest because Newman's VOICE DRAINS OUT. My entire body goes absolutely still from my feet to head. Not head to toe.

I can smell it, too—the sticky sensation of sweat that takes over my hands. They start shaking a bit, too. It's not a whole lot, but enough to freak me out. So, I use this particular hand and wipe it across my forehead, which is, indeed, greasy from sweat...

This strange RINGING sound pops into one ear, tunneling through my eardrums and directly into the other ear—

It sends my binder falling over my desk. I wiggle around in my chair, failing to find a zone of comfort. I hear the slap as the binder hits the floor, which puts a stop to the RINGING.

My eyes scope around, only a few heads in the seats in front of me turn. Before anyone offers to help, I descend to my knees and reach through the opening at the end of the desk and the floor. However, a pair of hands gets to it before me—long, black and metallic silver painted fingernails.

# Bianca

"Dope pic."

I scoop up her binder. She elevates back into her seat as I hand over her binder with the badass van Gogh cover. Yesterday, I saw one of those memes of the work, but get this—the bottom of the artwork actually had moving water and it was so rad!

Rad? What the *fauck*...

Wow, Alex is right—we are picking up the high school lingo, or the stupid lingo, as I like to call it.

"Thanks," her mousey voice whispers back. It takes me a minute before I spot the empty chair next to her. "Oh, Coolio and the Gang!"

I circle back around, squeezing by the freshmen who were late—Newman probably thinks I'm one of them. Although, some assholes in the front holler at me as I slide into class, afraid I am late. It's probably the fur coat and shades—FAKE fur. People tend to lose their shit whenever they see me wearing this.

Like fuck off PETA—I love animals and would never purchase real animal skin. Shit, not even leather pants get my panties all twisted and soaked.

Too much...right?

Guess that explains some of the snotty looks and scowls, even from the girls.

Whatever.

I sit at the end, adjacent from...

Shit, I'm an asshole that didn't even introduce myself properly, "Hi…"

What the *fauck*…She is staring at me long and hard like laser beams are about to zap right out of her doll-size eyes.

"Uh," is all that comes out of her mouth, "you're sort of sitting on my bag?"

# Erica

The girl who had screamed at my taxi driver was sitting on top of my tote bag. Literally. She picks up on my cue, as my eyes lower to the—

"Oh, *fauck!*" She worms off of it, allowing me to slide it onto my lap. "My bad. Well, I guess this would be the perfect timing to say that my name is *not* asshole. Even though it should be at this exact moment."

She gives a nervous giggle.

I hear Newman's voice babble on from the ear facing away from...from...

"Bianca," she says and sticks her hand up, pushing it towards and then pulling away from me, probably confused herself if we should shake hands or not.

Guess it is my final call when I put out my hand, "Erica."

Should I tell her that I saw her cursing at the driver the other day—?

"I'll be pairing you all up into pairs, based on your answers," Newman starts passing out papers; whoever is sitting on the end of the aisle leads the way.

I see it as soon as she tilts her binder cover upward—the blue textures and golden hour reflection stare right back. The same van Gogh replica is also on her binder cover, but on the backside.

Who would've thought...?

My eyes return to the projection screen—the ad is still up. I read silently to myself the bottom text:

Photographers take the photo!
Writers tell a story of the work!
A poem or a short story!
Partners get to pick!

Do you ever get that feeling, like deep beneath the surface of an ocean feeling? The deeper you go, the chillier you would think it would get. Only, it is warm. So, warm it's familiar.

That's the exact feeling I get as I'm reading the ad. The long-awaited process of getting back to work. Getting back to...myself. My true self—Erica in the sky with her camera...

The stack of papers goes to Bianca, and she passes the rest to me. Time for work.

---

If a bell were to ring, it would. But right now, it is just me walking over to the library, until—

"Yo! van Gogh!"

As I coil around, I swear Bianca nearly collides with me. I squint, preparing for the head-butt; but nothing like that happens because she is still, well, talking—

"Fun class."

"Yeah, sure was."

Jesus, I can hear the crickets. Please, stop...

Thankfully, the bypassing students and faculty fill-up the empty air between us. And her cell phone, which goes off for the second time. She checks it, but does not pick up—

"Well, I'll see you tomorrow!" And she smiles and sashays off. I hear her yell into the phone, "Wad up, homeboy!"

Man…

She is *totally* Janis Joplin with that grungy, high pitch tone. Pretty much everyone around us watches Bianca as she sashays by, her hair mimicking the movement of her hips.

---

The clinks, clanks, and moans from the other students are making me reread and reread this question, staring up at me from my table—

Do you have a particular project in mind? If so, what is it?

My answer…

____________________________________

Well…

I'm SCREWED.

As I press my back against the red metal chair, my head does the opposite and finds itself buried in my hands. Now, I am sitting up straight again. The air feels heavy like my shoulders and it forces me to take an extra look around—yep, nobody is at my table but, again, it is common in college since everyone else closes themselves off with the whole, "FUCK OFF," attitude.

As my eyes find their way back to my unanswered first—and failed attempt—assignment for Newman's class, I can sense the climate change as soon as I hear…him—

A burp.

It stings the hairs in my nose; not to mention the insane and I mean INSANE amount of cologne that he must have poured all over his body. God…it's stronger than stepping foot into a Bath & Body Works. I usually hate that place—holidays are cool because of the buy five or seven for twenty bucks (I still have bottles from high school)…

He drops into the seat in front of me, tuning me back into the 'now'. He slides his black JanSport backpack across the table. It rams into my arm and compels me to look right at him. With short, bumpy black hair and a black T-shirt, it is no surprise that his sunglasses are matching his attire for today. Although, it does pique my interest why on Earth he is wearing glasses in a setting where the glass double doors serve as the wall for the commissary…my stomach churns.

He tilts down his sunglasses and digs what he sees…ME. "You look new," he says and leans onto his elbows, coming closer to me. "Fresh meat."

Immediately, I pack up, not even taking another second or two to unwrinkle the sheets of paper that I jam into my binder, then into my backpack. There is no way in HELL that I am going to sit in this session with a wannabe Hannibal Lector. Seriously—the ASSHOLE has the nerve to whisper creepy shit and is, NOW…licking his fuckin' lips! Da *fauck!*

"Ah, come on!" he raises his voice, making the hair on the back of my neck rise. "I just got jokes, *yo*!"

YO?!

The nerve…the fuckin' nerve he has! I don't even bother taking another glance at him because I'm afraid if I do…I'll say something that will come off as sexist or one of those feminists who says they don't hate men, but really DO, and well…

I just have enough on my plate already. My back is already to him. As my eyes escalate from the blue carpet with gold shapes on it, I hear another boy's voice yell across the open area, "Hey, Josh!"

I stop dead in my tracks. Oh, no…not here. Not now—

I feel my eyes enlarge—

No. No. no—

The side of my neck starts as a strum, like the chord of a guitar. And then, it just speeds up. So does my heart, tightening and tightening—

As I watch…him…coming from the double doors—he is wearing his letterman's jacket—the sunlight behind him darkens to nighttime. It is a different era for me. High school. That…That night…

My eyes shut, and immediately, I see myself—

> Flashback to my old bedroom. I am more youthful and innocent. A fourteen-year-old teenage girl, who has a life filled with so many opportunities ahead of her, is just sitting on the beige carpet of her childhood bedroom. She is smiling as she opens up...that shoebox…that sits in front of her—

"Wad up!"

My eyes shoot wide open as my heartbeat slows down. I notice that the yellow, green, and blue color hues are no longer in sight. Well, at least in my sight. It is still bright out—the sun is striking through all of the windows. I am in the same spot as before. The only new element to this scene is the boy coming into my crystal-clear sight from those set of double doors…

"Hey! Paul, where the fuck have you been?!"

All the dots connect when Paul…okay, so his name is Paul…walks toward me, towards the other one—the asshole—Josh. So, HE is Josh…

Ironic.

I catch the slightest glimpse of Paul eyeing me to Josh. I tug at the top of my backpack straps and hurry out, headed for the set of doors adjacent to the ones Paul had entered from. I can still smell that cologne and it almost seems stronger, as that clip of his tongue goes off—

"Awe come on, mami!" the ASSHOLE catcalls. "Don't be like that!"

Creep.

I let the doors hit me on the way out—AH, that fuckin' hurts!

---

I spy with my little eyes: shadows of the feet that pass on by, other students—or, in the so-called correct political terms, my neighbors—who are headed off to a late lunch, or an early dinner, or whatever social event that will keep them preoccupied. I did hear some heavy objects being lifted, dragged, and banged against the walls earlier. But I don't mind. It covered the tears that turned into thicker, ugly and disgusting, heaving tears as soon as I got back to my dorm. Well, more like ran back here. I got some curious and worried looks earlier...

My backpack sits in front of my bedroom door like it will keep a monster out, regardless of the door being locked or not. Not all of my picture frames are up—the James Dean one with the "Dream as if you'll live forever, live as if you'll die today" one is leaning against the door frame, beside my desk and the Projects box. The box is still taped up.

My knees jostle around, as I fail miserably to find a more 'comfortable' sitting position. My bed is made. It feels sturdier than it did with just the mattress. I'll have to look into a new one—I DON'T want Dad and, especially, NOT Mom's help. God…she would just love that.

I have a stare-down with my cell phone. Conflicted. Tempted. Conflicted. And tempted some more…

Screw it!

My spine unravels as I sit up and cross my legs, my butt hides my feet for now. I pull up the contact list, scrolling and scrolling some more. Until I see it and it sees me—Josh and his number. Staring at it...so many flashes come to my mind, speeding up my pulse. I dial and find myself tensing up. My shoulders practically touch my earlobes, and my fingers clench forward into fists. My breathing stops all at once as soon as it rings and rings, and then:

"I'm sorry, but the number that you're trying to reach is no longer in service—"

*FUCK.*

My belly pops out, no longer sucked in. I hang up and, all-together, I drift down onto the bed, as my arm does with my cell phone. I exhale from relief, staring up at my starless ceiling.

This was a routine.

> I remember waiting and waiting for him to call, just to be sure that hitting 'block caller' was accurate and not bullshit. It wasn't. Never was. If he did call…I wouldn't know. So, one night—it was late, real late—I awoke from a nightmare and had instantly reached for my cell phone and dialed—out of service. For a while there, dialing and dialing him, just to be sure that he was no longer existent. But…I know he still is.

My phone ringing perks me up, startling me. I choke on some saliva as I lean onto my elbows to see who it is—no name, but a local area code number. Before I go to answer, something tells me to wait—my instincts, I suppose—

*It's not him, Erica. It's not Josh.*

Finally, I breathe and just answer, "Hello?"

"…Hi. Is this Erica Mantes?"

"It is."

"Hi," the boy's voice chirpers up. "This is Alex from the 'SoHo, This Isn't A Musical Shop'"—I sit up. "We received your resume. My boss and I would like to invite you to an interview. When can you come in?"

That music shop in SoHo—the one with the artsy theme, an artist's dream, and every hipster racist's worst nightmare. Think Amoeba on Sunset Blvd…?

# Alex

"And you must be…." I check the clipboard, just in case, since I called the previous interviewee by the last name. "…Erica."

"I'm—"

We shake hands—man, her grip is loose, a big no-no for a pre-interview. As soon as our eyes meet, she breaks focus right away. Immediately, our hands release from each other; mine is a bit clammy. She wipes hers onto her jacket, briefly, thinking I won't see it.

"Sorry," she says, squeezing onto the strap of her purse. Her tone appears shakier. "I didn't catch your name."

"Alex"—Ah, the boy with the chipper voice on the phone earlier—"Assistant manager. And let me guess, you were expecting someone older, bald, and probably fat too."

It breaks a smile on her until two of her bottom teeth find their way onto her lip, preventing the smile from turning into laughter. She skims around, and I notice her eyes going straight for the obvious picture on the main wall, next to the spiral staircase. It is a ten-foot framed picture of Prince in the middle of strumming his purple guitar at the Super Bowl. Awe…poor guy…

He was one of my favorite rock stars.

"Janet's upstairs. Ladies first," I say with a grand ol' gesture.

She hesitates and adjusts the strap of her purse. It is not just any ordinary purse; it's the kind that Bianca wears herself—"I ain't paying for that expensive shit," as Bianca puts it whenever we pass by those big store names. I think one of those fancy-schmancy stores is called Tiffany's, no?

I spy with my little eye the clothing patch of Andy Warhol's Banana cover album on the front side of her over-the-shoulder purse as she quickly bypasses me.

Holy…shit…

A Lou Reed fan.

I hear a chuckle and catch my co-worker, Hector, shaking his head at me as he rings up the two remaining customers at the register—the girls, think older, too due to their…well, if I must say it—their boobs—were coming at me pretty aggressively earlier. Until…well, until the Lou Reed girl had walked in. She was impossible to NOT notice. I saw her. She saw me right away.

# Erica

The hippie vibe was even heavier, going up the staircase with the fringe and beaded curtains becoming a choreographed routine as Alex led us down the hallway.

I think he was trying to sneak a peek at my ass with the whole, "Ladies, first."

Bitch, please. You really thought I'd walk in front of you the entire time. Men…

I glimpse over my shoulder, but he is not there. I assume he is standing outside the doorway. He and Janet have an interesting lingo with each other—she calls him an asshole, and he calls her "man" or "dude."

Interesting…but…

Janet, who still looks like the wild child she never grew out of—probably the type of chick who did all sorts of drugs with all the big names at Woodstock, sits across from me in her beanbag chair, scanning my resume. If I didn't see the burning incense sticks on top of her desk, I'd think she was smoking out before Alex and I had headed in. Maybe that explains the door-less door, and a beaded drape instead.

The beanbag chair brings an interesting vibe to the office, which outlines her aura with that long blonde hippie hair of hers. Besides, the office does NOT look like any other office. Not to mention that upstairs is just as busy as downstairs with the towers of used and new books, CDs, DVDs, vinyls, and a selection of artwork replicas. The vibrant colored items are overexposed. The walls are orange, at least the sections you can see through all the dozens and dozens of posters and hanging picture frames of—you name it—artist's artworks and of artists. She definitely has a big fetish for Hendrix…

That intense feeling returns to my throat—nerves. I wipe my hands onto my black slacks, thankfully out of sight due to all of the paperwork and paper racks on top of her desk. Oh, wow…there's another burning incense stick. What is that…pineapple?

"So"—*Jesus, why is Janet yelling*—"Why music? Says here that you've volunteered at a few museums in high school, not to mention you're a photography major at NYU. Fancy Schmancy."

Oh, no…please tell me that she isn't a *hater. Fauck…*

"Pop Art," it blurts right out of me. "There's a lot on vinyl artwork."

Now she seems interested and perks up, her elbows coming forward onto the desk. It's amazing, too because her beanbag chair is so…short. Her eye contact makes me peer away and I spy with my little eye a nearby vinyl on the wall: The Animals' *Retrospective* album.

"Ah, yes," she says and dips back into…well, her head leans against tower number three bookcase that stands behind her, "Eric Burdon. We smoked a joint together, after one of his stints with War."

HA, I KNEW IT!

*"Spill the Wine."*

"Dig that girl."

*"Boogie Nights* soundtrack."

"Great movie. Paul Thomas Anderson."

"Great filmmaker."

This smile breaks across her. Janet is…sold.

"So," she says, her volume dropping, "what do you think of today's music?"

Ah, shit, is this some sort of trick question? And all I can do is…SHRUG. FUCK!

"Oh, come on, Ms. Erica. It's not like I'll fire you or anything." And she does one of those head tosses back to let out a HAHA. "Today's music, in my opinion, and pardon my French, is shit if you'd ask me.

Snap.

"Yeah," I then agree. "It's not my type either."

"Well, anyone who wants to get their foot in, and has good taste in music, I fully support…"

There is this super long, way too long, silence. Until she laughs and tells me: "Congratulations, you got the job."

Uh…WHAT?!

My cheeks are burning, and I cannot find the words to speak. Unless my throat is preventing anything from escaping.

"Alex will take it from here—Alex!"

"Dammit, Janet!"

Hey, *Rocky Horror Picture Show.*

He slides right in like Morris Day. Janet digs it, mocking back that 'squawk' move from "The Bird."

And then, suddenly, his eyes go for mine—

I look away and at Janet for her to be my anonymous cock blocker.

Thank, GOD…she is, but is unaware as she proceeds, "Please give Erica the appropriate paperwork to fill out so she can bring it to her first day...this week?"

Oh…OH! That is not rhetorical.

"This week is great."

---

Hector closes off his register, giving me and then Alex a look. That kind of LOOK. Ugh!

I write faster on my application. Done! I go to Alex, who rings up one of the last few customers a few feet down from me on the counter, "Here you go!"

Oops, my voice came out more chipper than I'd expected. NOT that I'm excited or anything to see him—

"Done already? Damn Speedy Gonzalez.

It's just that he doesn't look like the kind of guy who would work here with his skater boy, possibly wannabe, appearance. And short black hair—

Fuck. My cheeks feel flushed, so I turn to leave. A split of a second later—whatever that is—the overhead speakers start blasting "Spill the Wine" by the Animals. Whoa…

"What?" he tries to act all surprised, even glancing at Hector for an answer. "Hector! Did you do this? Sound familiar? Burdon and War."

Hector just shakes his head. "No, I didn't put this on, Alexander. You know I only dig 'Pony.'" That last comment of his busts him up as he leaves through the downstairs beaded curtains. Talk about both a cock-block and wingman opportunist all meshed up in one long-ass awkward situation.

Alex doesn't stop moving, though. "Walls are thin, so I overheard. Janet has me wait outside of her office during interviews. You know, assistant manager so...Lou Reed. Dope."

He leans in for a better view of my bag, making me think that he was trying to cop a feel at first. Jesus…I need to chill out. But I also gotta go, "Anyway, it was nice meeting you. Bye."

I walk out without another thought or the slightest glance over my shoulder like one of those cliché moments in the movie, where the girl has to drop a hint—not that I'm trying to hint anything at all…

I hear Burdon as the bell rings above the door and slams on my way out:

*...Spill the wine/Dig that girl...*

# Bianca

Oh, sweet baby Jesus…

Professor Umbridge heads for the podium. "Good morning, everyone!"

Mrs. Newman says sounding all wide awake. Bitch…I'm low-key all kinds of jealous of her. This damn coffee is still making my eyes itch.

And I am already late—

"Ouch."

"Sorry," I say to the chick in the pink frilly top; it also has glitter. There is definitely a Britney Spears vibe to her outfit, not to mention that her hair is a dirty blonde, paper-y, like sandy beach. If that makes any sense.

Anyhoo…

At the podium, Mrs. Newman pulls up a list of paired-up names on the screen.

Oh, there she is! I see that chick from the other day—that real cute brunette who is short and wearing a Zeppelin T-shirt underneath her gray zip-up jacket. So, I wave over to her. Of course, she is in the back of the classroom again in the same seat as before. She has to double-take on me before removing her backpack from the empty seat next to her. I urgently make my way over, having to squeeze my fat ass over from some dude who has his ass sticking out in the middle of the aisle. *Like bro…come on!* Get the *hottie thottie's* number later and then bang her after class or whatever, but for right now, move!

I take the second to the last seat on the aisle. Of course, she would have the end seat—something about her vibe today says that she wants to be left the fuck alone. But when I smile at her, she gives a small one back.

Perfecto!

# Erica

Janis Joplin drops her bottom into the chair beside me. Her Starbucks Grande-sized drink never loosens from her long acrylic fingernails as she takes a sip. I'm assuming that she is the double espresso kind of girl. I can see the thin line of steam floating about in the H20 air, sucking us into the precious hot warm smell of another goddamn expensive drink.

I just have my gray and black striped thermos with me. The coffee is already cold. I could use a refill.

"Hey there, dope *twinsey*," she says. "Like fuck me, right? Taking a class this fuckin' early."

She sips. Some chick in a pink shirt that reminds me of a cupcake shoots a glare at me and then at Joplin, who is already on her mission to the next tangent.

"Just one hot sec." Newman disrupts my trail of thoughts as she points a remote at the projection screen that only shows a blue pop-up error message. She gives the remote a few clicks.

Technology.

"Ah! Perfecto!"

Interesting choice of word for this dull morning. Man…am I just not in the mood today. And it is only 6:59…7:00 am. Right on time.

Newman faces our way, but her eyes never divert from the computer screen atop the podium. The actual projection screen displays two lists of everyone's names, side by side. Mine is up there…somewhere. I am already searching for my name, but there are about fifty other people in this class…shocking, too, because most hate art to begin with.

"Please raise your hands, so you and your partner can sit together." Mrs. Newman opens her mouth and starts speaking, as does—

"Imagine," Bianca says, and leans to her side, closer to my way. Jesus…she almost gave me a heart attack for being so…in my face, "If you and I are partners."

Mrs. Newman calls out, "Jocelyn Strand and Adam Rodriguez," and I spy with my little eyes…

"...Erica and Bianca."

My eyes do some searching, as well as others. But only the girl next to me—Janis—locks hers with mine. A smile creeps on her, just one side, crooked. Only she makes it appear cool. It is the moment when I also notice the second irony of ours. Perhaps you can call it 'official meet cue,' when I spy with my little eye…the van Gogh cover artwork that is on the front cover of her binder.

I catch her eyeballing the replica of "A Starry Night" on the backside of my binder. What are the odds…

"God, I love him! But, cutting your ear off for some gal…not the best decision. As they say, some bitches be *cray-cray*."

If I was the one sipping on the coffee, I probably would spit it out by now. A chuckle slips through my lips. For some reason, that almost makes her choke, forcing her hand in front of her mouth like she needs to force out a sneeze, but is too prim and proper to do so. Okay, more like forcing back one of those sneezes in the middle of family dinner like the annoying "let's go blow a few hundred bucks on brunch and play pretending to do small talk."

"Shit!" She scans around as I do, but Newman did not hear, since she is reading down that long-ass list.

"Where are my manners? I'm Bianca. And you shall be my fellow van Gogh fan…"

And she rolls out her hands like a man does for his dancing partner to courtesy and get their groove on.

Whoops. I'm just sitting here, staring back at her. "Uh, Erica."

"Well, nice to meet you"—her tone lowers—"Uh, Erica."

She is being sarcastic. I got that. She lowers her hand first so my hand drops, too. I wait for her, well I'm just not sure how to…approach the subject…our soon-to-be project…

"Say," she interrupts my mind wandering off further into its deep, deep abyss, "Do you have class afterward?"

No. Why?

"Well, we should go over some ideas," she continues as though she read my mind because my lips are still zipped tight. "Plus, I can use a refill."

Bianca gives a long and loud slurp, finishing off her coffee with a burp. I catch a whiff of the caramel macchiato. A few heads turn her way, especially that girl in the pink. I laugh a bit. Bianca can finally sense a set of eyes on her—

"Oh, hey there, Britney Spears."

It makes her jaw drop, as well as forces her to turn back around—the girl in the pink blouse. Bianca just returns her attention to me and shrugs, "Oops, I did it again."

College isn't so bad now.

---

There is this low ambiance vibe to the café—perfect for the artists—which Bianca practically dragged me to as soon as Mrs. Newman, Professor Umbridge according to Bianca because—"You know because they're both short, round, and fat!"

She had no, and I mean ZERO, shame saying that one aloud. But Mrs. Newman *does* hide some shade of pink in her outfits every day…so far. I don't know. I'm keeping my eyes alert on that one for a bit.

My spine straightens out whenever someone or a group of the ideal definition of hipsters meander on by joining their group of friends or sitting by their lonesome selves. Well, there are more people flying solo today. The place consists of nothing but warm yellow-brownish and reddish-greenish colors. A few bookshelves compact the walls like the entire student body from Hogwarts barfed on them.

We have a table in the back, adjacent to one of the counters with the creams and sugars and a built-in trash bin.

"Ah, California," Bianca's high-pitched tone draws me back into the here and now. "Fancy schmancy. But y'all got some shitty ass freeways." She giggles, and takes a sip from the oval-shaped mug that holds her hazelnut coffee. It smells thick and homely, like a perfect gingerbread house. Very Christmassy.

I'm still nursing my herbal green tea. The light splash of honey is soothing to my nostrils as if clearing up a bad head cold.

"Yep," I answer, although her comment was a comment and not a question. "But it's not too bad, though."

The loud gushy sound from one of the distant coffee makers makes me flinch like the rush of wind from an ongoing subway train. It nearly knocks over my plastic cup with tea even though, it is half empty. The walk over here got my taste buds dry. Plus, coffee would've just dried them out even more. I mean, caffeine is not good for anyone in general. It isn't good, at least not recommended, for anyone who has what I have…

Oh, no. That tightness returns, forcing me to sit up even straighter. I take a long, slow sip from my straw while Bianca picks up the contest flyer from the table, "Winners to be featured at the Museum of Arts!" she mocks with widespread eagle wings. "Can you believe it? *The* Museum of Arts. It'd be pretty cool to win, but too much pressure, right?"

Pressure?! Yeah, if it is less than the compression that pulses back and forth in my throat, working its way up and down my throat…I think I'd rather take that kind of "peer pressure."

"So," she proceeds through quickly and with loud slurps from her hazelnut with extra coconut milk drink. "What notes did Newman give you from yesterday's handout?"

Oh, that's right.

I steal a glance at the sheet of paper on my binder, covering a portion of my van Gogh artwork. "It was…just a suggestion."

My eyes are already on the last question of the handout:

**Do you have a particular project in mind?**
**If so, what is it?**

My answer:

*A photography collage.*

And Newman's feedback:

**What kind, though?**

Fuck, is she *serious*…?

My gaze lingers too long on some bookworm who does a double take on me from across the café. As a smile appears on him—

I look back down at the paper. Fuck. Fuck. FUCK. I need to be careful next time.

"Oh!" She gets me this time because I jolt in my chair, starting from the feet up. "I'd almost forgot!"

Bianca pulls out the in-class assignment. She is grinning, too. Something is up with her. She gives a quick and off-beat drum roll with her free hand onto the table.

"It's OFFICIAL!" she reveals, facing the assignment my way. "I'm officially a Hogwarts student! They have a Harry Potter class here. Can you believe it?"

That is pretty cool. It does make me smile.

"For your G.E.?" I must ask her, receiving the paper from her. Shit, no joke on the true hardcore questions on Harry Potter; not the film version, but the books, for the lifelong fans.

"No! It's actually for my English class."

Interesting…and my face must say it because she preps up, pressing her weight down onto the table.

"I know, *right*! I'm still amazed that I got into it."

I won't lie…I'm kind of jealous.

"What about you, any cool classes?"

No.

"Just G.Es," I say. God, I must sound like Eeyore. The inner thoughts come off as a 'Fuck off' kind of attitude.

"Yuck!" Bianca even sticks out her tongue for the raspberry sound effect. "Stupid G.Es. Fuckin' bastards!

Oh, wow. I laugh at that one, louder than I should have since a few heads turn our way, but quickly recover and return to their own business. Bianca puts down her drink.

"Say, you have a nice smile. Very white teeth."

She gives a forced smile, and her facial expressions scrunch up like she is trying harder and harder to sniff out the shit. I close my mouth and sip, even though it is now just ice and no longer herbal green tea. Man…my chest feels tight again as I exhale.

"Oh!" It hits her. "I'm not like hitting on you or anything. I'm straight."

Noted.

"I didn't think you were hitting on me…"

Yeah, even I don't buy that. I sound way too unconvinced. Bianca's phone rings, but she ignores it. I don't think she hears it…

"You can take that call if you want."

Instead, Bianca rejects the call and starts texting. "It's just my friend. I'll call him back later.

Him—my fingers tighten around my empty plastic cup, making it give a loud crackle. Thankfully, it does not explode right here. Bianca's phone BUZZES and, now, she has no other choice but to answer it this time. "Ah, *shitburger!*

"Is everything okay?"

"Yeah," she says ten octaves lower, so obviously, things are *not quote-unquote okay.*

"I forgot I have this thing across town. Shit, I don't think I can make it in thirty."

"Maybe reschedule?"

"I can't." Now, she sounds and looks more flustered, as she is shifting in her seat. "I made the appointment two months ago.

Whoa—her eyes remain on her cell phone, mid-reach of grabbing her belongings.

"Oh, I hope everything's okay." It is all I think of to say.

"Oh, it's not *that* kind of doctor." She has said too much; now, embarrassed. Finally, her eyes avert to mine at this odd, off-balance slow pace. Before I can say anything, or even sit up and make the chair squeak, one of the distant coffee dispensers gives a loud gasp to fill the long, awkward silence amongst us. Well, at least to me.

"Let's meet before class tomorrow," she insists. "Bring a list of ideas or something you're already in the works with."

Right…Man. I can already picture the slimy mess that will soon make the crease marks poke holes into the handout from yesterday. My grip tightens on it, forcing my mind to slip back into its state of an abyss, where all my surroundings blur out to form a white tunnel in my farsight. Bianca is unaware because she is already back at texting, lost in her own world. Only, she seems more structured.

"Yeah. Yeah, that sounds good."

This time, my body does jolt. My knees accidentally hit the bottom of the table as soon as a blast from the distant coffee makers give a loud slurpy *GUSH.* It smells like burnt oil now, making me want to gag, for some reason. I take a long sip from my empty, watered down herbal green tea.

# Erica

The place looks more like home, although it doesn't quite feel like it…

Many items are up, including my calendar, with the first two days of school crossed off. Finally, it is a relieving, yet overwhelming, moment.

The shoebox is on top of my bed.

However, for the past twenty minutes or so, I have been pacing back and forth like a house cat all wired up after eating the wet food from a can. The side of my face sweats up and I briefly jerk away from my phone, but I cannot hear Mansell. So, I must press my phone back against my ear, returning the bottom half of it against my jawline, which tightens at the thought of having another attack…

Just breathe, Erica. *Breathe…*

I inhale and, somehow, manage to say directly into the phone, "I don't know. Guess, it's just personal."

"You don't have to share it," her concerned, soft tone echoes from the opposite line. Her soothing voice does help, forcing me to take a seat at the edge of my bed. But…I'm still so tense—my spinal cord tensing up from top to bottom like a puppeteer is demanding me to obey by a set of strings…

"But," the higher pitch tone of hers hauls me back into the conversation. "I know you feel this need to do this for the showcase. Why is that?"

My eyes find the Audrey Hepburn portrait that hovers over my bed; that quote just screams at me: *Remember, if you ever need a helping hand, it's at the end of your arm. As you get older, remember you have another hand: The first is to help yourself, the second is to help others.*

Yeah, no shit, Hepburn. *No shit…*

"It…" I practically choke up, "It just deserves to see daylight."

I can sense her thinking to herself, "Good," which makes me swallow the lump that was tensing up my throat like I had gulped down a web of cotton.

"You know, Erica, you're always more than welcome to call, but if you want something regularly…"

Oh, no. I can already tell where this is headed to—a.k.a. the big ol' talk with a therapist.

"…it might be a bit difficult with our time zones."

"Yeah. I figured." My teeth find their way to my thumbnail and, accidentally, I hit too hard and *crunch*. Luckily, Mansell does not hear my big "ouch" that popped out. With no shame in the world, I suck onto my thumb with the cut-off hangnail.

"There is someone I know closer your way. Do you have a pen and paper?"

"Yeah."

I grab a nearby pen from my purse and the sticky note pad from my desk which is a complete disaster, considering my laptop has all the tabs open for my online courses and student school portal. I have yet to answer any emails or read through anything. Luckily, most of the assignments are just the routine rundown of what the class is about and what is to be covered and learned and even applied to our own lives throughout the semester.

Also, the blank Word document stares back at me—the showcase guidelines.

I overhear another loud group of—whom I am assuming are—friends or partygoers, considering the late hour. After all, it is New York City—students pass by like lightning bolts. They are all shouting and hollering, young and alive and filled with such energy and happiness…

Funny thing—my windows are closed, not even slightly cracked open.

Mansell gives me the name and number, but it is almost a big blur. All I see staring back at me is the name of my soon-to-be new therapist: Dr. Zimmer.

In between writing, I catch a glimpse of the unopened Polaroid camera on my desk then the Projects box that remains isolated in its corner, away from all my other belongings…

---

The moon is in full bloom, reflecting its shine through the slight parting of the curtains that drape over the two windows in my bedroom…dorm.

I'm sitting in the middle of the floor; the moss green and brown checkered carpet keeps my butt warm. God, the color is hideous—you'd think that living in the symphony of New York would've paid more money for a different design or whatever—

I practically jump up as soon as a nearby door sends a quick vibration throughout the four corners of my dorm, followed by footsteps distancing further away. I'd like to think that my imagination is on point: it is a student with bookworm glasses returning home after a late night, scampering down the hallway, practically shouldering every bypassing student in this dorm; barely managing a stack of books or keeping their shit together.

Upon me is the Projects box, and it is now open, adjacent to some magazine clip-out collages that I had cropped out sometime, far, far away, back in high school…

I set the clip-outs down and return to the pile of Polaroids that sit diagonally from them. My old work: the outdoors and sun amongst the clouds. Good memories.

My fingers shake in-between the shuffling of Polaroids—one by one—but I keep going and looking, regardless of the nerves that I can feel itching up my chest, taking over, swallowing up part of the air that travels through my lungs…

Breathing…

And breathing…

"Yo! Tracy!" Some random chick screams outside my dorm and shouts as she runs off. Well, at least I'm assuming those are her footsteps clunking on the floorboards down the hallway. "Wait up! I don't want to miss Hogwarts."

Ah, I did see a flyer earlier for that—a *Harry Potter* marathon theme, because what else works best with a group of freshmen going off and leaving their loved ones behind…

Well, I feel like a freshman all over again, especially since my chest size and body frame have remained the same, just based on these older Polaroids. Yikes…no wonder the cafeteria lady had called me sweetie a few times.

I sigh and finally set down the Polaroids in my hands. There are still a few more to get through, a trip down memory lane again…

But it hits me hard. All I do is eye the Projects box and the camera on my desk, back and forth until it appears that morning has soon arrived and I'm still sitting on the floor with my legs crossed one over the other.

# Bianca

I spy with my little eyes—

"Yo! Erica!" I holler baller from across the classroom. She kind of glances around and slowly sticks up her hand, as though she is terrified of throwing up the Nazi/Asshole Hitler sign by accident. God, what a sick fuck! Last night's homework on him for History 101 – World History. Yeah…more like History 101 – Let's Talk About Assholes.

*Jeez.*

I feel a few eyes and heads turn away from me while the wind picks up as I drop into the seat next to her. Of course, she has the aisle seat per usual, not to mention that her backpack sits on her lap. Man, she is more uptight than a Stepford Housewife (except that Erica is actually…nice). Quiet, but so far, she is the only person who has said more than a couple of sentences to me since this semester had started.

"What?" she says and peers around because my dumbass forgot that I was staring at her without blinking. Therefore, coming off as a *creepo* like one of those dudes with buck teeth and thick glasses.

"Oh, nada. Just dazed out I guess." I take a sip of the last half drop of my frappe from Starbucks. Alex laughed at me when I was begging him to go there with me this morning. He called me a basic bitch. I called him the only wetback living in New York City. He flipped me off. I double birded him and won. Ha!

"So…"

That captures my full attention because even her face mocks that prolonged look—you know, where the person sort of resembles a turtle as they open and close their mouths. Jesus, girl just spit out what you want to say to me or ask me…

And then I notice what she is already holding—a plastic baggie with a bundle of Polaroids, ones that are already well developed. Finally, my eyes retrieve to her as she speaks, "It's some of my work. To just give you a better idea."

Ah, yes, what Newman had advised us the other day. I reach out to one of them, studying it and turning it around for a better look. God damn…she got an eye on this Erica chick.

---

Man, they need a new coffee machine. It just sputters on and off whenever the damn hipsters want a drip-drop-top-top drink. Okay, that's not *really* a thing—I just meant another drip of coffee.

"So," I start, "why Polaroids?"

I flip through Polaroid after Polaroid, catching a nervous glimpse of Erica who quickly brings her hazelnut latte to her mouth as if I did not notice. Man, wonder what is up with her….

"You can't Photoshop them," she finally responds.

She needs a drink-DRINK instead of this coffee shit.

"Which is good?"

All she does is nod and take another gulp of her drink. Her fingers remain enclosed around the cup as if winter came too early and she forgot her mittens at home.

Her work is beautiful, very poetic, which amazes me, considering van Gogh has thrown up all over her binder with his "A Starry Night" and the "Screaming Man" sets. Her voice is certainly aligned with peace and hope, just by her upper or straightforward aim at the outdoors. Most of them are of the morning sun parting its way through the clouds in the sky and reflecting down onto the ground, trees, and flowers.

But I ask her anyhow, "Why though? The Polaroids instead of film or digital."

After a long pause, she straightens herself up and tosses a fallen strand of her brunette hair behind her shoulder, "It's all real. Natural."

"Unlike a housewife's tits!" Whoops, that one just sort of slipped on out. I think she is mad, considering that her soft smile has, well, hardened and is out of sight—at least from me.

The coffee machines give a hiss and sputter in the distance. For some reason, I huddle in closer at our oval table in the back corner and set down the Polaroids, adding them back to the collection that is displayed out on the table like pieces to one big puzzle.

"I like this one." I point to the one with the rainbow reflecting and hitting directly into the heart center of a cloud in the sky. Her aim is upward. She was probably lying down while taking this particular one.

Now, I spy with my little eye—a smile returning on her face. She looks appreciative. I know this means a lot to her, which is why I now sit up. I down my coffee and wipe my sleeve across my mouth. She just waits for me. By her wider pupils I can tell she fears what it is I need to ask. To have an answer before we proceed onward.

"I do have a question. Well, two. Are these for a backdrop or is this an experimental piece?"

"What do you mean?"

"Well, your work sort of has the whole Avant-Garde thing going on. That's what you're aiming for the showcase, right?"

Okay, now I feel like I'm ramblin' because she goes all silent again. Thankfully, the coffee machines sputter out—well, one of them do—and it draws some attention and a small crowd as one of the baristas goes into mechanic mode to fix it. He does, but Jesus, do people really need to clap for that.

"That's what I wanted to talk to you about..." is all she says as my gaze meets hers.

# Erica

Underneath the table, out of Bianca's sight, I wipe my hands onto my jeans. This is it. The moment of truth to tell her…everything. But…

Shit, that tightness becomes tighter in my chest and all I spit out is, "So, what ideas do you have?"

I must look like a mess because the four corners of my face are clammed up. I'm disappointed and feel my shoulders dragging their way downward like Charlie Brown. God, not now. Please don't go back up.

My shoulders, ultimately, return to their normal stature. But that heaviness sits with me, almost like a mixture of sadness and just overall numbness…

But Bianca seems unaware of all my up and down reactions because she also has a similar expression as me…

She sets down the Polaroids.

"I don't have any ideas," she confesses and finds a way to look me in the eye—I see the guilt that holds her back for a moment. "I was trying to brainstorm last night, but nothing. I don't know, maybe it's writer's block. God, that's probably the last thing you want to hear. I'm officially the world's shittiest partner."

I don't think that, though.

"You're not," I say louder than usual. She smiles at that, but I can sense she doesn't quite believe what I just said.

She looks over her shoulder for an instant. I do too, well the direction in which her head and eyes are directed at the coffee machines that are being worked on. It holds up the line while three more baristas come out from the back and take down orders from customers in writing. I guess they're going the old-school way.

"To be honest, the last time I wrote anything, besides homework, was in high school."

Whoa. Okay, now that was more than a confession…

I lean in, pressing the rest of my weight into my forearms on the table. I can tell that there is so much more to say, but it's a slow build for her.

"I know, how hypocritical," she blurts and pats her hand onto the top of her head a few times. I'd say that would've been painful, but her Janis Joplin curls (wait, no, she doesn't have curls) are so up and out there that her hair might be serving as a mattress. "Writers are supposed to write every day. Well, my apologies to Stephen King."

She leans back in her chair, her arms already crossed. I feel…bad like this is her truly being honest with herself and a potential new friend. Wait, did I just really say that? I mean, this is adulthood and in adulthood, I've heard that people are fonder of having more colleagues or acquaintances rather than friends. Supposedly, it has to do with that whole not wanting to get "hurt" thing.

But I get it. I'm already living with that mentality of not wanting to ever EVER get hurt again. At least…not like that again…

I feel the sharp coldness hiss through my teeth as I catch my breath.

"High school…" I then say aloud and meet her sight. "Everyone has a story to tell from those days."

She bobs her head, agreeing with me, "You keep in touch with any friends from high school?"

I decline and shake my head from side to side. Hell fuckin' NO!

"Yeah, me either," her tone lowers and lowers. "Girls can be so cruel to each other."

Oh, for sure. So, true.

"But at least those bitches all got fat!"

I laugh at that one, too.

"High school..." She dawdles off, twirling one of her long ends of that seventies hairdo. "Not bad for the theme of our project."

Yeah...

"You know the best part about high school: love." Her cheeks tint to a rosy pink, all bashful and nervous, taking a stroll down memory lane of what she probably thought was everlasting love…

I get the feeling. I thought I was once…well, yeah. It was ages ago.

"I know, how cliché," she goes on, crunching up from the TMI details of her life, "but everything about it just makes sense. Love thy neighbor. Love thy self because we are fuckin' awesome! We all deserve someone."

Bianca smiles to herself...oh, nostalgia!

Until:

"But I was the one chasing him, until the day he found his balls and decided to chase me back."

I guess that's kind of cute, well for the tweens and teens.

"But calling someone else's arms home...It's the best feeling in the world, knowing that you're not or never were alone. It's true—you really do *know* when you find someone special because they were made just for you."

That was really sweet. It sticks with me, as we sit in the stillness of the café with, now, working coffee machines—there's a, "Woohoo," from the crowd.

"Man!" Bianca shakes her head and breaks off a piece of the—what should've been a bigger piece—chocolate chip cookie, "That was some Jim Morrison shit right there!"

It was.

"Who's the guy?"

She takes a moment before answering this or deciding to break focus from me, "Brandon. He dumped me after we…you know. He freaked out. Said I was too young. Like three years makes a difference. You know, no matter how much time flies by, you don't ever forget your first."

I feel my eyes draggin' themselves to the table before I even have a chance of connecting or trying to with her.

"What about you?" she asks. "Have you ever been in love?"

No. No. NO. No…?

I shake my head and my teeth find their way to the closest fingernail—

"Don't!" she couldn't it say any louder. "Bad habit. Trust me."

I believe her and obey. My hand drops and returns to its place on my lap. I watch the wheels spinning in her mind to the beat of a hamster's wheel, as a smile slowly creeps on her, "Say, we should hang out."

"Um, aren't we all ready?"

"No, I mean like *really* hang out."

And before I can ask—

# Erica

The spotlight reflects down upon Bianca, right on cue as she belts out Chromatics' "Kill for Love."
Her voice is fuckin' AWESOME! I mean…wow…who would've thought there is all this drive and passion for a song. The song has so much meaning, as I watch from the closest circular table on the dance floor. She sways side to side, getting lost in the intoxication of the lyrics:

*…Everybody's got a secret to hide/Everyone is slipping backwards…*

It is a small crowd tonight…I mean, uh, afternoon. I'd be surprised to see one more person walking in. This place that she'd dragged me into looks a hundred years old. Smelly, but beautiful. The color palette is red, pink, and purple. So beautiful and fresh. Young. Youthful.

*But I killed for love…*

I can resonate so much with the meaning of her lyrics. Well, her side to the lyrics of this song, especially how much into the performance that Bianca is. There is something so meaningful, sad, and survival about it…

"Aye! You again."

It makes me flinch. He makes me shake.

Alex approaches me, stopping at my side. He looks so different, dressed in, what is probably one of his many favorite band T-shirts that sticks out from underneath his flannel. He removes his earphones and stuffs them into his backpack, which he loops around. For some reason, his gaze never goes to Bianca.

He gives a tug at his backpack straps as well.

I do a double-take on him, as we both overhear the microphone about ten octaves LOUDER, "Alex!"

We both look at Bianca. Ah…they know each other, especially once she smiles and throws up her arms into a mixture of martial arts and gang signs.

"Wad up, homeboy!"

It must be their *not*-so-secret handshake, in "spirit fingers" considering that she never leaves the platform in her white platforms.

"I thought you were working!" she says even louder into the microphone, which sends the ringing hum of feedback throughout the room.

That awakens a passed-out drunk at the bar and rises a few heads as they turn away from their engagements and towards the platform, where this young spinning image of Janis Joplin carries no shame in the game; even when she takes a misstep but catches her balance.

"Not til' later!" Alex responds, as his fingers loosen around his backpack straps.

*Ba-da-da-da-da* the beat of the song repeats, giving Bianca just the perfect amount of time to chime back in, "Good! I see you two have already met…"

*Jesus.*

If I could, I *would* smack my face with my palm. My sight never leaves Bianca, who smiles as she raises the microphone back up—probably tipsy—as she resumes her singing.

*But I killed for love...*

I see how close his arm is to me against the table. It electroshocks my nerves. Automatically, I sit up straighter. That's when I catch him taking pictures of the show with his cell phone.

Photography…

The memories...

The song ends and Bianca is already receiving a few rounds of applause from the audience, including some, "Yays! Honey!" or my favorite, "Get it, girl! Suck that dick!"

Bianca curtseys, all into it, shooting me a smile. It makes me feel warmer and slows down my breathing. I have the feeling of my fingers unfastening from the top of my jeans.

---

The strumming of the guitar jams throughout the overheard speakers in the lounge area. I shift around, bumping my knee against the table. But it is out of sight. Well, out of his sight. Alex sits across from me. He gives one of those smiles where it's half up and half down.

Thankfully, the *clinks* and *clanks* and pool table sounds keep us preoccupied with addressing the big ass elephant in the room. So, I decide to give this a shot and open my mouth—

"Fellows!" the next drunk karaoke singer ascends the steps to the stage, well it is more of a platform, considering that Bianca made it look smaller and less clunky-sounding because of her high white platforms…

Speaking of—I hear their two-step rhythm approaching.

"What's up bitches!" she hollers a few times and practically scoots Alex over, so he is sitting closer…to me.

Shit.

Immediately, I grab hold of my small purse and shift it over to my other side. I don't know why though…it's not like I think Alex will steal anything. How come I do stupid shit like this?

*Killin' in the name of!*

*Ba-da-ba-da…*

"Ciao!" Bianca gives another holler over her shoulder. She turns around, her back towards the stage in our circular booth. "Gawd! I just love Rage Against the Machine." Bianca snaps her fingers, and the nearest waiter stops by.

"Wad up, *homegirl*!" he mocks, getting a laugh from Bianca and a smile from me. "Let me guess…cranberry."

"Hell no! Let's go with a cucumber cocktail."

"You got it." He turns towards us. Alex declines and raises his glass of water. I just politely shake my head.

Damn, that karaoke singer is rockin' out, lifting, and double kickin' his leg out and grabbing a hold of the microphone stand like Steven Tyler from Aerosmith. Well, most of those dudes did that. Mick Jagger still does that at his shows, from what I hear.

Bianca immediately gets the convo moving, "So, Alex!" It makes him snap out of whatever daze forced his attention down to the table.

"Erica, here, is a photographer."

Shit…

"A Polaroid photographer," she adds on, right on time, too because the waiter returns with her cucumber cocktail, which looks good—a cloudy kiwi-green.

I'm still the center of attention. At least, it feels like that, due to the sweat that forms around the circumference of my face and the tip of my back. *Fuck…*just breathe, just breathe. My fingers lock around the bottom strap.

"Bianca…" is all I can say, never looking up at anyone.

"Erica here is an *amazing* photographer."

Bianca…please.

"I believe you."

I look at him. His gaze is already on me. I immediately peer away. Whoa, what the hell was that?

"Hey, Erica!"

Jesus, that makes me shake again. I clasp hold of my chest, well, the center of my purse strap, for that one.

Bianca sticks out her chest and mimes flashing her tits. "Show us your pics!"

There is an emphasis on the 'c' for the 't' sound (like "tits").

Whoa, no—

Before I can shout that aloud, I stop her from pulling my backpack purse. I politely shake my head, *No*. Bianca pouts.

"Hey there, baby girl!"

"Ricky!"

Bianca spins halfway until she bounces up from her feet and practically jumps into the arms of this burly gay man. There's no other way to put it—he has the sass and class like Beyoncé. It is not my taste in music, and, to be honest. I sort of hate that stuff.

I just see it now—Ricky has a cosmopolitan for Bianca. I'm assuming it's on the house. Well, shit, then I should try and get one, too.

"Oh, my!"

"Peach," he…or she (I don't know the proper term) chimes in. "

"You shouldn't have! But I already *got's* my cucumber." And Bianca downs the rest of it, well more like tosses it back.

I catch Alex shaking his head, biting his lip to not laugh—

Not that I was staring, or leering at him, or whatever you call it.

"You keep killin' them my little Rock star." Ricky gives each cheek a pinch; yep, including her "peach" as he calls it, a.k.a. her ass.

Bianca drinks to that, chuggin' back her now empty Cosmo. Dang girl!

Ricky eye-fucks the fuck out of Alex. I double-take on that to make certain that *my* eyesight isn't tripping. Nope…I mean, yeah, he was just checking out Alex who could just shrivel up there in the booth and die.

"And for my little prince—"

"I, uh, work in a bit," Alex says, never breaking focus from the empty glass of his water. Until he looks up at him and keeps it that way. Ricky takes the hint.

In recovery mode, Ricky turns to me, "And for—"

"What? Oh, no! I'm good."

Bianca comes between us and throws her arms over my shoulders and Ricky's bum, "She'll have what I'm having!"

It is too late to defend myself. Ricky winks back and struts on out, giving his big booty a shake. Bianca fist bumps and sort of does this giddy-up dance routine, cheering on like it is her own Magic Mike show. Magic…Mary?

"Ah," Alex finally breaks the brief silence, "a *When Harry Met Sally* reference.

Bianca gasps. "I know! I just got that."

By the smile that comes across Alex, I assume that was a hint of sarcasm from his end. I can feel Bianca's eyeballs burning a hole through me as soon as I glance over my shoulder. We are both seated. This time, my ass is on the edge. I can still smell the malt liquor from Bianca.

"Erica," she sounds so concerned, "relax. Ricky never cards us." She indicates with her finger. *Come here*. I do. And sort of in a whisper tone, "But, he does want Alex's d—"

"Jesus, Bianca."

Poor Alex, choked on that one, and now has a puddle of water to clean up. I pass over my unused napkin. He quietly tells me, "Thanks."

I feel my upper lip curling up.

"Don't bring sweet baby Jesus into this!" Bianca pounds her hand onto the table, mocking a judge. "Besides, we all know it is *da truth*—oh, damn! I love this song!"

I swear, she has the personality of a Chihuahua.

Bianca coils around, facing the stage where a very intoxicated man is painfully belting out, "Tear You Apart," by She Wants Revenge.

*...As I whisper in your ear/I want to fucking tear you apart...*

"Ciao!" Bianca gives a few more mariachi screams. "Yay! I want to fuckin' tear you apart, too!

Bianca laughs and dances around a bit in her seat, forcing the red velvet cushion to give a few squeaks and one big ass squawk. Must be old. The intense, raw smell of this place is like an old bottle of whisky lit on fire. Alex just shakes his head at her.

My eyes wander back and forth between them, piquing my curiosity even more.

I sit up and decide to give this small talk a shot, "So, how do you two know each other again?"

"We live together," Bianca keeps her attention our way and flattens her bottom down onto the cushion.

Okay…

"Oh," is all I can think of before going in for the big and obvious question. "How long have you been dating?"

In unison, their eyes shoot up at me like I'm some creature from another universe. Bianca starts laughing too loud. Alex chuckles and reaches for his cup of water, drinking—what appears to be—melted down ice.

"Oh, God no! No offense, buddy."

"None taken," he agrees with her.

"People always assume that because we've been attached at the hip since kindergarten."

"We went to the same after-school day care called, Fun Club." He rolls his eyes at that bullshit name—sounds lame.

And with a big old sarcastic gesture, Bianca sets her hand—oh, look long black sparkly acrylic fingernails—onto her hip to indicate, what I'm assuming to be, seriousness or her adult mature side. "Girls just can't control their emotions, right?"

Alex tosses a rolled-up napkin at her. Bianca tries to dodge it, but for whatever reason, she moves in the direction in which it hits her. Then, his attention goes back to, uh, me…

I peer away as if looking for the check. I can already sense him being closer, not to mention the movement of the cushion. Now, he is no more than twelve inches from me.

"So, why Polaroids for the project?"

He never diverts his attention away from me, even when Bianca chimes in: "Because they're real. Natural. Unlike a housewife's tits!"

Wow, I can't tell if she's drunk, or it's just a mixture of decompressing from a long, stressful day and her extrovert personality. The complete opposite of my awkward self. Oh, right—Alex. He is literally waiting for an answer, especially when Bianca picks up the drink menu and brings it closer to her face. She eyes me the entire time, her pupils dilate as she glimpses from me to Alex and back to me again before she decides to "take another look at the menu." Like she is going to order a third drink. Well…

"Well," I finally answer, "you can't Photoshop Polaroids."

"Which is good?"

All I can do is nod and reach for my untouched glass of water, suddenly in need of curing my rush of thirst. Underneath the table, my free hand loosens from the top of my jeans, out of their sight. Alex holds my gaze. I can feel his breathing on me, brushing my way. God, why can't he just go talk to Bianca.

Oh, no.

My pulse vibrates and shoots its vibration down my arms and to my hands, almost making me drop my cup of water. I think they notice what is going on, especially when I decide to jump up from my seat. "Actually, I gotta get going."

"What? Why?" Bianca sets down the menu. "We just got here." If she were a cat, I think her ears would be pointed downward.

"It's just a long walk from the dorm," I lie, because the GPS on my phone says that I'll be there in ten minutes. God, I hope they can't tell. Thankfully, the mix of *headbanger* music and drunk karaoke from the off-key singers drown out my thoughts.

"Wait, you live on-campus?"

Oops. Thought I told her that part. "Yeah. I do."

She is silent, thinking over something until, "Cool. So, meeting up won't be an issue, unless your roommate—"

I can tell that I am a deer in headlights. I feel the rush of blood drain from my face and into my feet. I have already said too much.

"Oh," Bianca mumbles, figuring it out. "There is no roommate. Why do you live alone?"

"Bianca..." Alex gives her a look like, *Shut up.*

"What? I'm just curious."

And she has every right to be. She's right. Why do I live alone?

# Bianca

*Few times I've been around that track/*
*So, it's not just gonna happen like that/*
*'Cause I ain't no hollaback girl/*
*I ain't no hollaback girl/*

"Can we please listen to something else?" Alex says, gently removing his side of the earpiece.

I don't care, but I'm still getting my boogie on in the streets. Alex sighs and decides to push the earpiece back in. Now I feel bad.

"Okay," I interject. "Fine."

After scrolling through a few songs, he finally looks satisfied as a smile creeps on him to one of Velvet Underground's hits.

"Leave it," he demands.

Okay…

I obey as Lou Reed's voice adds a slow-motion effect to the hustle-bustle life of New York City; Times Square, with its three-piece suit men, classy dressed women, and tourists with the cliché equipment—phones out, cameras out, and—what is that…a selfie stick?

*Jesus.*

*Sometimes I feel so happy/*
*Sometimes I feel so sad/*
*Sometimes I feel so happy/*
*But mostly you just make me mad/*
*Baby, you just make me mad/*

My feet are no longer jamming to the beat of the song. I am just one of the very FEW people on the sidewalk who matches Alex's stroll. I sneak a peek and notice that his eyes are shut. Man, he is really lost in the music. I tug at his arm when a fire hydrant pops up midway—

"Thanks," he says, now fully awake.

"Of course, buddy!"

# Alex

And then I hear through the black abyss: "No. Fuckin'. Way!"

Before my eyes open, I feel my body being hauled three or four feet. Bianca slams her hands onto the nearby glass window, pushing' her face up against it. *Ewe.*

I remove the rest of the earpiece pulling from my ear during the abrupt movement.

She gasps again; her breath creates its own halo of smog on the glass window to some vinyl music shop, my work competition. Okay, now they are *really* showing off with the Kurt Cobain theme.

"I. Need. It."

I chuckle, "Don't you already have a copy?"

"You know me. One for the wall. One for the shelf—"

"And one for you to stare up at on the ceiling. Yes, I *do* know you too well."

"Well, music just went to shit after the nineties!" She projects, turning around to face the crowd as if there was one watching. Everyone is just minding their own business.

"And to the girl who'd begged me to go see the Jonas Brothers with her."

"It was a weird time! I was sixteen and just horny."

Uh, huh…

I bust up with laughter, which embarrasses Bianca for a moment until her still posture makes me stop laughing and smiling.

"What..."

She heads out, taking my end of the earpiece with her. I have nothing else to do but follow her along the sidewalk—this time, on the side closest to the shops and dives.

"What are you doing?"

"Oh, nothing, brother-o!" "She watches me as her eyebrows furrow, until they change into a straight line." "You just look happy."

She smiles at me until she pulls a *Bring It On!* moment and gives me spirit fingers, trying to make me laugh. It doesn't work. If anything, I just feel a sense of frustration tensing up my shoulders and the back of my neck. I take a deep breath.

"Sorry," she says. "I was just commenting on how you look.

And I get that. Really, I do. But I don't know...something is just irking me right at this very moment. And not having the answer or answers is just making my palms clam up. Thankfully, she can't tell. Otherwise, Bianca would panic herself. Ever since that one time...It just freaked her out ever since she had to call the ambulance that one time while we were coming back from a morning stroll after breakfast.

"Okay!" She coils around, stopping directly in front of me. "Fine. Caught me red-handed. I'm talking about—"

"Erica. Yeah, I know."

Well, I just connected the dots. The grin on her was the last giveaway.

I start. I can hear a two-step game shuffling behind me. She eventually catches up and loops her arm through mine, resting her head against my shoulder.

Now, she is following my lead for ONCE. I still love her though. She's been here with me through thick and thin.

"You know…there's this thing called talking…"

I know. I know that…

"She doesn't have a boyfriend," she continues onward and probably onward some more after this, too.

She catches it before I do—me sighing and feeling this pressure, clenching up my insides and teeth, "How do you know that?"

"Ha!" She releases me to toss her arms up in the air. "I knew it! You L-I-K-E her. And I'm a girl. Remember, we *know* this stuff."

Now we come to a stop at the intersection of two nameless streets, but the noise has died down—very few tourists are in sight. Just the sound of taxi horns and construction work. The smell of oil roams to one side of us. The other carries a floral scent from different perfumes and colognes that combine into the air and come at us with a mixture of…everything.

"Well, here's where we part! I'll see ya later."

I hand over the rest of the earpiece to her. "Yeah, it is."

She puts her fist out. Then I do so we could do our NOT-so-secret handshake. Afterward, she practically twirls away to the opposite side of the street. Before I call out and run up to her—considering that people can't drive here EVER—she turns around, her back to me. Thank God.

"And Alexander!" she screams over her shoulder. "Who would say no to a face and body like that!"

She thrusts her hips in the middle of the street, bumping into pedestrians who walk by her. One of them seems to scuff and pick up speed, while the other just laughs and does a double-take on her. What an old perv.

Well, it beats when Bianca pinches the sides of my face like I'm an infant.

"You're too much!"

She cracks up and skips away. I remain standing at the edge of the sidewalk, watching her go, making sure that she reaches the curb. She does in seconds and gives one last look over her shoulder for a big wave, practically leaping into the air. It makes me laugh.

She disappears with the passing crowd.

---

God, it's slow tonight.

I'm ringing up the last customer, hopefully for the night—most definitely it will be. Hector is already on his phone, checking the scores for the latest game—GO METS! (His words).

There she is. The new girl—Erica. Quickly, she glances away from me as soon as we make eye contact. Huh…weird.

Before I know it, I'm circling the counter and my feet echo the bass beat of another White Stripes song…not that they need a bassist.

"It's their best one," I tell her since her fingers remain on the vinyl in her hand—VELVET UNDERGROUND & NICO'S 1967 ALBUM COVER (the one with the banana). "Except, I dig the one with Warhol's name at the bottom." I notice that my arm is practically over hers.

"Uh, yeah," That is all she says before placing the album down on the shelf in front of her. Then, she pushes the cart, moving on to the next shelf that needs to be stacked and refilled with other pieces of vinyl, CDs, and paintings.

"So, Bianca told me everything there is to know of your guys' project. Sounds interesting. Different."

She resumes work. I notice how she keeps her distance, even glances at me.

"It seems cool," I start again but this time, cautiously, "to just put all of your energy into one big project, rather than getting distracted with smaller ones in-between. Bianca's real pumped up about it. Bet you are too."

She is still for a moment, eyeing something on the bookshelf before she fully looks at me to say, "I gotta put this..."

She sets the vinyl on the shelf adjacent to my waist. Briefly, we make eye contact, until a familiar SONG starts playing. Holy…it's—

"Reed!"

But she already knows that.

"Yeah, I took some music classes at Columbia. Reed became my hero."

She is back in the zone again—I'm not sure if she is purposely ignoring me or just…stuck in thoughts.

"There you are!" Janet comes storming my way; guess, you could say that she's cockblocking me. "We have a new P.O.S. associate. Show Stacey the ropes."

That last part was all for me. I glance over my shoulder to see a blonde chick, who looks no more than sixteen, lingering in front of the counter. Jesus, Hector…he's already checking out the poor girl's ass and she's unaware. Please, don't turn around Underage Girl. Man…Hector.

"Right away, ma'am."

Before I depart, I glance from Erica to the new vinyl records in her hand and back at her. She's already looking my way, like, the expansion of her pupils gave a heads up that she saw something interesting…that caused me to notice the Polaroid theme. For whatever reason, I give her a quick smile and head out. I never quite know if she returns the smile. But she probably does see when Stacey perks up, grinning practically as soon as I inch closer to the newbie.

# Erica

"So…"

Yes…

"Alex, huh?"

She literally does the whole 'wink, wink, elbow, elbow,' while her smile is spread back into a grin like Jack Nicholson from *Batman*. Aww…Heath…

"What about him?" I ask, avoiding eye contact with her on purpose.

I shiver because this quick adrenaline rush throbs throughout my body, starting at the center of my chest and giving an eagle wing spread like petals to a rose. It reminds me of *American Beauty* in a way, that scene where Angela is all leg spread on the ceiling above Lester, watching him like some angel.

"Oh, nothing," she says with that long roll, giving each vowel an extra twist of its salty, spicy flavor. "Just thought you two hit it off a bit."

We wait in line, more like lingering like everyone else. There are one…two…five people in front of Bianca and I before it is our turn to speak with Mrs. Newman, who is at her usual spot, leaning against the podium.

Not to sound mean, but I am kind of curious how sturdy those things are since Mrs. Newman is, well, not quite on the skinny side.

But who am I kidding…neither am I.

"The guy digs you. You know that, right?"

*Uh…what?*

I give her my undivided attention.

"God, he's going to kill me for telling you that."

That's all she has time for because it is our turn to speak with Mrs. Newman, who types everything into a file. "Hey!" Her eyes move fast, bouncing from us and back to the computer screen in front of her. There is only one click before she seems to find us. "Aha! Erica and Bianca."

"That's us," Bianca speaks on our behalf.

"So, what do you got?"

And silence…

Mainly because I refuse to look at either one of them for too long. Bianca takes the hint, again. She speaks up for me, "High school."

"And the college life too?"

The stillness paves its way back to us and it's because of ME …

By the time my eyes return upward—Newman's level—she is already blinking at me with those oval-shaped pupils.

I peer at Bianca and for the first time, she looks scared, anxious, just wanting me to say something—

FUCK. How long have I been staring right back at them in this cold-hearted silence?

"Uh, no," I couldn't blurt any louder and sloppier—I swear, some of my spit just smacked Newman on the nose. She squints and slowly rubs it while I just ramble on and on. Jesus, Erica... "It just might feel crammed, if we do both high school and college."

Newman has her chin resting atop her fingers. Her eyes linger off to the side; up toward the ceiling, lost in quick deep thoughts "Oh-KAY. So, Bianca"—and finally the attention veers back to Bianca, thank GOD—"You'll be writing about Erica's work on high school. Erica, what are you using?"

Damn it! Why, WHY is she facing me again? I mean, I know *why* but...Bianca is more of the speaker.

"Polaroids."

"Because Photoshop is only used for the Bravo housewives with the big tits." And she clutches hold of my forearm. "Sorry! Habit for jokes."

It makes me chuckle because this look of terror won't leave her face. She didn't offend me or anything.

"Anyhoo," Mrs. Newman chimes in, forcing Bianca and I to break eye contact and our complete attention returns to her. "That rules out my next question about editing and Photoshop. Great!"

Oh, GOOD. She clicks something. I hear the mouse give that soft click as her hand maneuvers the cursor on the small computer screen. For some reason, I'm relieved that the bigger screen, the one that my classmates and I take notes from, is turned off. I don't know...something about my name being up on there just makes me cringe. Shit, I'm probably wincing already.

Shit.

"My only question…"
Uh, oh.

"…is if you own a Polaroid camera, Erica?"

Uh…

"Oh, yeah," Bianca's tone jumps a pitch higher, "how come I haven't seen it yet!"

With Newman and Bianca both staring at me for an answer, I feel a tingle reddening up my cheeks.

---

The sun crisps its way through the nearby window at the end of the hallway. My neighbors continue on with their lives, whatever it is that keeps them holed up in their dorms, in the shared bathroom, or with each other. Some cute blonde giggles and runs by, nearly colliding with Bianca, who could just kick her ass with that glare she shoots at her like—

"HEY! You almost knocked me over."

"Sorry!" the girl shouts back, still giggling as the boy chases her until the door shuts on their way out—into the bedroom.

Finally, the door to my dorm unclicks. Before I push the door open, I look at her, "It's a bit messy."

I can tell that she doesn't give a shit, but I do. I really do.

"Oh," she practically sings aloud and flags her hand up in the air like that "Single Ladies" dance thing that Beyoncé does.

"Nothing can be messier than mine. Oh, come on!"

Bianca lets herself in. I have no choice but to follow her…

# Bianca

Man! I don't know where to even start. There is no shame in telling her either—

"Looks like Picasso threw up on your walls."

I know she is thinking the same because she does not attempt a snarky comment or even a quick eye-roll like, "Fuck you, cunt!"

Oh, damn...I haven't thought of that word in like, ever. It's fun to say—cunt, cunt, CUNT.

Erica shuts the door, her back to me as I roam around...

# Erica

I close my eyes, *breathing—*

"Whoa!" her voice echoes through the deep, deep abyss that I slip into. "Now, this is a pretty cool-looking box. Shall we see what's inside?"

I twirl around and see that she is already at my desk holding the Polaroid box. Bianca is about to open the box and I flock approximately two to three feet to stop here. "No! I got it—"

"Whoa! Now that is creepy as *fauck*!"

She is like a cat who sees a shiny inanimate object or a red dot of a laser pointer, frolicking away from the desk and off to the nearby picture that has hologram heads in jars. At least, she gave me back my camera. Shit, that scared me—the thought of her using it first. For now, I'll just hold onto it, fastening my fingers around it.

"And who be dis from?"

Oh, she's asking me that. Her finger rests a centimeter or two away from the head jar picture. I know she'll keep it there until I give her an answer.

"Tony Oursler," I say and remain in place.

Bianca's gaze lingers back to the picture. She gives it one final review of the eyes and bobs her head, impressed A LOT. Then, she scoots off to the picture beside it. All she needs to do is point to it and I know what she is asking, "What is this?"

It's an eerie still live portrait. A horizontal one.

"Gregory Crewdson."

"It's intense."

"But inspiring."

"How so?"

I just assume that her look is an approval to go on. "Just makes you wonder what went on in the photographer's mind while taking that picture. You can even feel it, just by looking at it."

I find myself trapped in this hypnotism because of this still life of a woman standing in the middle of the road, making you wonder and ponder what it is that she is waiting for. Whom she is waiting for…

"Why so serious," Bianca's gurgles close in my ear. I'm surprised it doesn't scare me to death. It does snap me out of it and back to reality. My fingers loosen around the box, no longer gripping onto it for dear life—my own sacred treasure.

My eyes start stinging. I think she can sense it because I beat her to the punch. "We should probably get started."

"I'll never know either because I refuse to make any eye contact with her."

"Camera time!"

Bianca does the MC Hammer move. I can't help but laugh and suddenly, I find my fingers popping open the lid to the camera box. Out comes the most beautiful and perfect camera. It is a lot to take in, that fresh car scent, to the heavy, yet, silky texture of the object. Like hips on a small body frame.

"Is it planning to speak or something?"

*Jesus...*

She needs to not do that again. That one made the hairs stand up on my arms. I decide to click the button on the right side of the camera—my right and Bianca's left. **Click** and out prints my first brand new Polaroid.

Just...wow.

That was it. A moment marked down in the history of my life. I smile because it is good to be back.

We finally look at each other. She smiles and mine grows wider.

---

The next thing I notice is the rush of time that follows—it is our own time-lapse as we sit, stand, and sit again going through the Polaroids, piling up my desk with them; new Polaroids with new items and new faces. All brand new.

I find the speed of time slowing down as soon as my fingers take hold of the last Polaroid, studying the sun between the clouds...

My interpretation of Heaven. I smile to myself. I'm ready for tomorrow.

# OCTOBER

# Erica

Next to the open Projects box on the floor are decks and decks of POLAROIDS. My work. My first true love…

The great outdoors; close-ups of items and locations; the sun, the clouds, and the sky; and a school portrait of myself from—I think—from the second grade. I'm only assuming I was that young because of the ribbon-tied pigtails, a.k.a. the days when my mother used to dress me.

Bianca's humming some tune—I can't quite put my finger on it, but it sounds familiar A LOT—brings me back to the here and now as Mansell would put it. We are sitting on the floor because of the more spacious room for our work. Wow…our work…It's still new to me to say or even acknowledge myself. Bianca looks up from her composition book. I immediately look back down to the floor, moving around a Polaroid or two, like pieces to a puzzle.

"Well," she couldn't shout any louder with a loud slap—I see that she has closed her composition book. "I'm thirsty!

Bianca packs up. Now, she has my undivided attention. "Um, what are you doing?"

"Leaving, and so are you."

Uh…

My hands leave the Polaroids that are sitting on my lap. Now, I really can't break focus from her. "But we have a lot of work to do—"

"Work?!" She is already on her feet with her hands on her hips. "You see this as work?

I mean, well, yeah…I mean, no in terms of work. I don't know. I don't know.

"Look," she then starts on a tangent, "we got a lot done today, just like yesterday, and the day before that. We can use a break."

Okay...

Suddenly, she gasps which yanks me out of my train of thought. "We should go get some cosmos!"

That small twitch of the eyes and jaw lowering to open reminds me of Rob Schneider from *The Hot Chick* after his body switch with the Queen-Bee, Jessica. Spoiler alert.

"Look, I appreciate the invite to..." Shit, this is it. The moment of truth. Finally, I allow myself to breathe, exhaling out the gust of air that was clogging up my lungs. "Look…I don't party."

Doing that must've unclogged my sinus too since I catch a whiff of her bold perfume. What is that…Chanel? No, wait! I got it. It's Estee Lauder's "Beautiful." I only know this because it's something that my mom wears…

Mom. Dad.

I should respond to their calls and texts. Speaking of—my phone gives that notification ding. I check and see that it is none other than my mom…

Mom.

"EWE!" Bianca's high-pitched tone drags me back to the here and now. "Party? Who says anything about parties? I HATE parties."

Wow, she looks pissed off. Weird, she did a complete one-eighty with that last comment of mine. Shit…I hope I didn't offend or piss her off. Fuck. Fuck. FUCK.

I would do this. I always do this—

"It just gets old," she finally speaks. "You know, waking up and feeling like shit all of the time. Then, for whatever reason, doing the same shit all over again. It's not for me like it used to be."

Okay, now she did another one-eighty. She looks…upset, not the kind where she is about to cry, or, scream, or anything but a look of regret. Like she had fucked up a friendship or some other important relationship.

I'm all ears because she hasn't exactly stopped pacing around the room, which is making me feel on edge. My fingers are tingly and so are the bottoms of my feet, forcing me to stand up to meet her eye-to-eye. We are on the same page because we should be.

"What can I say, I like karaoke and sometimes a drink boosts my confidence to get up on stage."

Oh.

"I, uh," it's all I can say. "I work, uh, later though—"

"I know." And trust me, she DOES. "Alex told me."

Alex…

Did he really?

# Bianca

"Ciao! YEAH! SING IT SOUL SISTAH FROM ANOTHER MISTAH!" I scream from my chair, my ass is going up and down— sitting and then standing, and then sitting again.

The group of drag queens cheer on their depressed soul sistah from another mistah, who just sings her little heart out to Rage Against the Machine's "Killing in the Name."

*"...Fuck you/I won't do what you tell me/Motherfucker! Yeah!"*

My lips curl around the edge of my glass, sipping the rest of my green cosmopolitan. Damn! That is sweet as fuck—green apple, only it is called "The Apple of My Eye." I can already sense the inevitable as soon as I spy with my little eye…

Erica has yet to drink her blue cosmopolitan. I mean, yeah, I did order it for her—Jolly Rancher. But she has also yet to touch it. Shit, probably has yet to smell it, either.

Ooo! Here's the best part of the song:

*Fuck you/*
*I won't do what you tell me/*

"I should really go," she shouts over the music.

"Oh, come on! A break doesn't kill ya. Yah know?"

I can sense it and then see it— Erica is still unconvinced. I set my drink back down onto the table and scoot in closer, accidentally bumping my knees into the bottom of the table. "Have you ever crammed in a last-minute paper or study session?"

She is watching me, but she blinks a few times before responding, "Yeah."

"See, now that's last minute! We're ahead of the ball game, right now. We already have a theme, and you got the Polaroids. I think we're off to a great start! Most groups won't even start their projects until the last minute, hun...Oh, my God. Did I just call you hun, like Paige from "*Degrassi*?"

Oh, man I sure did! HA! That's super funny and lame at the same time. But for whatever reason, Erica doesn't seem to get that. I perk up because I can just see the imaginary lightbulb going off above my head. I act quickly and reach for my red pleather bag—it's so shiny. I pull out the composition book from one of the two pockets and immediately jot something down.

"Ideas just pour out for you, don't they," she says. By the time I look up at her, she is already peering away…almost in guilt…

She bites her thumbnail.

"I'm journaling. Believe it or not."

# Erica

"I find myself staring at the journal dates." It piques my interest just as Bianca stops writing. Her gaze shifts from side to side, in deep thoughts. When she finally builds the courage and stares me dead in the eyes, I catch myself inhaling, which straightens up my body.

"Remember my appointment three days ago?"

*Yeah, yeah, I do. I remember that…*

"Well," she says with the tick of her tongue, "it was with a therapist. Dr. Zimmer."

Wait, what?

I sit up straighter than a number two pencil.

I remember that name… Zimmer… Zimmer… Mansell… Mansell…

# Bianca

Wow...

I just said that. And I keep going without a stop. "I know that's a lot to say aloud, but I just wanted to be honest with you. I know people aren't supposed to flash the, 'I go to therapy,' card but, it's been helping with *this.* A lot."

*This* as in the writing.

I feel a strong scratch burning its way up into my nostrils, hitting the flight of my nasals. *Fauck*…it hurts. When I finally meet Erica's sight and really look at her...like really look at her…Something in Erica's eyes is a giveaway. No way…

"Oh, my God!" I just blurt and her eyes slowly raise to mine. Her teeth let loose of her bottom lip. "You're a therapy baby too?!"

She stutters and I can't quite make up the words because I reach for my glass. It shuts her up. It's my cue to raise my glass. "This calls for a toast."

And she listens.

"To all of the damaged, crazies, twisted, fucked up, and, 'Dayum that girl got some issues.' Fuck the assholes who only feed off of stigmas! We are fuckin' awesome! We're extraordinary."

And far beyond ordinary.

I push my glass midway, perfectly aligned a few inches from the tabletop. Erica watches my hand and glass as if Toy Story is going to invade and set it to life. Convinced, Erica smiles and then picks up her Cosmo.

"To the extraordinary," she repeats, and we **clink** and hold our glasses together.

To the extraordinary ordinary.

# Erica

I like that…

Extraordinary ordinary.

The extraordinary ordinary.

---

Oh, man…

These are so expensive.

I keep scrolling through the Amazon page, accessing different links, and then circling back to option one and then two, and now…three.

Polaroids.

Why…Why, must you be so expensive?

There's a mini ***SWOOSH*** as I push through the magenta beaded curtains, officially entering the shop. Back to work. Happy student, happy…

Yeah, I got nothing. Work is a drag lately, BUT it does pay for things such as the Polaroids. I hit 'checkout' through my Amazon account—THERE, done!

The new stack of Polaroids will be here in two days. Thank you, Amazon Prime!

I feel my chest rise an inch or so, letting out a sigh. Relief overcomes me because my shoulders descend further away from my earlobes. By the time I reach the main floor, I slide my phone into my back pocket. I see Alex from the corner of my eye. He is already looking at me until that is—

"Hey, Alex!"

I only see Stacey frolicking his way. I reach the cart that is piled up with CDs and I think a few vinyl's…Jesus, whoever put this together is going to get me in trouble. Janet hates when they're not separated…the CDs, DVDs, and vinyls.

I can still overhear them, "Well," Stacey's voice goes up ten octaves higher, "I'm ready to learn."

"Yeah…yeah, I bet you are," I hear him say.

I can sense his eyes on me, and, for whatever reason, I want to double-check—NO.

Shit...He sees me, and I see him. We just hold contact for a moment. He gives a crooked smile. Okay, Alex...get to work now. Just show Stacey the ropes of the POS system.

"Erica?"

Janet comes walking my way. I try to look busier and randomly put a CD next to a vinyl. Shit—FUCK! Ugh, I hope she doesn't go all anal on that. I mean, yeah…

"Tom called in sick," she continues. "You free this weekend?

For whatever reason, my eyes scroll slightly to the right of Janet, and I spy with my little eye: Alex's gaze finds mine. Lingering…

"Earth to Erica."

Shit.

"Sorry, Janet. Um, yeah, I'm available."

Alex smiles before resuming work. I know he heard that. And I don't stop looking at him.

# Alex

*The night is young,* as the expression goes, something my grandparents, the old-timers, would say. People are out to eat, getting drinks, and mingling.

And there she is…

Standing at the edge of the sidewalk, double taking on the speeding taxies. She goes through something on her phone, so secretive as soon as I catch up with her from the shop. "Hey!"

Immediately, she puts her phone away, spinning around to look at me. I notice that her eyes flicker from wide to wider, eyeing me to the skateboard that I pop upward so I can be on ground level with her. I remove my earbuds.

She seems nervous. "Hey..."

Her tone is quieter too because of the car honks and random civilians calling each other assholes, dick, and even the c-word in one scenario…What a dick, whoever that person was.

"So," I try my best to sound chipper, "Where you off to?"

"Home. Why?"

"I just wanna know where I'm walking you."

A smile breaks across her face. But she hides it, shrinking its size by biting her lip. She glances away. I think I had embarrassed her. Shit…

"Don't you have to get home," she speaks, breaking my brief zoning out.

"Ouch! Trying to get rid of me that quick, huh?"

"I wasn't." And off that side glance, she leaves in the opposite direction.

I follow, walking and holding my skateboard. "Hold up."

"I just assume that a guy like you has places to go."

Whoa. Was that a *diss?*

"A guy like me?" It's all I can think of. "What does that even mean? Believe it or not, I pick and choose who's a part of my life. Only the special ones make it in."

We stop at the corner of another sidewalk, as she turns to look at me. I half-circle around and, finally, meet her in front. Now, we are eye to eye. Well, if I stood a bit lower, which I do. It makes her laugh for a moment. She does that thing again with her bottom lip, biting it to prevent herself from smiling or busting up furthermore.

I wonder why…

"I really don't get you."

She makes a face. "What's to get?"

"Your hot and cold vibe. It's like you want to talk to me, but something is holding you back."

That takes her by surprise because she now sounds slightly defensive. "So, now you just know my life story—"

"I'm trying to."

There's a brief silence between us as I stare back at her, and she stares back at me. We hold this intense look as if she is trying to read me; figure me out at this moment. Even with the speeding cars and other chaos of the New Yorker life, the overcrowded and oversized pedestrians zooming by, and unwanted smoke that blows into our faces, it is still an intimate moment for us. Well, for me it is…

---

She walks. I skate at her pace. She steals another side glance at me as soon as I ask, "...Warhol the Artist or Warhol the Music Producer? Just curious."

"Someone's been studying." Ah-ha, she's impressed.

"When it's important."

This time, that side smirk remains. She shakes her head, chuckling.

"What?"

"Nothing. Nothing." And she notices that my eyes are not on the road. "Are you sure you're not going to fall off?"

"Expert here! Been riding since I was a kid."

"Uh, huh."

A challenge, eh?

I pick up a few miles and do one of my most famous tricks—okay, so I stole it from a Tony Hawk game when PlayStation was a bigger hit. Well, maybe it still is. I don't know. Just as long as it gets her attention and I keep it by the time I stop to turn around…

She is smiling and shaking her head at me. I knew it! She's impressed. I puff out my chest and bow.

"Oh, God!" she busts up and covers her mouth from doing so, but it's impossible. Her teeth keep flashing. They're really white…

"Well," she says. "This is, uh, me."

She gestures as we come to a stop at the front of a building. My eyes scope upward. I see that we are already at NYU. Man, this building is fuckin' tall! It just goes up and up. A lot of people are here. Some of them even squeeze on by us, parting us further away for a brief second or two…

A lot of dorm rooms. A lot of…beds…

"Ah, already? We were just getting started. And you still haven't answered my question." I jump off my board and tilt it upward so it's touching the interior of one of my hands. I take a step forward. She does not move.

"Oh. *That*."

"Yeah, *that*."

I wait. She is already zoning off in thoughts.

"Well," she finally breaks the ice between us, "both inspire me."

"You CAN'T pick both, you know."

"Oh, you can, too! Besides, Warhol never fails as an artist or as a music producer."

She just smiles. And so do I.

"Well," I finally say; my cue was the car honk from a taxi driver, "it was fun hanging out with you. Goodnight, Erica."

I give her one last look—not the creepy, checking her body out kind—for something. Anything.

She breaks focus and stares off into the hollow world of traffic, impatient drivers, and students. Most of them pass by, inconvenienced by their last-minute paper to finish, or study group to catch up with, so they can ace that bullshit exam. Man…for sure, that is something that I don't miss.

"Goodnight, Alex." And she turns on her heel, leaving me stranded with nothing but a skateboard in my hand. I smile and she catches it over her shoulder. She returns the favor.

# Erica

"Hello? Erica?" my mom's voice echoes in the background, in perfect unison with the oven timer that goes off in the background.

"Hi, Mom." The stress sends me over the edge because it feels like I am swallowing a pill that is ten times larger than its size. The pill squeezes through my esophagus. If only I were taking a pill, to begin with.

*Breathe, Erica. Just relax…*

"Hi, sweetie," Dad shouts over the commotion.

"Hi, Dad. Yes, Mom," I grit through my teeth, "I'm here. Still here."

I'm still in my work uniform, making a poor man's attempt to try and shuffle my way out of it. Mom…She just keeps talking and talking…

I spy the new Polaroids from the corner of my eye. The two short piles sit on top of my bed. *Randoms*. No sign of people. No sign of Bianca…and Alex.

"…I just wanted to check in dear," Mom goes on.

*Dear?*

"Cathy." I hear Dad say in the back, an attempt to have my back. Only he backs down. The irony.

"Well, it just seems like we haven't talked in a while."

*Great! So, now it's not my fault. Figures.*

"I've just been busy," I can feel the twinge of anger flare-up. "You know. A thing called school."

*Like she'd ever get it, considering that her Ms. Teen Pageant days were her ending peak years.*

There's a clanking sound on her end, which stirs my attention. Before I can say anything, shit let alone fuckin' breathe, she beats me to the punch, "Busy…Are you getting sleep?"

*Oh, man.*

"Yes, Mom. Yes. I'm getting sleep—"

"Well, that's new," she snaps. The NERVE.

I run the back of my palm across my forehead, which is already clammed up from…her. "Why would you even ask me?"

"Cathy, give me the phone," Dad says, but I cut him short.

"You know what, I have to go."

"Why the rush?" Mom interjects, probably grabbing a hold of the phone back from Dad. Poor Dad. *How the hell does he put up with her bullshit?*

"I have some homework to do, Mom! So, I'd appreciate it if we just end our conversation here—"

"And you didn't finish that earlier?"

That's it.

Man, I don't feel so hot now. I force myself to sit at the edge of my bed until my body just falls back. Eye to eye with the ceiling, as Mom and Dad's brief—not so silent conversation about me—plays over as I just lie there in complete silence.

"Cathy, come on."

"You know," Mom starts up, "I'm not too happy with this whole part-time job either. I don't want you to overexert yourself. School *is* your job."

"A lot of kids work Mom because most of us WANT to." I lean up to my elbows but then, it just hits me.

Tension.

The headache starts in the middle of my forehead, just above my sinus. It doesn't hurt *per se* but just gets tighter and tighter like a rubber band being rewrapped over and over again around someone's wrists. My freehand—the one that is not pressing the phone to my ear, practically losing balance from the shakiness of my arm—decides to curl up into a fist.

Don't speak. Don't speak. PLEASE.

"Is money an issue?" Mom disrupts my silence. "Do you need more? We'll wire some more over—"

"NO! I don't want any money. I didn't ask for it. So don't go down that route and pretend that sending me over more money is going to solve anything. It WON'T."

*Fauck.* That felt great to say. I'm even panting. It takes a second or two until I'm able to catch my breath. I feel the corner of my lip curl up.

But it is only for a moment. Too short of a moment. Mom just knows how to get the final say…like always…

"Rob, get the checkbook."

"Cathy—"

"Mom…"

"Robert, the checkbook!"

"Jesus!" He could give up but refuses to do so. But not for me…for her. For her…like always.

I wince as soon as that weird RINGING makes its way back, stifling its way through my eardrums and circling back in and out like one of those spinning theme park rides—the ones where everyone typically pukes. I feel that way. I run my hand across my face, swiping up the dots of beaded sweat from my hot skin. Weird, I have no fever but I, suddenly, feel exhausted like I'm about to be…sick.

I rest a hand against my chest, just an inch or so above my breasts, trying to breathe. Inhale. Exhale. Inhale. Exhale.

And soon, my mom's voice is completely FADING OUT as the RINGING continues and progresses, forcing me to become paralyzed in place as a speeding car, followed by a few car honks—taxis, I presume—and cursing and snarling echo back to me from the world outside of my tomb.

# Bianca

"Yo, what's wrong home skillet from another millet?"

Erica looks up from her the mounds of Polaroids displayed on the desk, spread out in stacks of twos and threes. Some of the Polaroids are upside down with a number handwritten in Sharpie on the back; all in numerical order. Pretty pictures. Rad for the class…

Oh, shit.

I *was* speaking too loud. The Regina George of the class and her sticks of plastics eyeball our way with one of those 'looks.' It makes Erica look away and she quietly resumes work. Those bitches—HA! What a total Janis Ian moment.

Newman glances away from her computer in front of the class to scout Chatty Cathy. I clear my throat to cover up my tracks, but I do get some saliva going down the wrong pipe which, then, forces me to give a legitimate cough to prevent further suffocation. The plastics in the class individually turn their heads away from me with a dirty look; the blonde, and brown, and blonde, and brown hair doesn't make them appear innocent. They could belong to a cult with their similarities from their pastel-colored outfits and flat-ironed hair.

*What bitches.*

I hear Erica sigh and it whips around my attention to her. She is no longer holding the Polaroids. She has stopped working. Only the hum and some shuffling and low-tone discussions in the other groups are what keep a complete standstill of silence between us—Erica, and I.

I can tell that Erica's mind is elsewhere. I notice underneath the table that she is sliding her palms back and forth on her jeans...

"Do you need any help?" I finally ask, pulling my laptop screen down; it is an official break from typing.

"No, I'm fine. Just, uh, thinking."

Yeah, too much, girlie!

I spy with my little eye—the camera between our desks. I reach for it. She straightens up in her chair. Just as she is about to speak, I figure out the flash and turn it off, snapping a picture of Erica. Shit, it was louder than I'd expected. Damn, this version is no joke with it being refurbished to the original Polaroid cameras, a.k.a. the vintage kind from the seventies.

"Now, I think we've solved our little problem." I watch as the Polaroid develops, the corners sticking to its tan-brown crisp like the Polaroids from the seventies— the parents' days. Erica takes the Polaroid from me just as the outline of her body starts to get color. I'm a bit surprised, especially when Erica rips up the picture.

"I don't like having my picture taken," she tells me and only me.

I can see how it affects her, but I give a small laugh, trying to make a joke out of it. Hopefully. "Well, who does? No one likes to have their picture taken. Unless you're in porn."

I reach for the camera, and she jerks back, almost like I was about to hit her…

We hold contact for a second. She is the first to break focus as if…embarrassed. Cautiously, I move in and bring the Polaroid up for aim. Erica is still refusing to look up and pose, or smile or, something. So, I practically sit on her lap to snap a selfie with Erica.

"Oh, come on now. Put a smile on."

And she does! VICTORRRRRRRYYYYYYYYYY.

I snap a selfie of us and quickly retreat to my chair as soon as Newman eyes us. "Really girls," she says.

"Sorry," I mouth back, although I doubt, she can read that far. Not that she's stupid…

Anyway, I examine the Polaroid and eagerly watch as the color starts fading to life. Ewep! This is so cool.

"I probably look like shit," Erica chimes in, giving one of her long sleeves a tug. Man…what is up with her today?

"No. You *don't*." I even show her the Polaroid for proof. "Damn, don't we look fuckin' happy. Just like friends. I say you make a pretty darn beautiful subject—"

"You're just saying that."

She really has no idea. I turn towards her, lowering the Polaroid to the desk. "Erica, a lot of guys look at you as you pass by. Like a lot of dudes. I mean, they're probably looking at your ass or tits—"

"Yeah, right," she says all bashfully, her cheeks turning pink.

"It's true. You might want to pay some more attention next time."

And she doesn't say anything further, but she has also yet to check around and notice the blondie in the back corner who's checking her out. Even from afar…

The guy stands little to zero chance. Even someone like Alex, who's up close…little to zero chance. She sure is a hard one to crack.

# Erica

*Say a word for Jimmy Brown/*
*He ain't got nothing at all/*

Ah, Reed. The blood gets pumping into my ears. Well, Reed is singing over the intercom. As chill as Janet is, she still doesn't allow headsets or headphones on the floor during store hours. Thankfully, she has great taste in music.

I set one of the many mixed, out of alphabetical order, vinyls onto the shelf in front of me.

My back is toward the counter, where Hector yells, "Next," every other minute.

It is a packed crowd today. Usually, it is not *this* busy. But I guess it is, considering the one-hundred and something degrees outside in this fall weather.

Well, I guess September is still considered 'summer' like California. Back home…

The heaviness refuses to escape my shoulders which stand taller, uneven like a magician's trick gone wrong. Jesus…Polaroids seem to skyrocket to the moon and beyond. Never back. Fuckin' thirty bucks flat for a box of eight…EIGHT. Not eighty.

Shit, I can taste the lukewarm salvia that builds its way up to the back of my throat. Or maybe, it is working its way back down. Double shit! I don't know. I switch back and forth between the Amazon Impossible Polaroids package link to my checking…

Double SHIT.

Fuck me. Why the hell did I go overboard with the new posters and pictures for my dorm—

*And this is what he said/*
*Oh, sweet nuthin'/*

*Breathe, Erica. Jesus Christ. Get to work before anyone notices.*

And I do. Well, I think it looks like work as I push the supply cart to the end of the shelf and start restocking again. What the hell…Why did someone knock down the CDs…

You know what, whatever. I'll just scope it up. One by one.

*She ain't got nothing at all/*

Yea, yeah. I get it LOU.

I ain't got nothing at all with these Polaroids.

---

I take a breather, forcing myself to lean against the sun brick wall behind me. It's hot. Too hot. But I needed to get out of the shop for today's lunch break. Even though I forgot my lunch.

Shit, where is my mind these days?

My eyes never leave my phone. Mainly because I don't want anyone coming up to me. Beside…I've been having those thoughts again. The kind that just sort of has…I don't know. It is hard to explain. All I know is the nervousness…it triggers for me.

I inhale deeply again through my mouth so no one can hear me; just so I won't make it obvious. That's the worse—drawing unwanted attention. I already have enough stressors going on, including the fact that both of my pointer fingers and thumbs shake as I scroll through my text messages with Dr. Mansell.

Our last text exchange was the morning I had arrived in New York, thanking her for her farewell and blessings. A blessing for my new life…

"Hey, Alex!"

Slowly, my eyes ascend. I see Stacey practically bounce up from the bench, across from 'Tom and Jerry' (I forget who is who), as Alex steps out of the shop. He barely makes it to the bottom of the three-step staircase that leads up to the shop, before Stacey goes frolicking over to him…

Tom and Jerry talk some smack. One of them—the taller one with the curly hair—gives a whistle which makes Stacey blush. Or I'm assuming it does because she gives them one of those, "STAUPPPPP," looks. Jesus, how long have I been staring?

"You like totally saved my life back there," I can still hear her saying; probably twirling her hair too. "When that douchebag was just yelling at me because I couldn't get the register to open...crazy, right? God, I must've looked dumb."

Oh, God kid…you might as well get on all fours with your legs spread wide open for the butter.

I dab at the corners of my forehead, since I refuse to step into the shadows, because I would have to cross the small lot of cement, placing me in everyone—including Alex's—sight.

Yeah, I'm good.

"No," he says to her, sort of stuttering and hesitant. "You didn't."

I ram the second earbud into my ear, turning up the volume on my phone for "Goodbye Horses," the version from *Silence of the Lambs*. But I can't get to the first:

*Goodbye horses.*

The next thing I notice is a silhouette standing in front of me. My gaze tracks them up, going from the shadow of two feet to the black high- top converse, black pants...thighs—

"Hey." Alex leans against the wall with me, pressing his back into the direct sunlight and scolding red bricks. He winces for a second and has to take a step back from the bricks. I try to not smile but he returns one to me…

"Well," we both overhear Stacey, but only I look over Alex's shoulder and see her straight across. She's already reaching for the handle of the door. "I'll see you back inside!"

Alex waves over his shoulder as Stacey leaves. Poor girl, she has ZERO idea. I remove my earbud just as Alex tilts his head closer to tell me, "Is she gone?"

I double-check to make sure. "Yeah."

Alex gives a long sigh and rests his head back. Dang, guess he doesn't like her. I mean, why else would he be asking me if the coast is clear. Why else would he be over here…with me? Wait, why not her—

"She's a cute girl," it just rolls off my tongue. *Jesus, what the fuck, Erica…*

"Eh." He makes a face and shrugs. "She's not really my type."

Huh?

He turns his head to the side, facing me; his body follows. I break focus and look down at my phone. I, I don't know for what exactly. I guess to text Mansell or maybe to check the time. Oh, that's right! I got to get back in since Janet is so old-school. She *literally* wants us to punch in for arrival, departure, going and coming back from breaks.

"I'm curious," his soothing tone draws me back to the here and now. "What are you hiding over here?"

"I'm not. Hiding."

I jolt as soon as my phone buzzes off in my hand, almost dropping the damn thing. I can sense that he never looks away from me. But I look away from him because the flashing, three bold white letters capture my attention and hold it, robbing me from the now: MOM.

I reject it, well not hitting the actual red button but the down arrow so she can't tell that I'm...rejecting her. I just don't want to talk to her. I can't get into it.

"You all right?"

Oh, right. For a moment, I'm surprised that I forgot about...him.

"Yeah," I answer. "Yeah, I'm alright. Why?" Whoa, I hope I didn't sound annoyed or ticked off because he straightens up and it almost seems like he has taken a step or two back...away from me.

*Great. Nice one.*

"You just look a bit preoccupied. Wanna talk about it? I'm all ears."

By now, he circles to the opposite side of me. He makes a weird face. Well, a few of them. I don't get it until I find myself chuckling. He smiles back and presses his back against the hot bricks.

"See," he picks up where he left off, "life is not always so bad when you just smile."

# Alex

Her smile brightens. Nice teeth—very crisp and white. She's really…beautiful. I just get the sense that she doesn't know it. Or, at least, not enough people have told her.

"Say, what are you doing later?" I ask her.

"Um, going home."

"On a Friday night?"

"Yeah. Why?" Her teeth are no longer flashing. Shoot, I don't know if I pissed her off or something. I mean, chicks often get mad or irritated over the smallest things. Okay, now that was a douche thing to say. Okay, maybe I should just ask her. Can't hurt…

"Well," my tone is all scratchy and dry from standing in this heat; that sun...

And then, I decide to do something about it. I reach for her arm and tug at it to step into the shadow underneath the overheard of the building, out of the sunlight. At first, she sort of gives a flinch and her eyes get wider like she is about to scream. To be honest, it freaks me out for an instant, and I release her wrist. But then, she reaches out for my arm, resting it on there as we step into the cool shade, draining out the other voices and streetwalkers who hustle by, even though the gate and other brick buildings keep them out of their sight.

"Sorry," she says and removes her hand from my bicep, almost dragging it down for a second longer until she seems to notice and steps back. "I, uh, was just caught off guard."

Oh…kay.

"Come hang out with us. We'll get coffee or whatever you like to do on your downtime."

"Oh…"

Oh?

"I mean, I was going to text Bianca and see if she could work—"

"Great! You guys can work at our place before we hit the town."

Now that gets her quiet. She keeps peering away from me. I don't think even wanting to look at me anymore. Shit…I must've fucked up. Maybe that was too…pushy? Aggressive?

No, wait…girls like the whole direct thing. At least from what Bianca tells me. Although, she still prefers going to the gay karaoke bar instead of a bar *bar*, where she could get hit on. But she claims that she's too "bro-ish" and scares and turns off dudes.

"Well,"—her tone carefully rises—"I don't have my Polaroids. And I had to reorder some more. To be honest, money—"

"I got you."

That…surprises her?

Huh. I thought that sort of thing/offer works.

"I can't have you do that…"

"Well, that's too bad...." I tilt sideways to meet her standoffish posture, one wrist crossed over the other, while her free hand is wrapped around the other wrist. Locking herself away. "I heard

Lou might make a special appearance tonight. Not him for obvious reasons. But still…any Reed fan would *kill* to be there."

She is quiet and still. There is this look on her, making me wonder if she wants to laugh at me or with me. If that makes sense. Shoot, maybe the whole leaning my head against the white brick wall is a bit too much—

"How about tomorrow night?" she suggests.

# Erica

602…

Yup, this is the right place. A lot of bricks. A shit load of red bricks with a mixture of white in it. Oh, wait…that's bird shit. "$8.56, miss," the cabbie tells me.

Right. I pull out a ten and just tell him to keep the change. I get out. Cabbie zooms off, just as my left foot exists the cab. Yeah, probably the only downside of this city life—assholes are at every corner. I give my backpack a tug at the straps, adjusting and tightening it closer to my body like it's some sort of cloak.

The neighborhood isn't…Okay, it's shady as hell. But I guess that's expected with someone from the 'nice part' of town who steps foot into the lower east side. Not to mention every other crack in the sidewalk and the off-balance tree stump that is working its way through most of them. Okay, all of them since the concrete seems lighter than the cement. Weird…

I sound like my mom.

"Crack is WHACK!"

I look over my shoulder, back at the 602-apartment building, and see Bianca skipping down the steps. Every other step and magically landing on the balls of her feet with no injuries, not to mention…she's barefoot.

"Wad up, chica," she hollers and yanks me into a hug; her breasts press deep and hard into my brittle bones—no big titty committee here. More like the itty-bitty titty committee. "Come on! Let us go. Welcome to our palace where all the magic happens. And by that my dear friend, I mean action. As in Bianca hasn't had any in *weeks*."

She gives the heebie-jeebies shake, sticking out her tongue in disgust. Her arm remains around my shoulders, linking me in as we, simultaneously, walk up the steps and into apartment building 602 under the radiant, hot sun. I squint as I glimpse up at the sun…pushing its way through the cotton candy clouds that scatter about in the sky.

---

"Kara Wanker?"

"Walker," I try to not shout at her, lowering my phone with a photograph of one of Kara Walker's artwork. Walker is famous for her artwork where she uses cut-out cardboards and displays them on the walls at her exhibitions. She also incorporates the use of lighting, usually from the ceilings, which give her art pieces an extra glow. The lighting creates an illusion to ones' eye, therefore, the cardboard cuts-outs of her characters, such as slaves, appear to be moving shadows on the walls. It is something to see in person and how Walker uses the rise and fall of slavery, including the power status of slave owners.

It's quite moving, I must say.

Only, Bianca doesn't seem to get that…at least not yet.

"So," she says, twirling the end of one of her many curls, "She's basically telling a story within a story…"

"Yeah. Stories. Kara Walker does the construction cuts-outs, manipulating into shadows with awesome lighting. She uses the index cards to tell a brief story of her work. Often, they're quotes."

"Interesting...I dig. I dig it, a lot."

A sense of adrenaline pumps its way through my system, rushing and reddening my cheeks. "What?" I must look dazed and confused; my feet paralyzed to the wooden floors as if t quicksand had stopped its work at a midpoint.

"OH, nothing. I just recognize a lot of these." She stops twirling her curl and picks up a few of the index cards from the coffee table in front of the red sofa. "James Dean. Lou Reed. Jim Morrison. Brando. And Audrey Hepburn. Your top favs, I suppose?"

Most definitely but, instead, I just nod and smirk.

My eyesight never leaves her. Although Bianca is already trapped in this dazed and, somewhat, confused mindset. Still twirling her curl, just going at it. I scope the place quickly, noticing just how bare the walls are. They're an off-white and…yellowish color with a 5 by 7 picture here and there of the little girl and little boy versions of Bianca and Alex. No sign of a Mom or Dad…

"Cute Halloween costumes," I say, pointing to the one closest to me—a picture of Bianca and Alex, who must be no more than ten or eleven years old.

Bianca has her arms linked around Alex's neck, sticking her tongue out at him like she is about to give him a wet willy or something, while Alex's face is all squished up from crying or laughing, or maybe both, knowing how Bianca must have been as a kid even. Probably just as goofy.

"Beautiful home too," I add.

"We manage. It's just us, though, pretty much. Alex's dad works a lot. He's usually gone by the time either of us gets up."

Alex's mom? Before I can ask, Bianca rises from the floor to inspect the circle of Polaroids on the floor. She eyes my Polaroid camera bag, the empty plastic baggie, and laptop that sit on the coffee table and then back to the half-written and blank index cards that are either sitting underneath one of the many Polaroids or…still sitting in the small stack of pile adjacent from Bianca's right foot.

"The Animals," Bianca says, referencing one of the quotes on the index cards as well as disrupting my trail of thoughts. For some reason, I see that my fingers are loosening from the bottom of my shirt. "I see why Janet had hired you."

"Well, I was thinking since you're the writer, maybe you can type these up in a cool font and we can present some of our favorites on a slideshow for the class presentation." I think that made sense. I don't know, my tongue is all dry and feels swollen. I nibble on it for a second to make sure that it's not growing. It's not.

"*True*…but when we *win*"—her words make me gulp—"we'll have them displayed all bold and colorful underneath the Polaroids in picture frames."

"You really think we'll win?"

Does she really think we'll win?!

"Nothing is impossible, even the word itself says, 'I'm possible!'"

She was holding the one index card that had it in writing as she said it. I smile and add, "Audrey Hepburn."

Door UNLOCKS, or I think I hear it. My eyes and head find their way glancing over my shoulder, centering in on the doorway where only the first half of the actual hall is visible. I hear the rattle of keys.

Bianca keeps talking, "It was on a birthday card that Alex got me last year."

"Heard my name!"

And that's when he walks in, still in his work uniform, stopping dead in his tracks as soon as he sees me. He smiles at me. I can't help but return the smile until I immediately peer away, staring back at the floor. Back at the Polaroids.

"Jade!" he sings.

Before I ask, Bianca leaps up and down, making the apartment room rattle a bit. "ALEXANDER!" she sings right back at him. Somewhere, there's a *THUD THUD*—probably from a broom or the end of a pole—telling us to shut the FUCK UP.

We burst out laughing.

Alex drops his backpack onto the chair in the corner next to the doorway. Bianca goes back to the floor, giving one of those, "OH! THE HEAT," as her hand touches her forehead. I laugh even more, which forces my face to go red. At least, it feels like it since it is fucking hot now.

"Edward Sharpe and The Magnetic Zeros," Alex chimes us all back in as he pops a seat on the end of the suede red sofa—not the fancy suede, but the knocked-down version of it…God, that's something my mom would have said. "Surprised you haven't heard of them, Mrs. Reed."

"For your information, I *have* heard of them." That gets a cackle from Bianca, who sits up, leaning on her forearms to watch us like Alex and I are in the middle of some match…

Okay, maybe we are.

I continue, "They sing, 'Home.'"

Bianca hollers and half mimics an ape. "Our anthem! You should see us rock the shit outta that song. Shit gets motherfuckin' LIT."

She goes for the hidden liquor cabinet underneath the shelves with glassware, paper plates, and some unorganized utensils. Wow, what the fuck…I'm becoming my mother. Jesus—going straight for the exteriors of something, rather than the meaning beyond it. Because to be honest…I got a feeling that it is really Bianca and Alex who only live here. I mean, I guess their dad…Alex's dad…just wires over money or stops in now and then to leave a check. I mean, Alex can't be making that much more than I am at the shop.

"I'd love to see it," I tell them, which stirs their interest. Bianca freezes midway before popping open a half-empty Jameson bottle. "You know, your guys' rock anthem. Live."

They literally couldn't be any closer, both saying, "OH," and then cackling up like I'm a clown entertaining them. Well, I guess that does exist—the whole twins can read each other's mind thing. It can probably go the same for two people who've known each other their entire lives (or, at least their childhood and teen-hood like Bianca and Alex).

Man…they do get each other. Bianca is over there throwing up gang signs, taking a sip here and there from the Jameson bottle. Alex hands her over a nearby Coke bottle, meaning to swap with her (probably to pre-sober her up, or something). But Bianca just grabs the Coke bottle, pops open the cap, and takes a sip from that, too. It becomes a two-time rotation of sipping Jameson and then the Coke before she comes around to me and lifts up both bottles.

I shake my head, refusing the offer.

"Ah, come on," she pesters. "It's the only thing that gets me up on stage." I must look shocked because then she adds in, "What? You don't think I get nervous?" She giggles, still managing to do some more sipping. She winces and makes that disgusted face, sticking out her tongue, again.

I can't help but laugh. It's pretty ridiculous, sort of funny, to see. It gets her going too. She looks at me for a second before glimpsing over at Alex. "What?" I ask.

Bianca and Alex hold this look with each other. Some kind of secret, not-so-secret, mindreading thing. The whole 'twin thing'. Their faces say enough when Bianca speaks: "Well, it is duet night..."

And then I'm tempted to bolt for the door—my fingers reaching for the backpack straps on my shoulders; only, they are not there.

# Bianca

"Blush. Blush. Blush. Now, pucker!"

Erica does, but she's all hesitant like she needs some sort of approval or something. I have to help her out there since she keeps hesitating. I cup my fingers around her mouth, forcing it into fishy lips.

"Pucker," I repeat, trying to not squeeze her bottom lip too much since her eyes are all bold like black olives.

She does a few times. Ah! There she is—the Snow-White beauty of them all. Erica is very pretty, but I don't think she...gets it. I guess she's just insecure and shy in general...but there's something about the way she was carrying herself into my room just minutes ago. I nearly had to convince—BEG—her to let me do her makeup. At first, she sort of looked offended like a school bully passing by and knocking down her untouched tray of food.

But I feel fly as FUCK. Shit, I'm so glad that my fashion sense kicks in...at the thrift shop. Ha! I just got my own "What/What/What" lyric part to Macklemore's "Thrift Shop" song.

*Jesus...it's been forever since I have got that.*

"Uh, Bianca," Erica's quiet tone kicks up with each syllable.

"Yes," I try to match her, leaning closer and setting my chin on top of her shoulder.

"I don't look...well, you know...It's not too much—"

"No! No!" I circle in front of her, blocking her mirror reflection from seeing her real-life self. "You look amazing *girl*."

I turn around and smile at us in the mirror. "We deserve to feel bold, beautiful, strong, sexy, and extraordinary."

Only, she allows the hesitation to overcome her again. There is little to zero reaction from her, so I'm not sure if she lets my words sink in. Probably not. She just stares eye to eye with herself for a SECOND before they drift away, down to the floor from what I'm witnessing through the mirror. The biggest furniture in my room and the whitest too – everything else just sort of reeks from the off-white…what is that…yellowish colored painted walls. Yeah, Alex and I have been meaning to get that fixed.

Oh, SHIITAKE MUSHROOMS!

Alex is waiting for us.

I pull Erica by the arm, which startles her—a short gasp escaping her lips, and hustle and bustle our way over to one of my many clothing racks that surround my bed like sex warriors. "Outfit time!"

# Alex

I eye the clock on the wall. The minutes seem to tick by, but it has only been two minutes since I last checked for the time. I line up the three shot glasses on the countertop—oh, man what is that! I grab a nearby…napkin! Napkin works. I give the counter a quick clean and pour three shots.

"What is taking you guys forever?!" I have to finally ask because now, this is getting ridiculous. But again, I remember the times with Mom and how long she and Bianca took to get ready, even if it was a quick grocery store run…

"Darlin'!" I hear Bianca charm her way in; more like shimmering in because of…that dress. It's like some sort of…gray—no, not gray—metallic shiny thing. I don't know what the fashion people would call it. She just looks like a disco ball. I know she has that same design in red, too, but she only wears that one for getting laid or 'trying to find the D.'

So, I guess tonight…it's all about impressing…

"Whoa," it just escapes my mouth.

Erica walks in, behind Bianca who gives her arm a tug. Bianca even double takes on Erica; I am assuming that is to make sure she doesn't ditch her. I got to say, the ladies sure know how to make a *vavoom* entrance. She looks…different. I see her arms and legs for the first time. That sounds weird, but what I mean is that…

She should show some more skin because she looks really…HOT.

"I KNOW!" Bianca takes a step forward to do that—yep, she's doing that whole leg pop, or as she refers to it 'the Angeline Jolie Oscar leg pop', "We look awesomesauce!"

Shit.

*She* sees that I'm checking her out. Think, quickly, FAST. I reach for the nearest glass and go to the sink. I force myself to drink the glass of water. I down every drop of it like my life depends on it. Once I'm done, my eyes return to them. Bianca has this disgusted look on her face, usually when she has too much to drink.

Yep, she sticks out her tongue and gives her body a shake. "Ewe foo! That glass was on the dirty dishes side."

Shit. It WAS.

Man, I don't think I could get any worse than this.

I catch Erica looking my way again. As soon as I catch her eye, she looks away. Bianca's nonstop talking is sort of keeping the awkward thing from interfering: "One for me. And one for—"

"Oh, no," Erica demands, waving her hand at the shot of tequila.

Bianca would have dropped the glass, if not for my fast reflexes, practically catching the thing an inch before it hits the floor. Jesus, Bianca…

"Say whaaa?!"

"I just never drink," Erica says.

Okay. Now I'm with Bianca on this one.

"Yeah," Bianca adds in. "Me either."

Nice, sis! Say that while you take a swig of the Jameson.

She *would* do something like that.

Erica just waits for one of us to say something. I decide to—

"Well, okay!"

Bianca gets to it first. She pours us a shot and hands one to me. Then, she goes for the third shot and begins to fill it up. Erica is about to say something, until Bianca raises both of her shot glasses, "Salud!"

And now, we drink.

# Erica

They must hate the AC up in here because it is a SAUNA in here. I follow Bianca, who drags me by the arm. At some point, a mob of people waddle by—assuming they're drunk—causing one of them to booty bump into a friend. Before we know it, a chain starts of bumping and drinks going jittery in hands. Alex grabs a hold of me for security reasons. Of COURSE…

"Easy there, rider," he quotes one of my all-time favorite movies, *Giant*; James Dean last said-to-be movies in which he shot.

"More crowded than the other times," I have to raise my voice even more as we slither our way to the back…to be honest, I have no idea where Bianca is guiding us. Well, it could be the fact that everyone is at least four inches taller than me. I'm like a marching penguin trying to waddle its way back to its clan.

"Yeah. It's discount booze." He said, too close to me.

I force a chuckle, "Someone's drunk."

"Yeah. On love. You know that Beyoncé song," he says, circling to stand in front of me.

Through the small gust of smoke—wait, you can smoke in here—I see his Cheshire Cat grin…It's the first time I sort of…see him. The way the backlight puts this glow around him. Guess you can call it his aura; it's yellow like a gold star—

I catch myself holding my breath this entire time. I manage a cough. Perfect, too—Bianca hauls me to a stop, forcing me to do the same with…Alex.

I laugh, taking in our new semi-surrounding. Oh, good…we're at the back, the end of the bar.

"Ricardo! I'm home, *papi chulo*!" Bianca shouts, pressing her hips to the counter, practically leaning over like she is about to steal a few sips from the alcohol bottles. A passing bartender snaps his fingers at her to order her back. Like fate, Ricardo comes sashaying on out in the perfectly tight, booty-shaped shorts. He has on a matching black muscle tee as well. Damn, he looks hot.

"Bianca!" He sets down his tray with drinks that should be delivered, he meets Bianca halfway for kisses on the cheek as the French do, I guess…

Whoa, okay I'm feeling off. Maybe it's this odd, lukewarm temperature in the back of the bar, and the fact that…Alex and I still have a hold of each other's hand…

Immediately, my hand jerks away and so does my body. It catches him off guard as we awkwardly spread a few inches apart, sort of studying each other eye-to-eye. I can tell that he's trying to…read me, figure me out, if you must call it that.

For the first time in a while, I just breathe and breathe, never breaking focus from him.

"Get us a round, Ricky Vicky!" Bianca jumps in-between us and yanks Alex underneath one arm and me under the other. Oh, thank God! She shaves…

My nose practically buries into her armpit. It makes Alex bust-up laughing. My cheeks are burning; oh man, I'm probably all red now.

"Oh, no, no!" I protest, worming my way out from her arm.

"Yes, yes!"

"Bianca…"

Even Ricky looks a bit annoyed to be waiting, sort of a "Nobody leaves Baby in the corner," well that same analogy goes for Ricky by the tap of his foot and jaw misaligning when he gives one of those, "Mmmmhhhhmmmm."

"But Erica," Bianca pushes on this topic still, making a sad little lost puppy face (the one that gets her anything), "We've been working nonstop and deserve to cut loose. Besides, Alexander and I rock the SHIT out of duets!"

And before I can speak, Bianca twirls around to her boi—

"Ricky! There shall be drinks!"

"You got it, baby girl." Ricardo is in mid-pass of the Cosmos to a nearby patron at the bar—a very VERY slippery mess—when he gives Alex a wink. Wow…okay if he were a chick–*I'd be jealous as fuck.* Wait, what—?

Okay, someone is smoking reefer up in here because I'm not jealous. I'm not jealous at all. I mean, so what—it's cute that a gay guy has a crush on a straight guy—

Oh, Ricardo! Man, he is so…confident and *fierce* like Beyoncé.

He winks at Alex before twirling on his heel. But not before, he cocks his head to the corner and makes quick eyes with Bianca, me, and then Alex—he licks his lips all the way around as he holds contact with Alex.

By the time Ricardo retreats behind the beaded curtains with an empty tray, Bianca and I just lose it.

Bianca turns to me, "Look, just have fun. You like music don't you."

"Yeah…"

"Well…" She turns her body toward the small, dinky stage in front of us. Although there is a crowd going, most start to dance to the drunk wannabe acapella group's version of "Stayin' Alive."

Bianca squeals when she spots another bartender with shorts tighter than Ricky's.

"My Latina!"

"My Persian pop princess!" he hollers back.

And there she goes…skipping and leaping right into his big juicy arms. The dude must bench press at least three reps a day.

We stand in silence. I refuse to steal a glance at him and force my gaze to remain on the half-naked chicks who wiggle and giggle on stage. They are a lot skinnier and prettier than me—

"What?" I ask him because the whole, 'I can see you from the corner of my eye,' was getting old after ten seconds of knowing that he was doing…that.

"Do you have your camera?"

Ah, I forgot—it's in my purse. Usually, I tend to carry the bag in the open. Bianca said not to because it did not go with my outfit.

"Yeah, I do." I can already feel my cheeks spreading back into a grin because off of that look he holds with me, I already know what he is thinking. And I dig it.

"Ricardo!" he shouts over his shoulder. "Make it a double for me!"

And then I find myself sitting at one of the round black tables in the front row of the stage. Bianca and Alex down their shots as soon as Ricardo sweeps in with a tray. Alex gives a peace sign, a.k.a. requesting two more shots. He even points to me, but I shake my head.

They are a TRIP—Bianca and Alex belt out Edward Sharpe & The Magnetic Zeros' "Home."

He: Alexander.

She: Jade....

# Bianca & Alex

**BIANCA**

*Alabama/*
*Arkansas/*
*I do love my ma and pa/*
*Not that way that I do love you/*

**ALEX**

*Holy moly/*
*Me/*
*Oh my/*
*You're the apple of my eye/*
*Girl/*
*I've never loved one like you/*

**BIANCA**

*Man/*
*Oh man/*
*You're my best friend/*
*I scream it to the nothingness/*
*There ain't nothing that I need/*

**ALEX**

*Well, hot and heavy pumpkin pie/*
*Chocolate candy, Jesus Christ/*
*Ain't nothing pleases me more than you/*

**BIANCA**

*Home, let me come home/*
*Home is wherever I'm with you/*
*Home, let me come home/*
*Home is wherever I'm with you/*
*Take me home/*

*Mama, I'm coming home/*

**ALEX**

*I'll follow you into the park/*
*Through the jungle, through the dark/*
*Girl, I've never loved one like you/*

**BIANCA**

*Moats and boats, and waterfalls/*
*Alleyways, and payphone calls/*
*I've been everywhere with you/*
*That's true/*

**ALEX**

*Laugh until we think we'll die/*
*Barefoot on a summer night/*
*Never could be sweeter than with you/*

**BIANCA**

*And in the streets, you run a-free/*
*Like it's only you and me/*
*Geeze, you're something to see!*

# Erica

Somewhere in-between their duet, I sneak around, hidden amongst the small crowd that their performance draws in. Mostly, a lot of gays and a few drag performers even…

Quickly, my eyes find something else—ANYTHING—to focus on as soon as I see a lady in a red leather skirt sit down, dropping both her matching purse and…let's just say, *something else*—balls.

I raise my arms and up goes my Polaroid camera. The first snapshot is Bianca belting out more "la/la/la/LA'S/LA'S" in-between the Jade and Alexander duet breaks. Ricardo photobombs my next shot to deliver their next set of shots—

Someone behind me screams, "GIVE ME DAT DICK!"

I fumble for the loose end of my camera's arm-wrist cord—*Jesus, four-hundred bucks here.* I'm not mad at the random who screams behind me every time Alex opens his mouth to take over the Alexander part. To be honest, the gay guy behind me just practically wets his pants if Alex is even breathing—not my quote, his own; and now he's going into great DETAILS how he would let Alex just destroy him in bed…

They are cute together—the way Bianca and Alex play off each other. There's love in the air and NOT that kind, but the love where they just genuinely like being around one another. I guess that's common though, considering that they are childhood best friends…

Ricardo circles in to sweep up the other two empty shot glasses (clearly theirs and not mine) from the table. The green apple Cosmo is still full—I never touched it. Bianca had ordered the thing for me, but really, I think she wanted it since the first Jell-O shot was already kicking in for her.

"Another rain check for My Fair Lady?" he asks, doing a spot-on impression of Elle Wood's bend and snap. God, I hope I'm not homophobic for thinking that—he even asks me if he did it right.

I nod, assuming he did. I wouldn't know; I've sort of been out of the movie loop for a while.

**BIANCA & ALEX**
*Ah/*
*Home/*
*Let me go home/*
*Home is wherever I'm with you/*
*Ah/*
*Home/*
*Let me go home/*
*Home is where I'm alone with you.*

Something just hits me as soon as Ricky goes to pick up my Cosmo. "Actually...I'm drinking that." I approach the table and kindly reach out for my glass.

Ricky smiles and passes it over like a queen recruiting in her next entourage. Awesome…I'm digging the vibe to the place now. Well, that could be because I finally feel my shoulders and neck lowering in ease as I take my first sip of the Green Apple of My Eye Cosmopolitan—oh, HA I just got that.

"Attagirl. Now, the second one is on the house." He leaves before I can reject. But he snaps his head back 'round to add, "I'll bring out our pink flamingo straws. They're shaped like penises."

And there he goes, no shame whatsoever. God…I think I'm in love as he wiggles his way through the crowd, hovering his arm up so the tray is in full tower sight. He whips his head back, but he seems taller and slender and my God…He's very attractive. On fire…

Oh shit, I can feel the Apple of My Eye getting to me. I can't help but chuckle a bit, even when the microphone gives a loud crackle as I hear Bianca scream my name.

I whip around and our eyes lock from the three to four-foot gap that stands between us. I notice the song is coming to an end because the chorus beat is slowing down, meaning that...*Oh, man*—she wants *me* to *join in*.

"Erica! Get yo ass up here!" Bianca sings that part out, doing her best impersonation of Mariah Carey.

"Camera time!" Alex swings his hips as he chugs back the cranberry vodka that Ricardo must've dropped off a few minutes ago—

Oh, wait no...one of the gays bought it for him, a.k.a. the "I WANT DAT DICK" dude.

I bust up, covering my mouth, but the giggles still escape my lips. I feel two burly arms wrap around me. It freaks me out, almost sending my drink straight for the floor. I swear a scream slips out of my mouth, but I doubt it since...well, the bouncer just helps put me on stage to join Bianca and Alex. Bianca yanks me into her and Alex's proximity. I can smell the liquor on both of them, which heightens my heart rate...

I scope the place in front of us but can barely make out faces because of the overly bright stage lights hanging above the ceiling, aiming like the beams of a riffle. I feel my jaw tightening and my fingers curling into fists—fingernails pressing into my skin.

"Camera time!" Bianca shouts, squeezing herself into the sandwich (I'm the middle) and grabbing a hold of my camera. She levels it, implying that it is now my turn to take the picture…of all of us. I find the blood flow has stopped at the tips of my fingers, forcing me to a stop. A dead-end…

I'm assuming that Bianca and Alex take notice because they both move in closer and, in perfect timing, grab the end of the Polaroid base and hold it. It encourages me to try and relax my shoulders down by giving them a roll. Also, the button to take the photo of the Polaroid camera is eye level with me, so it is nearly impossible to back out of this now. Otherwise, I would feel like the world's biggest douchebag.

With one click, pressing together the two panels with my thumb and pointer finger, the Polaroid gives a loud click and a flash, capturing our first photo together.

# Bianca

I nearly fall off my chair—the red pleather cushion gives my bottom a quick jerk to its side. I clutch hold of Alex's arm. He is already pulling me up. So, is Erica—man, she looks worried like a ghost just drifted by or something.

"All good," I inform them with my hands out as if beads or something are dangling down from my long sleeves; I don't have on long sleeves. "All good."

I turn back to the stacks of Polaroids. Thankfully, my Blue Velvet Cosmopolitan missed when my arm decided to shake and spill most of the liquid. It is this gooey blue. Kind of gross!

"We look so *fuckin'* awesome! Awe, my sweet, Alexander."

"My sweet, Jane," he sings back; although, his eyes remain level to the centerpiece on the table. I catch him glimpsing up at Erica, which must be a cool effect, considering that the centerpiece is a dimmer candle. It is fake, but FUCKIN' RAD!

From the corner of my eye—just kidding, I am full-on staring back and forth at these two cuties—I spy a smile spreading across Erica's *face.*

My fingertips find their way to the last Polaroid of the stack. It sort of melts my heart, paralyzing me in place—it is the three of us, bound close together. We are all smiling, including Erica. Man…she does have some nice teeth. "We gotta take more of these."

"Of course," Erica says; she goes for her drink, but the glass is empty. And just like that—

Ricardo swoops in with a refill. Alex and I can't help but bust-up. Alex coughs and practically chokes on his ice. I'm assuming it's scotch on the rocks, but I'm also very very VERY buzzed so my brain is making all my memories mushy… musheeee… mush…

"You guys, okay?" Erica asks, finally taking a sip of her drink. It took her two hours to finish the first one, which explains her sober demeanor. She is sitting all…stiff…until her shoulders finally descend to an even level.

"What…?" she asks again—oops! I think I was staring too long; damn…these cosmoses sure do catch up with you.

"Oh…nothing! It's just nice to see you relaxed for once."

"Relaxed...Oh, shit," Alex then starts cracking up, "I'm *drunk.*" And now, he seems all paranoid because it hits him like a pile of bricks. LOL dude…you ain't driving or anything!

I just laugh some more. Erica takes a long sip of her drink until she settles back in her chair. Thankfully, her seat has more back support; it could explain why I almost landed flat on my face like a pancake. "You know," it then rolls off of my tongue. "I needed this. Really, I needed *this*. I've just been so overwhelmed sometimes."

Oh, shit. They have that look—Erica sits up straighter and scoots to the edge of her seat; Alex is already looking at me. He slowly lowers his drink to the table, all eyes on me. Damn…that was not meant to happen.

"Oh, it's nothing serious. Just that, well, Zimmer and I've been talking so much about my past. Growing up in that home...Oh, no, Alexander." I eye Erica. "He worries whenever I talk about my past, but I always tell him that it was HE who'd saved me."

"Saved?"

Oh, shit—forgot that she doesn't know about that...my history.

"Yes...saved. Alex's parents had adopted me a year after we met. We're brother and sister. He saw the bruises."

Erica steals a glance at Alex, who I can tell is upset because it shows...a lot, especially when he is halfway standing by the time, I finish speaking. "I'm going to get some water," he mutters and is then pacing out of sight.

My eyes linger back to Erica, who is utterly speechless. She grabs a hold of her drink but just holds it. I notice that her fingers are locking around the glass tightly. Extra *tight*.

"He'll be fine," I tell her, pushing myself up by bringing my crossed arms onto the table. "He just hates when I'm so blunt. And drunk when it happens."

"That's why you're in therapy?" And I see it in her eyes of connecting the pieces even more and more to get that finished product—voilà!

"Suppressed childhood trauma because my parents are low lives who didn't know how to take care of me. But that's addicts alright."

"Bianca,"—Oh, worry fills her voice, especially when she does that lean in thing so her tone could drop down to a half-whisper—"where are your parents, like at this very moment?"

I just smile for some reason, giving a nod. I reach for my drink. "They're long gone from here! *Thank gawd!* They're in prison, especially since the cops found their boogie sugar and Walter White snacks. Code for cocaine and crystal meth. By the way, have you seen, '*Breaking Bad*' ? It's one of the best shows EVA!"

*...What's love!*

And I spy with my little eye—the contestant on stage, SAD SACK. Poor guy, he's all fucked up while doing a sloppy version of "What's Love Got To Do With It" by Ms. Tina Turner. Man…he is so frustrated! Just belting all of his pain, anger, and vulnerability out into the crowd—

"I'm sorry," he chimes in midway. "My fuckin' bitch of a wife just left me—"

*Got to do/*
*Got to do with it...*

"Yay!" I scream, bouncing up to my feet. "Sing your heart out honey! Fuck that bitch!"

"Fuck that bitch!" someone in the front of the crowd chants.

Sad Sack tilts their glass to me as a salute and then down the rest of it. I do the same and return my bottom to the red cushion…

I only wish that I saw how tense Erica was sooner that night. She had a habit of curling her fingers tightly into fists…usually, they say that's the first sign. The first sign of a trigger event for someone.

# Erica

"...What? You gotta stay out longer with us!" Bianca pleas.

"Sorry, I gotta get up early for work tomorrow."

We are standing outside of the karaoke bar, waiting for Alex. He has been gone for a few minutes now, excusing himself to go take a whizz. Yeah, he is a bit buzzed. As for Bianca, though...

She is rockin' a hard buzz. One of the multi-million taxi drivers gives a honk as Bianca teeters her way to the newsstand with all of today's gossip. I have to steer her aside before she is thrust into the streets by the nonstop passing crowd. "Oh," she whines, eyeing the karaoke bar, "come on, Alex! I wanna go!"

She giggles a bit, too. And then it just hits me—hard and FAST. It is my own merry-go-round…

My hands are sweaty by the time I bring them to my forehead, which creases with more sweat. A tingly sensation strikes the tips of my fingers, working its way up my arms. This electroshock feeling sends a sharper shock throughout my entire body—

That *riiiiiiiinnnnnngggggg* echoes from one ear and out the other and back into the other, over and over again.

"Hey, Erica?" I hear Bianca ask, but I cannot see her. "Whoa…Dude!"

Black and white spotting is taking over my sight, tightening my throat. But…I…I can't scream or speak!

And then, I see her—Bianca. Now, she is standing in front of me. I feel the warmth of her hands on my wrists. She refuses to let them go…let me go.

"Hey," is all she says before...before *he* speaks and approaches...us.

"Yo!" the guy—*Josh*—speaks; the asshole who tried to pick me up in the dormitory. Fuckin...ASSHOLE.

"Uh, yo?" Bianca chimes in, taking a step closer my way. She's already...blocking me; a shield for the battle. My own armor.

"Wad up, ladies!"

Bianca is already reaching for my hand. "Come on, Erica—"

"Erica," he says as the lightbulb clicks. "I thought it was fresh meat."

"DON'T TOUCH ME!" I scream as he stumbles in closer.

Bianca practically pushes herself in front of me and accidentally twists my arm in the process. It sends a sharp pain throughout my arm, numbing it for a few seconds.

The asshole laughs. "What's yo deal yo? I was just trying to talk to your friend—"

"My cheeks are pinching to a red color because of her...bottled-up anger."

"Asshole," he laughs again, all amused and not backing off. He takes a step towards Bianca. I don't know how she doesn't flinch.

"No. No," I repeat. "I don't know him."

"Thought so." Bianca loops her fingers through mine, turning around and forcing us to leave his sight.

And then, he opens his mouth again. "Cunt."

Bianca stops dead in her tracks—no, no, NO.

"Hey," I tell her. "Let's just go. Ignore him. It'll be okay."

But it's too late because she releases my hand and approaches *closer* to him, practically eye to eye.

# Bianca

"I'm sorry, do we got a problem? *Asshole.*"

"Dayum." His chivalrous grin widens like the Joker. "You got a mouth on you. I'd like to sex in your city, mami."

He grabs his crotch. MotherFUCKER!

"Mami?! What, do you have mother issues or something?!"

"Bianca," Erica begs. She gives my arm a tug to 'just drop it and leave'…but I can't. Not like all of the other times when people like this little shit do…no. I won't let that happen.

People around us are probably listening in at this point. Shit, they're probably stopping to gawk, which could explain Erica's second and third plea that we should just GO.

"Man," he says with the click of his tongue, now all serious. "Man, oh…man. What did your daddy do to you to hate men so much?"

I swear my teeth give an audible screech, practically breaking them as I go to slug this motherfucker in the face—

"Hey! Bianca, NO!"

Alex stumbles in front of me, his body giving me a push backward. Fuck…he stopped me from turning this prick's face into a greasy ass pizza. Alex grabs a hold of my fist, holding it, and repeating, "Stop. Not worth it. Okay."

And I don't need to beg or preach any further. I just…nod. Shit, I'm so weak right now—

"Bianca!" Erica calls out after me as I storm off, removing one heel at a time because of the forthcoming vent on the sidewalk.

It gives me a semi-walk-of-shame Marilyn Monroe effect and lifts part of my dress.

Whatever.

# Alex

"Bianca!" I call out for her as well, but she is already halfway in-between the sidewalk and the crossing path that leads to the intersection.

"Ah, shit." the dude standing in front of me says. He reeks bad, too…like malt liquor and too much whisky.

The worry in Erica's tone matches the boldness in her expression. She looks weathered down. I reach for her. "Come on."

I slip my fingers through hers. She is already squeezing them back, half-circling around to be on my other side; away from this guy…

He hurt my friends.

"Good luck trying to fuck that!" he could not yell any louder. "You get what I mean when I say, 'too tight.'" He mimes the sexual gesture—

"Alex," Erica mutters, her nails start pressing into my skin.

"Asshole," I call him, letting Erica lead the way. The last we see of this guy he is stumble toward the brick wall, lurching for one of the bricks for support to stand.

# Erica

A few feet away, Bianca paces. She is *livid*.

Alex and I catch up; his hand never leaves mine…

"That motherfucker!" she screams, glancing at us until her eyes settle on Alex.

"I know. I know."

"I should've said something to him. I'm going to castrate him!"

Alex stops her though, just before she can race over to the club. I don't see the asshole…he must have stumbled off somewhere. Probably another bar. Or another poor chick to hit on…

The back of my neck is hurting. I try to straighten out, but I realize that I'm already standing tall. Somewhere in between, Bianca drops to the floor in front of the mailbox and newspapers. People take an extra look as they bypass. Some teenager flashes his camera at her—

"Hey!" Alex calls out, missing the tourist who runs out of sight. His hand leaves mine…

My eyes stay on it. It's a new…feeling. I don't hear anything but the footsteps of people and drumbeat of the nearby struggling musician begging for pennies. I don't even hear that *riiiiiiinnnnnnnggggggg* effect in my ears. Usually, it would go off like a BOMB.

I then hear Alex tell Bianca, "Hey! Bianca! Look at me."

I look as he tilts Bianca's head up. But she still refuses to look at him, "Alex, don't—"

"You're amazing," he tells her, eye-to-eye, cupping her chin; at least, it finally gets her to look, shut up, and listen. "Way more than you think. That guy's a prick. Look how far you've come already. You're one of the hardest working people that I know. You're passionate, dedicated, and persistent. But, fuckin' crazy as FUCK."

It gets a laugh from her and a smile from me. I remain off to the side, watching them. Seeing it. Feeling the energy from and around them —compassion, big genuine respect for each other. And I love it. Seeing that between them.

"You're *trying,*" Alex reminds her. "That's all that matters."

I can see the honesty in his eyes, never breaking focus with her. She doesn't either.

She nods. "It's a fucked up world."

He agrees, "It is."

"The assholes get by. We struggle. It's…bullshit!"

I agree with her. I agree with her no doubt. He drops to his other knee, more level with her. Those last words hit home for him, too.

She stares at him for a moment, tearing up. I know this because I take a step closer their way. "You've always been so good to me," she tells Alex and leans into him. He wraps his arms around her, too. I come to a stop, directly in front of them, lowering to my knees as well.

"Ah, shit." Bianca dabs at her eyes before she truly looks at me. "Erica..."

"It's okay," I say. "You don't need to explain."

And she really doesn't. She *never* has to…

I catch myself glimpsing away. My eyes lock with a passerby across the street, going on with their life. We almost exchange this look of reassurance and a farewell—a farewell that it's one in a million that we will ever see each other again. Ever.

"You didn't deserve any of it."

I know the silence seems longer than it is. By the time my sight returns to Bianca's, her mouth is parting ways. I cut her short, "Whatever your..." I pause. "Whatever happened to you."

I can't bear to say it…abused. And she knows it. Alex knows it, too. His eyes are already lowered to the concrete.

"I know. I'm still learning every day." Bianca gives an appreciative smile. This is hard for all of us.

And then, Bianca sits up, capturing Alex and my attention. "What is it?" he asks.

"Maybe we should incorporate everything into the project. The then, now, and what will become…"

She's saying that last part directly to me. For some reason, I can't find the words. Or at least they're stuck in the back of my throat—because I cough, too. Bianca ascends to her feet. Alex follows.

"Just think about it," she continues. "The then, now, and what will become."

And she looks from Alex to me again, smiling. "The awesome. The awesomeness of life. We are more than ordinary. Forever extraordinary."

I find myself nodding, but my eyes wander away as soon as Alex looks my way.

# NOVEMBER

# Alex

I find myself pacing outside before I knock on the door—

"Yes?!" Bianca hollers before my hand reaches the door. I swear that we are twins—that whole telepathic thing. "Come in!"

I do.

Bianca is lying down on her bed—a bedspread that matches with the deep purple curtains, if I must add because she would want me to. She's writing in a composition book, a.k.a. her work booklet. Her feet are kicked up in the air. She looks up, pausing for a moment, watching me take in the overloaded band posters and towers of CDs. Everything from punk to metal—no country or pop, because as Bianca would say it—

"Wake up, Alexander!" she couldn't holler any louder. She removes her earbuds. I catch the last verses of System of a Down's "Chop Suey". Damn...a great band from my middle school days. Well, Bianca's, too.

"Uh," it's the first thing out of my mouth, "nothing much. I was just going to turn in."

"Same." She coils up her earbuds and closes her composition book. I see that she has been jotting down sentences, not bullet points like she usually does. Wow...she was really into the writing session; a "poet's session" or "the non-LSD Jim Morrison sesh," as she would put it.

Bianca sets the items onto the end table beside her twin bed. She has this worried...look. Shit, fuck...I forgot that I'm just standing here in place now, probably making her wonder what the fuck is wrong with me—

I should really go.

"Stop worrying," she tells me. "Really. I'm fine, Alex."

And I believe her—really, I do. But…this tightness just remains on my shoulders, almost pushing me down to the floor. So, I take a seat on the edge of the bed. She scoots closer, joining me so our legs are dangling off. It reminds me of memories of her and me as kids; you know, those moments of joy and just pure…innocence…before all of the bad stuff had occurred. Before we took in Bianca.

During this thought process, she must have scrolled through her phone. Now, a song starts through the speakers,

*But mostly you just make me mad/*
*Baby, you just make me mad/*

"I'm glad you're going. To therapy." And my eyes meet hers. This appreciative smile spreads its own set of wings across her face.

"The place for freaks," she responds.

It makes me smile. She snorts. By the time we look at each other, the joke is done. Then, her eyes lower. I notice the shoebox on her lap. I…I don't recall seeing that after walking in—

Before I ask, Bianca sets it in the end-table drawer. Her gaze returns to me. She pats the spot next to the left side of her body and lies down on the bed. I join her, lying next to her. We remain in silence, staring up at the ceiling, compact with glow-in-the-dark stars and *more* band posters.

*Linger on your pale blue eyes/*

"You must have a nice time falling asleep."

"I sure do," she says.

I can't help but point out the Captain Obvious. "I see the Jo Bros are still a hit."

"Of course!"

God, it is weird to see those three still making Bianca's final cut, as she calls it—"Boys I want to touch but not fuck because I got's too much respect for them but they're still hot and smokin' aces."

"Who's the little one again?" I ask, to which she gasps and pushes herself up to her elbows. "What? I forgot. They all look the same to me."

"Racist much?"

We bust-up. Her smile fades. She lies back down, facing me. My eyes stay locked with the little Jo Bro—oh, right! It's NICK.

"I keep hearing your dad leave early in the morning. Still working overtime?"

I don't need to answer. I…I'm still having a hard time with it.

"Well," she intervenes my thoughts. "At least, we have each other."

It cracks a smile on me. I peer away from curly-haired NICK. She gives me a small smile, squeezing my hand back. "Are you working on Thanksgiving?"

"Nope!" And GOD, it feels great to say that. The first holiday off in…well, the first time since I started working more hours. Janet needed the help…

It never hurts to have the money.

*Linger on your pale blue eyes/*

"Why?" I ask.

"Oh, nothing." She shakes her head and turning onto her back again. Her eyes linger with the glow-in-the-dark stars (or, the Jo Bros).

She is quiet. It makes me lean up onto an elbow. "I just wanted to double-check." She takes another long pause before adding in, "We should invite Erica over."

She looks at me. I lean up onto an elbow for support.

I can see it in her eyes…the good kind, where you just know. "You must really like her."

"Yeah, I do. And so do you."

I find my sight going aloof, like not shut down or anything; just more…avoidance.

"I can tell." Her fingers tilt my chin toward her, so I'm forced to watch her for whatever she says further. "She likes you, too."

I see how serious she is.

"You're amazing, Alex. Remember that. Always."

I nod but find myself breaking focus from her…again. I take a deep breath. My eyes shut on their own. I feel the weight of her head shifting around until it finds a comfy spot on top of my shoulder. And then, I feel the weight of her head…the world…shift again. Without even checking, I know that we have returned to the stars…

"Goodnight, Alexander."

"My sweet, sweet, Jane," I sing back softly.

I grab her hand back. She holds on for dear life.

*Sometimes I feel so happy/Sometimes I feel so sad.*

Exactly, Reed. Exactly…

# Erica

It just screams right at me from the wall across from me:

**(December 14th) – Class Project Presentation**
**(December 20th) – Showcase**

The letters are even in neon colors so I don't forget. I make certain that I remember...a countdown. I find myself stiffening—my shoulders are just inches from my earlobes—until the air escapes through my parted lips. Just breathe...Fuckin' breathe, Erica.

I go to cross out today's date. T-minus one-month.

---

I swear this city will never sleep again.

The callousness of car honking increases. Tires screech on by; angry cabbies who just want to get to their next destination. You'd think they would like their drives being longer for more money. Maybe my mind is just in a messed-up spot right now...

I mean, like work was just...slow, I guess. I don't know. It was just weird—

"Hey!"

I remove one of my earbuds and see that it is Alex as I begin to turn around. He catches up to me before I fully can, standing to my left side. He is all bundled up as well and is wearing a beanie. Velvet Underground's Banana cover album is on it.

"What?" he asks, rubbing his hands together to warm them.

"I'm sorry. I just like these."

Shit—my fingers get some of his forehead. Damn it, why do I have to be so…bad at this.

He smiles. "Thanks, they're nice and cozy."

I cannot help but mirror his look; Jesus, my cheeks must be flaming like red Hot Cheetos. I have to admit, too—we both sort of forget that we are standing in the middle of the sidewalk, because some lady's big ass, beige bag rams into my left side as she bypasses. It sends me forward a few inches, practically shoving me into Alex.

"Nice!" he shouts at the lady in a cheetah print fur coat. She could probably give a rat's ass, considering she has somewhere to be.

Moron.

"So…" Oh, right. I awkwardly lean back; his fingers remain on my forearms. "Did you want—?"

"I have to get going." Fuck, Erica, just blurt it out any louder.

Alex is silent for a moment like a cat got his tongue—if that's the accurate expression. Shit, I can't think right now. I don't think the chilly air is helping me out right now. I have to tighten the flaps of my jacket closer, even though the buttons of the coat are secured up.

"Oh…righty then," is all he says. *What does that even mean?*

Oh, God. Not now. That stiffness takes over the back of my neck, wrapping around it like a snake. I can still breathe, maybe not as much with this dang fuzzy cream-colored scarf around me. Maybe I should just remove it—but yet, the cold air is bristling up my nostril hairs, so it would be stupid to do so.

"Take a break."

Uh, what?

"Well, I don't know about you," his voice slowly rises at each beat, but not like an acapella group or whatever; he just sounds more…enthusiastic, "but I could go for some coffee right now."

Before I can speak or move, Alex switches sides—now, he is on my right side. "So, coffee on the go?"

He tugs at his backpack straps and then I notice—his fingers are squeezing around the bottom of the straps. It must be…It can't be…

His own nervous/stressor tick.

# Alex

If I'd only know it was so crowded, I'd have probably picked a different spot. The only place Erica and I could think of was none other than Coffee Bean. The lady's request. I order my usual and Erica is sort of at bay with what she wants—her eyes scoping those bright and shiny signs behind the registers.

She finally settles on an Ice Coffee. "What?" she says, catching me watching her…probably for a bit longer than I expected. *Shoot.*

"Nothing. You're just one of those."

"What do you mean?"

I wave her off, finding my wallet before she does. I pay for our drinks. "What I mean is you're one of those New Yorkers who drink hot drinks in the summer and cold drinks in the winter."

"Isn't that like everywhere else?"

I catch the smile creeping on her. "Nice wallet," she tells me before turning on her heel, cueing me to follow her to the pickup counter for our drinks.

She was referring to the design—Velvet Underground & Nico's banana album cover with Andy Warhol's name at the bottom.

---

We walk, sipping coffee and listening to music. I lent her the right earpiece.

"Ah, Kurt Cobain," she says, digging the "Heart-Shaped Box" track. Nice choice. "They don't make music like that anymore."

"As long as it's not Courtney Love."

"Hey now," –We side-eye each other—"*Hole* has some pretty *sick* songs."

"Sick?!"

"You should listen to some of the things you say sometimes."

Her eyes linger on mine for a moment. But she breaks focus right away. I've noticed her doing that throughout the night. Well, the past forty-minutes or so. Velvet Underground's "Sunday Morning" is next on the playlist. "Well, I wonder who dis be?"

"How about you?" she asks, all serious like an answer to an exam. "Warhol the Artist or Warhol the Music Producer?"

Yea…for some reason, I thought she was going to grill me about my history or something. Her brows are still all furrowed like the question has been on her mind for, well, ages. "Well,"—I take a sip of my coffee, giving a pucker to savor the aftertaste of my go-to, peppermint mocha—"Well, both inspire me!"

She laughs. "What? They're both inspiring pieces of work."

"Yeah, I know." She really is amazing…

I'm just not sure if she realizes it. Again, she has stopped looking my way. We round the corner, meeting the doorstep of the main entrance to her dorm. The area is more compact. We sort of sidestep and get closer to a group of corner shrubs.

"So, this must be the place." I eye the twelve-story skyscraper. Unless I miscounted.

"It is," she answers, handing me back my earbud. "Thanks."

"No problem." I copy her and remove my earbud and wrap up the chord. We stand there; she looks like she has more to say. Well, I do too.

"Thanks for keeping me company. Really."

"Of course." As she is about to speak, turning at the same time, I take a step forward: "You know, listening to Velvet helps me get through stuff, especially after a long day. If you don't already, you should listen to music while working on your collage. Block out the stress. Just let the inspiration take over."

That word must get to her—collage—since I noticed she got all tense and broke focus with me. It has her in this funk like she is second-guessing herself.

"Sorry," she says, still having a hard time looking at me or anything, except at the sidewalk we remain standing on.

"For what?"

She could just shrug, but the look in her eyes already speaks that she is unsure what she meant.

"Well…fun date." I manage a smaller smile. Her eyes could not get any larger…

"So…Was it? Never mind."

"No, go ahead," I tell her, patiently waiting for her.

"Look, I'm not very good at…"

Oh…It makes sense. It's sort of been a while. And she's…embarrassed about it.

Erica glances away to both of her sides and I don't blame her—it is noisier over here, making it more difficult to really, ah…I just need to…

"Let you in on a little secret—same.'

She stares at me like I'm lying.

"Truth be told, I'm not so great at this either."

"You mean, dating?" she finally says it.

I nod.

"That's impossible."

…and I guess she said too much because now, she is red. Like, really red.

"I should probably go study—"

As she turns, her camera bag drops. We both go for it, our hands brush as the Polaroid camera bag falls into my hands first. I sort of do this side-sweep, dipping an inch or two rather than both of us dropping straight to the ground, while bypassing students enter and exist every few seconds from the dorm's main entrance.

"Uh, thanks. The reason why I should get a new one."

"It's good quality. Your camera…"

I find myself breaking focus and move the camera her way. My eyes meet the ground. The air strokes my nostrils, harsh and thick from the cold. The breeze creeps along my neck, forcing the hairs to rise and remain standing. Then, I feel the back of her glove touching my cheek.

My attention rises to her now. She is there, her bold eyes are already staring at me. Staring into me. It is…a bit intimidating. Her fingers don't leave my cheek. Instead, they find their way, cupping around my jawline. I can't help but sit there, sort of hypnotized by her. Her lips part a bit. I can feel my breathing speed up.

Then, she gives me a nod, her hand dropping as I go in and cup her face. We kiss for a long moment, a few seconds; maybe ten Mississippi's before we seem to detect the right moment to finally come up for air. We smile, still close.

"Been wanting to do that for a while," I tell her, running my hand through her hair.

She gives me another peck. It's sweet…She's amazing.

I hold her hands. She squeezes mine back. And at that moment, her hands stop shaking.

"I make you nervous."

"But the good kind," she reassures me before she leans in, and we kiss again and again.

# Bianca

"Lookie you!" I lean back in my chair, twirling the led pencil in my hand around and around like it's a daisy given to me by my noble Prince. "Someone's got a crush. Well, I think it's cute as fuck—"

"Bianca," Erica mumbles, glancing right and left; but I couldn't give two-fucks who hears! I mean this is my best buddy, Alex—ALEX whom she is into as he is into her as well.

Gawd! That is so motherfuckin' CUTE.

Erica resumes her notetaking. Okay, now I should get back to that, too. So, I do.

Newman is still blabbering on about the Campbell soup days of Andy Warhol. It is interesting; Jesus—Erica is practically drooling over every slide that Newman clicks on by and by…

"Warhol," says Newman, all mighty and macho with her stiff posture and hands neatly placed at the corners of the podium. Ha, she looks like a mini dictator. "Haring. Some of these names were once strangers, until the start of their own revolution."

And click click—next slide: Andy Warhol's Campbell Soup collage and Keith Haring's Dancing Cartoon Figures…Whoa, so many colors. Now, this is making me hungry.

I inch closer to Erica, lowering to my right side as she always gets the chair at the end of the row; she insists on it, she is always here early to make sure, too. Huh…I'd never asked why either; guess, she lives close by—Oh duh! She does. Campus life. Yolo!

"So…"

"Yes…?" she half-mimics and asks me.

"Well, since you and Alex had"—I then lower some more to mouth—"K-I-S-S-I-N-G, I take it that you're coming over for Thanksgiving. Sister-n-law."

And I could've seen this sooner—maybe—because the next thing I see is Erica literally staring right at me. Eye-to-eye. Soul-to-soul. Shit…

I triggered something for her.

# Erica

Bianca picks up her laptop. In the doorway, I stand with Dad. We are locked in a hug; primarily because he has an issue of not letting go of me. But I get it—he's happy to just see me.

"Still not going anywhere, Dad," I remind him…for the seventh time.

"Oh"—now, he releases me. His head corks back, just enough to see me—"I just miss having you around the house. That's all."

That makes me smile. Dad is…He just gets me, unlike...well—

"I can't believe you did this yourself," he chimes in, scoping my room. I try to follow where his eyes are going but the sun glares at my eyes. I go to close it, making the curtains touch. On my way over, I pass by Bianca, who is all set and ready to go.

"Now, you sure you're not giving away some credit?" Dad says to Bianca, who picks right up on his humor.

"Nope! This was all her." She sticks out her hip with her curled-up fingers over it like some wannabe trying to make it on *America's Next Top Model.* Oh, God…I didn't mean it like that.

*Shit.* I must've sounded like an asshole with that bad joke.

"But everything is just so…so crammed."

And I'd almost forgotten about her. Mom.

Mom stops at my desk, where the camera and Polaroids are scattered all over. Bianca and I had been up until three-in-the-morning (technically earlier), deciding which Polaroids were making the cut and were not.

Mom is not impressed.

"How do you even…find things?"

Really? She is REALLY going to put her fingers on some of the pictures with that…that disgusted look. What the FUCK!

"I manage," is the best comeback I can think of; not to mention that a singe of rage is filling up my eyes and I am struggling to fight it back. I watch as my mother prowls around until her eyes settle with mine. They linger with mine for a moment, just as her fingers graze over the Polaroid camera. It brings back...a lot for her and me.

She forces herself to peer away, and I know that it is out of force. Mom gets this tightness in her back, which forces her to slouch forward, rather than straighter taller. Only Dad and I can pick up on that. Dad…Well, Dad gets even quieter. He's avoiding any eye contact with me.

"Well," says Bianca, probably picking up on the damn tension due to our extreme physical distance from each other in the room; in general, "it was nice meeting you Mr. and Mrs.—"

"Rob," Dad tells her. "Call me, Rob."

Bianca returns the smile. I let out a sigh of relief. Thank God…

"So,"—there goes Mother again, fuck—"what is this project exactly about?"

That was for me because now she is facing me, a full-on villain if this were a movie. From the corner of my eye, I catch Dad shaking his head at Mom as if telling her to shut the fuck up. But she doesn't. Not even close to it.

"I'll see you later," is the last thing Bianca says in that room before Dad escorts her out—he insists; anything to get out of that room. Now, it's just Mom and I.

"Collage..." My mom's fingers continue to graze over the Polaroid camera. "She's talking about the one from..."

It still hurts to say.

"Yeah. Yeah, that's the one." And that hurts even more to admit.

"And the guy she'd mentioned...Your new friend, Bianca. Her roommate…Alex?"

That makes me break complete focus from her; my gaze returning to the window, where the sunlight streaks ever so slightly through the small gap between the two curtains that I had closed just moments ago.

"He's the boy you were exchanging spit with last night?"

Uh, what?!

My eyes might as well explode out of my head. I have no idea how I'm able to look her in the face, but I do. We hold eye contact and by all-mighty, we refuse to break it this round. Mom doesn't need my answer.

By this point, I am burning red hot—I could spy it in the small mirror reflection on the end table, adjacent to my alarm clock. I am literally on the spot; there is no way out of this one.

"I need to meet him. Tomorrow. I need to meet him."

Her eyes are begging me, all bright, bold, and watered up. Yet, I avoid the elephant in the room and start on another trail from hers. "But I already have separate holiday plans with them—"

"Erica, all I'm asking is for this one favor. *Please.*"

I tense, conflicted on my next move...

My fingers tighten even more in their fists.

---

Stacey is third-wheeling it with Tom and Jerry at the table. Those two guys are in another, yet again, deep discussion on life and the latest *Star Wars* movie. I only notice this because Stacey is, well, she's eyeing us every four—now, three seconds...

Alex and I are across the lot from the trio. I catch a breath, using the brick wall behind us as some sort of support for the right side of my body. "Meet the parents..."

"Yeah..." Shit, I can feel my cheeks burning up. "They saw us last night."

It takes a moment for him to get it; his moment of realization, a character pivotal moment as Bianca would refer to it because she is the writer. "Oh! *That.*"

Yeah, dude. *That.*

"That makes so much sense now. Are they like...conservative or something?"

Ha! God, I wish that were the reason. It's nowhere close, though. This heaviness takes over me, giving my neck a crank.

Alex matches my standing position, pressing the left side of his body against the brick wall. I can feel his breath instantly and the whiff of cologne that opens my nostrils. It's not like Old Spice or anything, but this floral scent. I think it's…lavender.

Similar to the essential oils that I had once used from Mansell's recommendation. She never believed in pills; well, with the exception at times.

"No," I then say. "It's nothing like that."

He knows that I'm lying to a degree. The fact that he is already holding my hand, slipping his fingers through my own.

"Then, what is it?"

But it is too late—the so-called cat has my damn tongue; from the corner of my eye, I see Stacey looking at us like full-on, her dead eyes watching us. Shit…she might be a spy if I'd not been mistaken. But this is it…the moment of truth; in fact, I can taste it crawling up my throat and sizzling hot on the tip of my tongue. It reeks of gasoline and tastes like cough syrup.

"Alex," it slips right out, my fingers breaking free one-by-one from his, "there's something I want you to know..."

But I cannot say it. It's like the damn cough syrup taste is clogging up my throat. Tension rises in my shoulders, pushing them upward. My neck is hurting from the takeover. I can hear the harsh exhale that escapes my parched lips.

Alex sees it all unravel in front of his eyes. He notices that my hands are shaking, watching as they go to remove the sweat from the four corners of my face.

"Erica—"

That weird RINGING is back.

Stacey, who is purposely leaning closer to Jerry—for obvious reasons—even notices the tension that is taking over my body. She is standing up.

"Hey, Erica!"

But I bolt away, rounding the corner of the brick wall that is no more than four to five feet from where we stand. Well, where we were standing. Alex follows me. I hear his footsteps grow louder and closer like a gust of wind whipping at my backside.

I am hunching over to catch my breath, gasping for the first two inhales through my mouth. My nostrils are refusing to open wider, preventing any of the air to travel through for more air…to just FUCKIN' breathe.

"Shit," I hear Alex as he stops by my side, leaning over to be closer to my ear. Well, closer to me. "Just breathe." And I do, as he helps me lean back and gently sets me against the new brick wall of the building; we are behind the dumpsters. Fuck…this is so fuckin' EMBARASSING—

"Just breathe in and out through your nose," he tells me, grasping a hold of my hand. "But slowly."

He demonstrates. I mock his breathing technique as best as I can—something that Mansell had once guided me through while having a trigger set off a panic attack. It was full-on body shakes and a sweat fest, too.

"What am I?"

Uh, what?

"Huh?" it's all that escapes through the inhale, inhale, and exhale, and exhale, and…oh, shit!

"It's a technique," he tells me, circling so he is now standing in front of me. *Sheesh,* intimidating much. "What am I?"

"Uh…Um, a guy."

"Okay. What else?"

"Um…a person?"

Did I really just ask him if he was human? *Oh my God,* I *did.*

"Good," he says, holding my hands that are clasped together like someone had crazy glued them. "And what's this?"

He's pointing to the wall behind me. I look at it for a moment before answering, "The shop."

Then, he takes my hand and sets it onto the side of my throat—my rapidly beating pulse.

"And that?"

"My heart."

"Still beating?"

"…Yeah. It is."

I choke up. My throat hurts, but this time from the build-up and the pushback of tears. I can't cry right now.

"Good. You're still alive."

That makes me chuckle as I dab at my eyes with my sleeve. Alex waits, leaning with me against the wall. I sink to the ground before he asks. He sits there with me, cautious about what he says or what to do next. But it worked…it worked; whatever he did and said to me just now. My breathing slows down further, but I refuse to look at him. I think he can sense that because the next thing I see is his fingers reaching over for mine. I lock our hands nice and tight, half scared half embarrassed to look up at him. And he helps, even more, brushing the fallen strands of my hair out of my face and behind my shoulders. But my eyes remain at the asphalt…

"You can go now. You don't need to…"

"Erica, I don't want to go."

He reaches for my hand. It makes me shift nervously, but not the kind that I just went through with him. No, it's different. But I already know where this is headed...

# Alex

"Alex, I can't..."

Figured she'd say that.

"...Bianca and I are on a deadline..."

Yeah, I'm not planning on going anywhere. Still here. Next to her. But I notice, through her one little piece of fallen lock of hair, a tear forms and then a few more.

"You can have any girl..."

I wish she didn't think that. Erica's body moves as she inhales and then exhales. Clearly, she is upset...and I'm not sure what else I can do.

"Well, now you know," she tells me.

"Erica, there's nothing wrong with you. We all have things that we're going through, and it doesn't make anyone less or more fucked up than another. Trust me on that."

That makes her look at me. She gives this linger gaze, sort of in a trance of dazed and confused but also, clarity. She can tell—I'm being honest; she's not damaged, fucked up, or has those so-called "issues." She's here. She's normal. She's...more extraordinary than she realizes.

"Okay," she then says. "I'll try. Take it slow, okay?"

"Okay."

Trusting me, she squeezes my hand back. Only, I find myself hesitating. I don't know why but I just don't do anything...at all. She then leans into my arms. My arms find their way around her, as she thanks me and squeezes me tightly. I know she appreciates it.

I just wish that I knew how to thank her back.

# Erica

*Oh, God. Thanksgiving.* The time of cheer and joy; a time of getting together with the family and 'enjoying' each second of company.

Families are pretty much wining and dining here. *Thanksgiving…*

I'm thankful for the clinks, clanks, and scratches of utensils and glasses from the other tables. It is somewhat keeping the silence away from our table. Sarcasm, I guess. That whole awkward silence. I sit in the middle of Bianca and Alex. He is to my left, and she is on my left. Wait—shit! I meant he is on my right. God, I can't think! I've just been so…

My food remains untouched. Dad has the end seat of the booth; he is next to Alex. Mom sits on the other end of the booth, directly across from Dad, and next to Bianca. Everyone is eating, except for Mom and I. From the corner of my eye, I notice that she steals a few looks from Alex and I; then I and Alex.

*Great.*

"...Well," Alex answers the question that Dad had asked a few seconds ago to snowball into a successful game of 'small talk,' "my pops works a lot of graveyard and overtime."

"He sends his hello," Bianca chimes in between her munches of Thai noodles. She even adds in one big, "Mhmm," as she slurps one into her mouth. At least, it gets a laugh from Dad.

I feel another jolt—Alex; his leg has been all scattered brain since we'd first arrive. My attention draws to him. Awe, he's nervous. I can tell because his left leg is still bouncing up and down; he rammed into me four times between the waitress seating us and our dishes arriving. But I didn't mind. I'm glad that he's here next to me. I squeeze his hand under the table, out of, what I think is, everyone's sight. Yet, I see that my mother is already watching us like a hawk on its treetop, chewing and then, taking a sip from her wine glass. The glass is still full. I guess she lost her appetite.

Alex has been far from Bianca's upbeat persona; she gives another slurp, apologizing this time. Poor, Alex…He just gives off this stressed-out vibe; like his mind is racing through millions of 'small talk' topics. Only, I notice that all of his energy is being put into the red cushion that we are sitting on; his fingers give it a pinch.

Holy shit...

"Well," my mother states, "be sure to tell him, 'Hello,' back."

That was a hint of sarcasm (it runs in the family), considering her glance at me, biting down into a piece of her bloody red steak. Bitch.

"And what about your mother?"

That holds Alex's attention. Bianca looks at him, waiting for him to react…she's worried. And so, am I. Before Mom asks again, Bianca sits up taller, setting down her utensil; I guess she has lost her appetite. "Alex loves music. *Spill the wine/Dig that girl*...No? No one's heard of it?"

Nice try, I guess.

Bianca shuts herself up by taking a few gulps of her water. She even calls for the closest waiter, requesting a second…nope, two more! Guess, she's nervous as well.

Now, it's Dad's turn: "So, where do you study at, Alex?"

"Um, Columbia. I mean, I was studying music there. For a bit."

And there's a big *clump*. We all turn to see Mom staring down at her steak knife that has fallen to the beige tile; the bloody red steak juice leaves a few splatters on the floor. Mom goes to reach for it, but a waitress beats her to the punch. Before either one of us gets a chance to chime in, Mom is already thinking ten times ahead, "Was? Are you taking time off? Or something."

Ouch—Alex's entire knee collided into mine.

"Sorry," he says, his tone dropping lower and lower with his shoulders and a frown on his face. What's wrong…?

"Well, it's common, Cathy," Dad is the only one with big enough balls to respond to Mom. "Time commitments can be—"

"I know, Rob, time is everything and draining. But everyone is busy. Period." And she drinks to that.

What is going on here…?

"Cathy."

"What, *Robert*? I just want to know who our daughter is dating—
"

Jesus!

"Mom…"

Alex sits back, his head leaning against the shiny red booth. I mock him, reaching for his hand. I notice his shoulders are all tensed up.

"Well, you two are dating, right? I just assume since your father and I saw you both making out—"

"Awkward!" And we all look at Bianca. She nearly chokes on her drink. "Shit! Sorry. Thought that was inside of my head. I tend to do that a lot."

When the waitress returns with two full cups of water, Bianca immediately chugs one back to shut herself up…*again*.

Oh, man…the family behind our booth is getting up to leave. Fuck—it *was* their joyful conversation and rounds of laughter that kept our table, well, happy. Fake happy. At least, our table—number eight our hostess called it—was blending in with the surrounding happy families at dinner. Now, we must look like a sore thumb sticking out; like one of those situations where someone is present but does not belong. In this case, it is my parents and me…and me…

"To answer your question..." Alex finally looks up, meeting my mother's lingering death stare. "We're just taking things slow. No pressure or anything."

Underneath the table, I feel his hand hovering over mine which loosens my fingers; shit, I had no idea they were already balled up into fists. He holds them. I squeeze his hand back, lacing our fingers; regardless of my mother seeing it or not. And when I finally return my attention to hers, she breaks focus right away and goes for the water cup in front of her. She drinks and drinks.

I notice a tear slipping from the corner of her eye as she does so.

# Bianca

That Cathy chick is fuckin' CRAZY!

Like no joke, there's no other way of putting it. I'm the first to walk out of the upscale version of this Olive Garden, finally catching a whiff of the night's air. It's cold—the kind where you want to cozy up with a mug of cocoa by a fireplace. Oh, man! Now I want some s'mores or something.

And then I see it—"Look!" I tell Erica and drag her ass on over toward the curb to look up. We watch as the beautiful nightfall shines bright with stars. "Camera time!" I give my hips a swing which makes Erica blush as group of dudes whistle at us. Uh, oh! Let's hope Alex doesn't catch that; or worse, CATHY. Ugh!

"Bianca…"

But she is already fetching her Polaroid out of her bag. She snaps a photo of the moon in the sky; a mini after- Earth in front of us. It's quite amazing to see—the way that the stars align and individually give a sparkle in unique shapes. It's fuckin' awesome. It's extraordinary.

And here comes Alex walking on over, his hands buried into his coat pockets. Of course, he goes to Erica first—ass, HA! Just kidding over here. I'm glad. He looks less…stressed out. Probably that stupid Cathy. Ugh! He just deserves the best. I sandwich towards Erica, while my left arm swoops behind her back and around Alex. I make Alex form the other side of the sandwich, gesturing to Erica to aim the Polaroid camera our way. Selfie time!

Only, I wished this time the Polaroid camera was a cell phone…

"Cathy!"

The three of us whip our heads around—fuck, here comes…Cathy. Jesus Christ, lady!

"No pressure?" she says, all hostile and practically out of breath herself; odd, the door is not that far from where we linger on the sidewalk.

Her question was directed to Alex, who is a deer in headlights; as well as Erica, she is turning red. I don't know if it's out of embarrassment or anger.

"Shit! Cat!" Rob practically skids to a stop. He sorts of gives his best attempt of ushering us further away from the wannabe Olive Garden. Yet, it fails. Sorry, Rob…

Cathy takes a step towards Alex, who loosely releases his arm from around Erica's waist. Oh…

"You said you two are taking things slow and I want—no, I *need* to know just what the hell the "no pressure" part means for my sake and her *own?*"

*Her*—She means Erica.

My head whips over to Erica and she looks pissed. I notice that her hand is trying to break free from Alex's. Shit.

"Cathy, what the hell? We talked about this," Rob almost begs his wife, who refuses to listen to him; she'd rather focus on Alex.

"Yeah, Mom," Erica grits, "what Dad is saying!"

"Erica, don't!"

"Whoa!" I step in-between the two; but at this point, I've always been Team Erica. "Jesus Christ, lady!"

"Excuse me?" Cathy barks.

"Ah, shit! My bad. Look..." Shit, I'm not making this any better. "Look, my bad. I didn't mean to call you lady. Not that you're old or anything—"

"Trust me, you're not making this any better for *you* or *him*."

*Him*, as in Alex. Now I *really* want to slap this woman in the face, but Erica. Erica—

Okay good, she's still standing; not that I didn't think she'd get sick...or something.

"Look, I'm sorry," Alex begins, "but I don't know what you want me to say."

Cathy shakes her head and then just storms off.

"Cathy!" her poor husband yells after her, unable to hold it back this time—the anger, shame, and maybe even guilt that he carries. I'd know those looks; it's something I once saw in Alex's dad's face when they took me in. I never forgot that day.

"Erica," I say, "maybe we should go. It's okay."

But as I go to grab a hold of her hand, Erica flinches and tosses her arms to the sides. She IS ready to rumble. 'It's not okay with me." And then, there she goes...

"Erica!" Rob calls out for her now but it's too late; he has no choice but to follow after them. "Fuck! Jesus Christ everybody!"

# Erica

MotherFUCKER.

"Mom!" I chase her down the sidewalk, squeezing my way through the dozens of bodies that fill up space. Shoot, just a second ago it was all cleared. "Mom!"

She's only a few feet in front of me. I pick up the pace, feeling the tension building up from my calves to my head—kicking up the adrenaline. It feels good. I feel good for the first time since she showed up. As I go to reach for my mother's hand, she comes to an abrupt stop and spins around—

"You can't be doing this, Erica!"

"I'm not doing anything, *Mom*."

"You're lying! To me, to your father, and to yourself. I can tell—they don't know. Alex doesn't know."

I find myself running my palms over and over my jeans until one of them grips tightly to the bottom of my shirt. The claustrophobic feeling does not get any better once Dad zooms into the situation; once again, his attempt at middleman and trying to peace the deal.

"What the hell was that? Why are you yelling—?"

"I'm not yelling!"

What the fuck…?

People are watching now. Fuck.

"You didn't have to be so rude back there, Cathy!"

Mom and Dad are going at it more now. Shit. Fuck. FUCK.

I take a step back; this sudden urge to disappear into thin air like a ghost. The living dead…

"Erica?" I can hear Bianca calling out…I think. It's hard to tell because all I see are spotted black and white dots taking over where my parents are standing, still arguing.

"I'm going back to the hotel!" Mom shouts even louder, her hand pointing down to the ground as if she is about to swing her purse at Dad.

"No, you're not!"

"I'm not going to play pretend and act like this is okay because it's not!"

Not, not…that word just echoes in one ear and out the other. That heaviness takes over my body, making it feel gross and fatigued. I'm…burning out…

"Erica!" I hear Alex, followed by a few footsteps and gasps and some more name-calling—

My name.

I go to dab at my forehead, but instead find myself taking a step back—well, my body forces me to—and the air feels…lose. I…I can't catch my breath—

"Honey!" Dad cries out.

"Erica!" Mom is next.

My heart pounds and pounds against my chest, ready to burst right open—a sharp pain screaming throughout my body like nails on a chalkboard. That loud RINGING noise returns and drains everything out, clogging up my ears. Gravity yanks me down to the ground; the world is spinning beneath my feet. One of my shoes slips off as my foot goes crooked and my body falls backward—head back until I find someone's arms wrapping around me as the sky above me stares down…

So…peaceful. The nightfall and stars transition into a dark blue sky, and the clouds flutter around like a sailboat reaching the horizon of a glorious sunset. Only here, at this moment, everything just goes BLACK through my sight.

Nothingness.

My heart has slowed down.

# THREE HOURS LATER

"I'm prescribing ten milligrams," the doctor tells me, scribbling it all down on that damn piece of paper.

My feet dangle off the cold hospital bed regardless of the nurse who's telling me to sit back and relax. There's this IV in my system, pumping in some nutrients and other supplements that my body was, according to the doc., "missing." Fainting is no biggie…except when it deals with, well, the obvious.

The doctor tears off the prescription slip. Oh, hell no—he's really expecting me to just, what, take that. No thanks! I don't plan on getting back on medication. Fuck that.

I just sit there. My eyes beam away from him, but they find their way back to that slip. Shit, his arm is really not going to move.

"Look," I say to him, leaning forward, never breaking focus. "I don't think I need that."

And I don't. I don't need that. He just wavers the slip.

"For what?"

And now, his arm lowers, as he inclines on his stool. "You do realize what you were having earlier was a panic attack."

No shit, bozo.

"Erica, it's only logical to take something to help reduce the anxiety. After all, with your records…"

Great, now he's flipping through my chart. But I could care less. I'm elsewhere…I don't know where exactly my mind is taking me to. It's just not here or…here. I feel trapped; the cold air sends a shiver through my esophagus, forcing the hairs on my arms and neck to rise.

"Erica?" his voice grows louder.

I look up at him; everything seems closer…Well, at least the edge of the bed is. Or was. The doctor helps me up; shit, I must've blacked out for a moment. Only, I don't think he knows that. Otherwise, it would be the death of me if a doctor saw their patient on the verge of blacking out; shit, I'd have to be here for another hour then. But I am safe now. Everything's…normal for now.

"Look. No."

"No?" he says and then, opens my file but not to double-check; just to state the facts, a.k.a. the other obvious. "Says here that you've taken Zoloft before—"

"Yeah. That's just it—I *did*."

I sigh—I just can't fuckin' keep talking about this; not to avoid…it. It's just too difficult to process one thing at a time. *Sheesh*!

"Okay," he breaks the silence with a louder tone, clicking his pen. "So, a no to prescription?"

"If I go back on the pills, I'll only have to relearn how to not rely on them. I don't wanna do that again."

I think he picks up on the borderline desperation in my tone and my overall expression; just from what I feel on the inside. The doctor's stern look remains on him, giving me another hard stare. He even seems uncertain what to do. Yet, he does not press furthermore with the questions and diagnosis.

# Bianca

We've been in the waiting room for a few hours now…

When I see Erica, I run to her, finished with my pacing, and grab a hold of her. She sort of winces—*shit!* I apologize but find my arms coiling around her even more; firmer and stronger. My grip refused to loosen.

"Bianca," she says, spitting out a piece of my hair that stuck to her mouth. "I'm fine. Really."

Yeah, bitch my arms ain't going nowhere. I'm not going anywhere. I can't just leave her; especially with Cathy standing over there with her arms crossed, leaning against the pillar that divides up the two chairs. Stupid twat…

"Bianca. You're kind of squishing me here."

Oh, shit I'm—a gasp escapes through her lips because, well, I guess my grip is somewhat suffocating her. Damn it. I pull back, just enough to see her and enough for her to breathe. She forces a smile as if she is telling me that she is fine…

But she is not "fine."

Who on Earth would be after…well, her panic attack? It sort of looked like a meltdown.

"Sorry," is all I can tell her.

"It's okay"—she gives another forced smile, eyeing over my shoulder; ugh, Cathy!—"I just want to go home. Now."

"Of course," I hear Rob agree.

My eyes never move from Erica, even when she unwraps my arms around her and steps aside, breaking free. She lingers about a foot or so from my side. I finally turn around and immediately see Alex stealing a glance my way. We both return our attention to Erica, who keeps staring down at the white and blue checkered floor. Thankfully, her dad is already with her, waiting patiently for her next answer or thought. God, he's amazing; he even brought coffee for Alex and me after he made a quick trip to the cafeteria about an hour or so ago. He's a trooper. In my eyes, anyone would be lucky to have him as a dad…

"Rob." And then, here comes Cathy, finally getting her lazy ass away from the pillar. "Call us a cab. We'll go back to your dorm to pack a bag…"

Uh, WHAT?!

Cathy doesn't have to take another peek, but it has become obvious that her remark of going back to the dorm…to pack a bag…not on my fuckin' watch…is crazy. She's insane.

"Why is everyone looking at me like I'm crazy?" she states. It's a rhetorical one—

Shit, she gives me a long hard, cold stare because I roll my eyes at her.

Whatever.

"I'm not staying with you or Dad." Erica's tone is so soft and so fragile that it piques my fear as if it is a moment of truth or dare.

"We can just drive her there, Cathy, and then—"

"Erica"—*click click click* go Cathy's Vera Wang high heels against the tiles—"You're not going back by yourself." She chuckles, one of those sinister laughs. In reality, the villain always fuckin' wins.

That's a dose of the real world, kiddos!

"Well, *maybe,* Cathy," I bark, "she doesn't want to go with you!"

"Bianca..."

"Alex, no! It's fine. Erica will stay with us." Oh, that's right, CATHY. I will play this staring contest with you as long as the hospital will allow us. I'm not backing away or sitting down, as Alex is trying to persuade me to at the moment.

"Well, I appreciate your admiration and looking out for my daughter, *Bianca.*" Oh, shit…she's throwing fuckin' shade now! "But that's not going to happen. At all."

I stand up taller, giving a smile. "Okay. Fine, I'll go stay with her then."

"Rob—"

"I mean if Bianca is willing to stay with her…What's the big deal, then?"

Yeah, CATHY, what's the big deal…*stupid twat.*

Cathy grabs a hold of Rob's forearm and does her best attempt of a whisper 'let me lower my voice so the kids can't hear me' shit. "Robert, we're going to keep an eye on her. We're her parents."

"And we're her friends. Practically, that makes us family too."

Wow, that just blurted right on out of me. It turns Alex into a nervous-nellie, giving me one of those cold 'I disapprove' remarks by stating my name. Huh, it's almost like he and I these days are mocking Cathy and Rob's so-called 'loving' marriage. They're better off as colleagues.

Dayum, I just compared myself to the bitch.

Cathy's eyes lower. Rob just stands there…silent. Okay man, this better be you just thinking of a better comeback jab at your wife…

But nothing.

Instead, Cathy is the first to make a move. She grips onto the handle of her purse. I guess it's Rob's cue, he shifts in place. He clears his throat. "I'll go get us a cab then."

Really…that's it, Rob? God, he's so pussy whipped.

I find my shoulders standing taller. This is the moment when I feel fingers grazing on my own—Erica is giving me this look, like a crossover of 'thank you' and 'just shut up and listen to her.' And…I do. For her I will. Not for Cathy.

"Alex?" Rob says. "I can use the company."

*Bad company…*

It's all that pops into my head. God, Alex turned me to that song by Bad Company last semester. It was the only song that sort of calmed me, I suppose. One of those metaphoric songs that you find yourself listening to…reflecting on life…and how far you've truly come.

I swear I can hear the crickets. Poor Alex…He's just so jumpy these days like a Chihuahua. He's standing still one minute and then in a blink of an eye, he's all fidgety and like, playing with the zipper of his jacket or going to bite his thumbnail—

I even stop him, pushing his hand down and shaking my head.

"Sure," he replies to Rob.

Alex exchanges one last look with Erica and me before he leaves with Rob. And she doesn't see me noticing—but Erica quickly breaks focus from Alex as she grapples a hold of my hand. I squeeze it back.

# Alex

Traffic. It's forever escapable and annoying as hell, too.

Rob stands at the edge of the sidewalk, waving his hand up every other second for a cab. Only, a dozen or so of them are all stuck in the traffic jam line, backed up. One of them honks back at Rob and demands him to shut the fuck up. Another cabbie gives his most convincing sarcastic response of, "Good luck."

Poor guy.

Finally, Rob drops his arm. "Unbelievable," I hear him say before he turns and approaches me.

It's his footsteps that catch my attention, snapping me out of my thoughts. I find myself straightening out against the pillar; my spinal cord hits the prickly part of it—you know, similar to the popcorn ceiling. Shit *hurts.*

Rob gets aligned with me, only he stands against nothing. I think I should offer to trade spots with him, but the words do not come out. My lips refuse to open. So, we just stand in silence; luckily, the sounds of the cab honks and cabbies, and people in general, yelling keeps the air from being completely dead.

Otherwise, I would've attempted to push myself through the pillar behind me to escape this long, awkward moment.

"It's a bad habit," he tells me. I look up at him and he gestures with his eyes—my fingernails; shoot, I was picking at them.

"Yeah, I know. I guess it's a lifelong habit of mine." I even show him the fingernails that I'd already begun to chew on. He chuckles, probably agreeing with me.

Rob zips up the rest of his jacket, pulling it closer to his ears from the chilled whiff of breeze that the sky sends tumbling our way.

I'm shivering myself, shoving my hands further into my pull-over jacket. I think it is he who allows a moment of silence before he starts again, "Cathy used to like parties. But nobody ever tells you that the first one will leave you with a chipped tooth and a fractured rib. She and her friends were dancing on the tabletop."

He laughs at the memory—it's a *good* memory, too, just by the smile that sits with him.

"Sounds awful. I didn't know there was a side of her like that."

"You know what they say: Disco was a hit back then."

My eyes break away from him, especially when Rob seems distracted again—I guess by a bad memory. I wince as soon as one of my nails jams into my palm; shit, I keep doing that lately—my fingers curling and securing themselves into balls of fists.

"I was the one who rode with her here."

*Here*, as in this very hospital. He doesn't need to point or say more.

So, I just continue to listen.

"Cathy and I were once New York natives. You know how it goes—getting married so young to start a family. It was a miracle when we had Erica..."

There's more, so much more to their story. I could tell, but now…Now, he's just confirming it.

"She's my little girl and always will be. I know she'll do good. God, she'll do great, *great* things in life." And then, he takes a step forward, making sure that I'm looking at him. "I want you to know that she trusts you and Bianca. She might have not said anything, but that doesn't mean you don't matter to her. You do. Just give her time and you'll see what I've always seen in her. She's an extraordinary girl."

God, I get it now…so much to resonate with. Rob sniffles, forcing a smile, while a few tears stream down his face. He excuses himself and paces a few feet away, retrieving back to the edge of the curb to give the hailing for a cab a shot again.

And then it hits me—my eyes also retrieve back to my fingers; they are no longer in fists, but free.

# Bianca

The night's air breezes into the room; Erica had cracked the window open just moments before she tossed over and knocked out. But it is not cold, rather a warm breeze. It's perfect weather, actually.

Erica has been all Ms. Sleepy Beauty over there; while I just lie here, flat on my back, staring up at the popcorn-free ceiling. The shadows of a few bystanders, who walk on the sidewalk in front of the dorm building entrance, bounce off of the white ceiling. Shadows in the night…

Shit be scary.

At least Erica is here. Otherwise, I'd feel like I was in an episode of the *Twilight Zone*. I swear if there are any nearby trees, that shit would be waving its long acrylic-like fingers at me. The shadows of trees are always outlined like CGI in a Disney or DreamWorks television show. The shadows have a mind of their own like a Tim Burton movie, crawling and reaching for the viewers to join their dark, twisted, fantastical universe. It is quite extraordinary, just thinking about it.

Yeah…I can't take this anymore.

Slowly, I find myself leaning up to my elbows. I steal another glance at Erica—she's still facing the opposite direction from me with her back toward me. I can tell she is sound asleep because the side of her body gently moves up and down as she breathes. I swing one leg over the bed and the other one follows.

I crawl to the floor in front of the bed, the back of my neck is touching the deep purple comforter that is half slipping off—

I catch the section—my side of the bed—before it completely goes overboard. Good…Good. But that does not wake-up Erica. Instead, she fidgets for a second, mumbling something, and gives one of those long stretches before snoring again. Well, it's a soft snore; not one of those manly kinds.

Relieved, I let out a sigh and lean back against the bed framing. I sit there to let everything sink in; and then, I push myself up to sit straighter and reach for my nearby bag. Luckily, there is no zipper or anything; just a flap to slip anything through the small pocket of the over-the-shoulder hippie-like bag. Erica called it hippie-like due to the sunflower and meadow theme going on with neon colors and overuse of swirly-swirls design.

I pull out my composition book, cell phone, and headphones. I see that I have a missed call from Alex and an unread text message from him as well. His text reads that he is bored at work, followed up with a "What time are you comin' home?" I think he misses my company; lately, I have been here a lot with Erica. But work is work. We need to get this project done. So, I avoid his text—I'll get back to him later.

I reach for the second bag, adjacent to the bed and in front of the desk chair—my laptop case. I remove the laptop and immediately Microsoft Word loads up to a fresh blank page. It is a start. I pull the composition book closer before I decide that it is best to just lay it on my knee. I type away, referencing the poem stanzas in my notebook, copying word-by-word into the document. Of course, I shove in my earbuds before doing any of this to focus and, well, relax, too.

*Alabama, Arkansas, I do love my Ma and Pa/*
*Not the way that I do love you/*

# Erica

Slowly, I awaken…

Turning over, I already see a silhouette sitting at the edge of my bed—Dad. I sit up as soon as the sleepy crust falls out of my eyes once I rub them out.

"Hey, kiddo," he says to me.

"Hi…Uh, what are you doing here?" I push myself up to my elbows before I sit up completely and push back to lean against the wall—still, no sign of Bianca.

"Bianca didn't want to wake you. She says you've been out for a while..."

I have. And…?

I take another scope around the room and notice: "Where's Mom?"

"You know her, bringing business wherever she goes."

The tone of disappointment also reflects on the exterior; his shoulders slump forward and his eyes divert away. I think this *is* his reaction to any mention of Mom. Before I can ask him…how he's been or doing…his phone gives an alert beep.

"Bianca says to check your email," he informs me, texting her back…

What the hell.

"I see that you guys text now?"

"Your friends are my friends."

It makes me laugh—what a dork! But Dad is watching me, no longer texting. To be honest, I don't think he even finished the text to Bianca.

"I, uh," it's all that comes out of my mouth. "I have some work to do—"

"You know, I could really go for a cup of coffee right now. It's been a while since we've last gone to Katz."

Yeah, it sure has.

---

Dad insisted that we hang out; or as most parents put it, "We need to talk" or a.k.a., "I know you need to vent to me about your shitty life!"

So, why not.

Katz's Delicatessen has been a favorite spot for Dad and I, as well as the group of tourists who are getting a KICK out of the famous "I'll have what she's having" table from *Harry Met Sally*. The elderly man in the Hawaiian shirt gives his best Meg Ryan orgasmic…expression.

It reeks of fried oil and salami. I swear, this place has a different smell whenever the bell at the take-out counter goes off.

Dad busts up laughing at the man in the Hawaiian shirt although, I DO find it funny, too. But I'm also finding my eyes retrieving back to my cell phone—Bianca's email which has an attachment of a completed draft of the poem. Well, as mentioned in her signature sign-off, it's only one of MANY drafts. She keeps telling me that a writer is always writing and then thinking and thinking, 'OH, MY GOD! That fuckin' SUCKED!'

Dad takes a sip of his coffee—they still serve in plastic here but at least, it's free refills. From the time I was a kid, Dad has always come here for the coffee and never the food. Usually—

I set my phone down, still impressed and quite moved.

"She wouldn't let me read it." Dad turns to me. "She said it was between you two only and you two only. Her words. Is it that good?"

"Yeah. Yeah…It's amazing."

"Extraordinary, as I see it."—I glimpse at Dad and this guilt has already consumed him—"Sorry, I saw a few lines after reading her email. I mean, she did send it to me, so it was an accidental look."

I know; I believe him. I do. Really, I do.

Dad gets all fidgety and red when it comes to something that can potentially turn into a confrontational situation. But it's me, *Dad*. Not Mom **your crazy wife**.

"Honey, they care about you. You know that, right?"

"Yeah. I know..."

I think. Then, it burns with a desire, working its way up to my throat and eyes. I start sniffling, holding back the tears by not making any sudden movement. But the tears still drop and drop, plopping down onto the plastic wrapper—Katz's version of a tabletop protector for the red cloth underneath it.

"Dad," I say before my eyes meet his, "I haven't told them. Any of it."

He's still listening, waiting for my next move.

"And the project…I don't want to screw this up."

"How are you going to screw things up?" he says, it's rhetorical because he leans forward in his chair, watching me. Yet, he is also distant at the same time, too. It's a bit unsettling…

"I just don't want to be a hypocrite, Dad. We know how that went when I told you and Mom for the first time…"

My tone had already diminished by the time I reached, "Mom." I straighten up, shivering at the same time, and take a breath. Dad reaches for my hand. He holds onto it for a moment, shutting his eyes to process…everything. Great, I'm triggering shit for him, again. I'm such an asshole.

"Give it time," he tells me. "Be patient with yourself, Erica. I know that's the cheesiest and lamest thing to say to your own child, but that might just be the answer to this all."

And I know he wants to chime in, "Trust me," again. Yet, he doesn't. He has rested his case. I never break focus from him. Instead, I try to let the words sink in and consume my subconscious.

But at this moment, I feel nothing. The pace of my heart picks up swiftly, enough to clam up the balls of my feet, to my fingertips and then to my temples.

# Alex

The breakroom at work is quiet per usual; except for the clanks, clinks, and other metal movements of my co-workers and I shoving our belongings into our lockers. They are small lockers, like the length and width of a size ten shoebox.

I see Stacey at her locker glancing my way. When I look fully at her, she pretends she was eyeing something else to play it off cool, so I don't think she's a creep. Although, I don't think that and never did, but I kind of want her to stop watching me at times…

She's also young, and I guess this is her first real job so…I think she's just trying to make friends.

Okay, Stacey…I know Tom or Jerry are not into you either. *Sheesh,* she's doing that whole laughing and gently slapping their arms thing as if they said something funny. I doubt it. Those two…Well, I don't think I've seen them talk to anyone else but each other. I guess they just put up with Stacey out of guilt. I've never seen either one of them bat an eye at her. Ever.

Oh, man. I sound mean right now but it's just that—Erica has been on my mind.

Just then, I hear small footsteps trying to sneak in and out—it's her. Erica pushes her belongings into her locker, which is four down from mine. That seems to be a lot but really, it is only about five or so feet of air that swims between us.

Her eyes stay glued to her phone like she is waiting for a call or a text…

"Hey," I finally say.

"Hi…" She quickly puts her phone away into her back pocket.

"I didn't think you'd be in today."

Shit, I shouldn't have said that…

This look comes over her, a mix of shame, guilt, and more embarrassment. "Yeah, neither did I."

She shuts her locker. I have to say something, but she beats me to the punch just as I go to take a step closer to her: "I'll see you later, Alex."

She just storms off in her not-so-quiet tip-toe grand exit, catching Hector's attention as he heads in. Erica practically brushes into him, but she apologizes. Hector looks at me, gesturing to where she was located. I just shrug and shrug. Too late for me to build the courage and spit out an answer.

Leaning on my locker door, I catch my breath, but this heaviness still weighs me down like a pile of bricks are being added onto the invisible backpack that I am wearing. Only, those are my shoulders and the small gap of skin between is burning from tension. I go to crank my neck, resting my hand on the side as I do a few reps.

Once I feel that is enough, I close my locker. For whatever reason, my eyes go over to the area behind me where Stacey is the last woman standing. She pushes the door to her locker shut, holding eyesight with me. This time, there's this compassionate reaction.

I'm assuming she feels bad for me because everyone saw that whole thing with Erica. Plus, I know if I can feel the awkward tension—not to mention how I'm all worked up—then everyone else can too. Shit, even Tom and Jerry give a pat on my back and shoulder as they pass me by like, "Sorry, bro/Ouch!"

I'm the first to break focus with Stacey, conflicted about what to do next. I just…stand there for another moment longer.

# Erica

The moment has passed; but maybe, just maybe, hours have gone by. I've been stacking the shelves for…ever.

Jerry and I stack together. It almost seems to come off in a rhythmic way; he goes first and then I do. He puts a record on that shelf; I place a CD on the other. And so forth.

It's kind of irritating how long we have been at this, neither one of us saying a word to each other. Except for a friendly, cordial-like, "Hello," before we started to work.

I don't even need to glance over my shoulder because I already know that Alex is watching me. Plus, I hear Stacey whisper politely, let's say that, to Alex every other minute that a customer is waiting on him. Guess that is him also waiting on me, too. We haven't spoken since earlier…

The bell of the door grasps my hearing, especially when that…voice rings a bell in my head: "What the fuck, Paul! This hipster *sheeeeet*."

I don't have to look. I already know that voice. And so does Alex once I hear him respond, "Uh, can we help you…?"

"Come on man," the second male customer's voice echoes before I finally take a peek at him…Oh, my God. It's the boy who was hitting on me back at the cafeteria and his friend. "Josh, come on."

*Josh.*

Say no more because I can already hear that ringing in my ear, clamming up my hands which refuse to let go of the mini vinyl that is supposed to go on the shelf with the others. Fuck, fuck, FUCK.

"Really," Josh says with such disgust, toying with one of the CDs in the nearby discount bin. "Everything is clean-cut? Where da fuck is the explicit shit?" He tosses the CD back in and digs through the others, eyeing Alex, who has already circled in front of the registers. "Hey man. Yo! Are you like offended easily or something? What the fuck—"

"Dude, come on," his buddy—Paul, that's right. That's his name—pleads, attempting to grab a hold of Josh's wrist.

Only, Josh retorts, and I catch him mumbling, "Faggot."

My eyes are already shut by this point. Tension consumes my body, making me think of that Freddy Kruger scene where he is eating up a young Patricia Arquette. He really swallows her up to stop her from screaming while all the blood and bodily fluids spill around her on the floor. This is what comes to mind at this exact moment. Shit…it's getting warm in here. Just breathe…BREATHE.

"Come on!" Josh chucks whatever CD is holding back into the discount plastic bin. "When we gonna blaze haze."

But I cannot breathe. The air tubes are clogged up or something. And I begin coughing. I don't move until my hand rises to cover my mouth. Only that does not work, especially when Jerry finally turns to me and approaches like a foot or so closer to me, asking if I'm okay.

No, Jerry, I'm not OKAY. Jesus Fuck. Now he's getting closer—

I stumble backward. Now the attention gets drawn to me. That weird ringing grows louder, forcing me to cover my ears as it all just hits me like a passing train—

*Me.* I'm sitting on my bedroom floor. The Polaroids are all spread out in front of me on the beige carpet. They are upside down, while a few of them are pushed off to the side, still wrapped up in a rubber band. Those are the ones that I have yet to look at…

Focus, ERICA. FOCUS.

My pulse is vibrating—I mean, beating faster. I can feel the beat of it against my neck echoing to my wrists. Both of the wrists…

And before I turn just one of the Polaroids over, I hear in the present-day world—

"Erica?"

Before I can see who, it is, I flinch and flee—turning around without hesitation and head straight for the beaded doorway. My body is fatigued. At any given second, I know it's going to drag me down. Then, I'm done. Crap, not here. Just wait until I get to the employee room.

"Hey," it echoes from afar and then, right into my ear. "Hey! Erica?"

It's Alex, but I already could tell. He has me stop about a foot or so from the doorway, a.k.a. the beads. Fuck, I just needed to get to those damn pink hippie beads and then I would've been out of here. Away from that idiot…

"Hey," he says quietly, holding onto my wrists. I can feel the pink flushing up my cheeks because guess what, I'm avoiding giving eye contact with him. It's something I'd noticed a while back from a session with Mansell.

I think he knows this look…Alex gives a quieter, "Hey," as if he is asking something else. He is and I know it is killing him. But Josh is already ten steps ahead, coming our way.

"Thought you two looked familiar." Josh stops at the end of one of the shelves, the section which Jerry and I had stocked up and restocked unpurchased items like two-days ago. He leans an arm against the glass counter that the registers sit on, tilting down his sunglasses.

Poor Stacey takes a step back, so that she stands opposite the registers. Hector comes out, stopping in the beaded doorway.

"Look at you," Josh starts up again. "Fresh meat found her some *meat*."

"Really?" Paul gives me a look, apologizing.

Poor guy…There is really something weird going on for someone such as Paul, who is just covered in a sweat of guilt and fear, to be friends with Josh.

Josh is probably just as manipulative and cold as he is with Paul, his so-called best buddy. What a fuckin' asshole. I can think of a few girls from high school who pulled that shit with myself and I… Paul reminds me of my high school teen self at this moment.

"Alex?" We hear the fear creeping into Stacey's tone. She is just as terrified as she sounds, practically pushing up against the wall behind the registers.

If I were not mistaken, I'd say she was attempting to push her way through that wall. Her knuckles are slowly turning white from gripping onto the table that sits beside her.

"Well, look at you!" Josh faces her and presses his body…his groin…against the glass of the counter. "Ain't you a cutie." He wiggles out his tongue at her—

It just ticks me off, something lights the ignition. "Hey!" I call at him, tossing Alex's hands off of mine. That was accidental, and I hope he knows that. But I…I can't let this piece of shit in front of me do…make Stacey feel at harm…

I'm shocked myself, realizing that I'm standing next to him at the counter. Josh straightens up, returning to his normal 5'8"/5'9" height. And then, I tilt my head to my left side—an attempt to block Stacey from his view. He just flashes a grin at me, tilting and leaving his sunglasses hanging at the bridge of his nose.

"Back off. From her."—Stacey—"Them."—Alex, Jerry, Tom—"And me."

"Alex…?" Stacey says again but this time, she edges a few inches to her right—an attempt to leave, far away from Josh.

"You should go," Alex warns Josh, taking a step closer to us. He stands in-between us, blocking me from Josh's view. I can only see part of Josh and his right eye wandering from me to Alex. I can see the top of his hair; he's about an inch or so taller than Alex.

"And what the hell do you think you're doing." Josh smiles and removes his sunglasses. Shit—that tightness is making its return, spotting out part of my vision from the corner and working its way inward-

Breathe, BREATHE, ERICA.

"Hey! Hey, *asswipe*!" All eyes go over to Janet, who lingers at the top of the staircase in the corner of the shop, a.k.a. the grand entrance to her upstairs office. She's carrying a small brown box. Who knows what's in it because she sits that thing on top of the railing and slams her hand on it…there's no cover.

Nope, it is just an open box.

"Who, me?" Josh points to himself.

"Yeah, you," Janet mocks him, making this ugly long face. It gets a chuckle from Stacey, and she sees me stealing a glance at her. "Get the fuck outta my shop!"

Paul is already at the door. Josh laughs and goes to turn around, back to Stacey, until there's a big slam—Janet removes her boot from the white railing; she kicked it. "Now! Get the fuck OUT!" She delivered that with rhythm, descending a step down to each word, "Get/The/Fuck/Out."

She almost sounded like an acapella group warming up their vocal range.

"All right! Ya damn ol' hippie." Josh exchanges one last look with us, scanning/creepin' on me. His eyes send daggers into mine. It creates this weird, eerie feeling at the pit of my stomach as he seems to zoom in closer on me…making me dizzy. The room is tilting on its axis—

I bolt out of there, loosening my fingers from Alex's wrist.

"Asshole," I hear Alex mumble before there are footsteps following me, followed by, "Erica!"

But I pick up the pace, barging through the hot neon pink beads and rounding the corner. I head for the metal door that goes outside to the courtyard, which is our usual spot for breaks. I feel my throat tightening, mirroring the tears that ooze right out from their sockets and dripping down my cheeks like blood.

"Okay! Back to work everyone! Fuck that fucker. Little shit!" is all I hear Janet half mumbling half shouting as I exit.

# Alex

After barging out to the courtyard, I come to a stop. It is empty out here. I don't see her, but I hear her sniffling and gasping for air—

Around the corner.

I rush over there. I swear that my breathing matches her own.

Erica uses the wall for support, leaning part of her body against it, including her hand, still catching her breath. Jesus, she's flushed as hell. I don't know what to do but just stand there and wait for her. But the ball is in her court. It would only make sense that she tells me what my next move should be. Even if I don't like it, I know that now is the time to listen to her…and what is in her best interest.

Once her breathing returns to a normal pace, straightening herself up but still leaving one of her hands flat on the brick wall, she opens her eyes and looks up to see me. Her shoulders move up and down in two-sets of 'one-two; one-two,' making me wonder if she is still in the process of having or coming out of a panic attack. Whatever the case may be, I have to go to her.

So, I do.

"Shit," she says, balking away before I can touch her. "I'm fine. Really."

No, she is not.

"Erica…you're shaking."

She already knows that. Erica turns around and leans back into the wall, pressing the back of her head on it which makes her look up at the sky. I copy her move. The sky is bluer than ever today with whisks of clouds surfing by. It's kind of interesting that the sky has swirls of yellow roaming around, yet there is still no sign of the sun. I wonder if she notices it, too.

"I'm just so...annoyed," she says, which makes me look at her. "I *hate* that guy. He needs to *get a life*."

"I know."

She takes a deep breath. I see that her fingers are still shaky. I reach for them. She leans into my shoulder, letting me comfort her for once. Her breathing is raspy, not harsh. I think…I think she's just overwhelmed with everything. Like…there is more to what had happened back inside with that asshole customer.

"Well, I'm here now." I pull back, which she does as well, to remind her.

It calms her. She can see it again—I've noticed this thing she does where she jerks her head back never breaking focus with my sight, she studies me.

It sounds creepier when I explain it but it's like…she's studying the facts of me, who I am and how I am acting towards her; *if* my actions and words align together. She's…trusting me more and more.

But this time, she is still embarrassed. I notice that she is wiping her hands over and over onto her jeans like some magic trick.

"You know, panic attacks are more common than you think..." And the shift in my tone has her listening again, waiting until I say something next. "Can I show you something?"

---

Hector grabs something out of his locker before we hear the door shut, followed by his heavy black boots trudging against the floor. I think he gives a head bob to Erica because I see her glancing back my way.

I take an item out from my locker—it's a small booklet. Now, it all just tumbles from there on…reminding me of everything that once was…hitting home for me all over again.

"I wanted to show you earlier, but it never seemed to be a good time."

She can see how difficult this is for me. Reaching for my hands, she says, "Alex, can I see?"

She doesn't have to beg because her eyes say enough. They never break away from mine.

After a moment, I pass the booklet into her open hands. Her fingers run over the band stickers on the cover. I've been collecting them since I was thirteen-years old. Now, I'll occasionally find myself placing a few more on top of the older ones as some tribute to my teenage—youth—days. I guess it's one of those sentimental moments for me…and maybe for her as well.

Erica finally opens the booklet, thumbing through the pages and pages that are compiled with some of my favorite famous and inspirational quotes/song lyrics/short entries, all in my handwriting. A few get a smile out of her like it flashes a good memory for once. Whatever it is…she seems happy for a moment. It's…nice to see a genuine smile for once.

"I started looking up random quotes one day. Ones that deal with grief and healing. It was something I'd started doing the day...the day they told us that she was never going to get any better."

Erica flips to the next page, and it almost paralyzes her. This heavy exhale escapes her lips; I think she's taken aback.

"Remember when I said I was taking time off of school..." I need to say no more, I think.

Erica holds this sad, lingering look with the photograph of my…my mother. It's a beautiful photo, regardless of the IV tubes attached to her and the fact that she has no hair and is very…She has pale skin. It's my favorite photo of my mom. I know…She'd still want me to see that everything happens for a reason. No matter how painful it is; at least for those of us who are left behind when a loved one passes.

"I didn't want to remember her like that, but it's reality. Hers and my own. She never stopped smiling, even when it was time." And I can already taste it—the shame, guilt, and, sadness that hits me all at once.

My breathing becomes shallow. I go to grab my backpack straps, only they are not there. I forgot…it's still in my locker.

"Oh my, God," she whispers, and it catches and holds my attention. "You get them, too…" She covers her mouth to prevent herself from saying anything further. I forgot about that tick of mine, too…I stop wiping my hands onto my jeans (it is my own panic attack).

She and I are more similar than I thought. But it appears that neither one of us want to believe it.

"Remember when I said, there's nothing wrong with you…"

"Alex…?"

"The attacks come and go, but they're manageable," I reassure her, squeezing her hand back. I know it's her way of consoling me…and maybe even herself in a way. "It's fucked. How the worst moments in life become that extra push to pursue something."

And that lightbulb flickers on for her. "Columbia."

"Yeah, Columbia. My mom's an alumnus. Alto singer. She used to sing to me every night as a kid. Even to Bianca."

"She sounds like an amazing woman."

She's so sweet. It gets a smile from me and her as well. "Yeah. She was. She was *fuckin'* AWESOME!"

Like me, Erica gives a small, 'woot, woot,' making us both laugh for a moment longer. Then, I have to tell her. "She would've liked you. You know that?"

"I would've liked her too." She leans into me, resting her shoulder against the side of my shoulder again. "Thank you for being here with me."

Huh, I can sense another vibe—guilt, I think.

I wrap my arms around her. "Moms," I say. "We can't live without them. They're always looking out for us. For the best."

Ah, *Cathy*; makes sense now, especially when she goes to bite her nails, already lost in deep thoughts. I remove her hand from her mouth, slipping my fingers through hers. I study our fingers from the way they both stop shaking a bit, especially hers. They become tight locked, bound together. For the first time, it feels safe…like home. I know she feels the same way, as she parts her head an inch or so back to look me in the eye. I lean in, and she kisses me first.

"Let me take you out after work," I tell her, in-between breaks for air. "We still haven't had a real date."

Yeah…I'm still surprised we haven't had one of those *yet*. And she gets all quiet on me, realizing it too, "Oh, that." Followed by more silence.

"The suspense is killin' me!" I say, making her laugh, and smiling even more.

# Erica

He's…amazing.

Alex.

I really like him.

As soon as we get out of work, I find myself running with him through SoHo. We spend the rest of the afternoon, slipping into the evening time, sightseeing, and taking pictures of the city life. The landscapes. The buildings. The trees in Central Park. The infamous bull…I'll leave it there.

I start with taking the photographs, while strangers and then, ultimately, Alex serve as my muse.

Listening to music together, sharing my earphones, my throat burns from laughing. My cheeks are starting to hurt from smiling so much.

Even when Alex swoops around me and I don't realize that he has taken the Polaroid camera out of its bag while we gaze out into the ocean on the Brooklyn Bridge. He's so sneaky, aiming the Polaroid camera at me and capturing me in the basic, typical tourist act. The flash catches me off guard. He makes me set my hands down, away from my face as I go to cover it and snaps my photo again.

I…allow him to. It's a first…

I pull him in, looping my arms around his waist, pressing my lips to his, hard and tight. He almost drops the camera, making me laugh again. He announces to the passersby how he'd never dropped a van Gogh's fan piece of work, the Polaroid being my so-called masterpiece.

I shut him up and kiss him again. I feel the camera hitting my side. At some point, I guess he takes a photo of us; the most basic kissing selfie…a couple's photo.

---

We stroll down the sidewalk, hand-in-hand, sharing an earpiece. Alex sings along to Tom Misch's "Memory."

He's so…I hold onto his arm tighter, watching him jump into the verses, all into it and spinning me around so I'm walking in front of him, backward as he serenades me.

God, this is so cheesy but he's really…sweet.

*…So/*
*Tonight/*
*I'm sleeping under the stars/*
*Cuz I feel it/*
*And you're climbing up with me/*

"Alex!"

Without realizing it, he swoops me up, carrying me from the waist up. I don't get him…still singing/rapping to me. At some point, my feet find their way back to the cement. I can't help but maul him right here and now, leaning into him, which almost sends us over until he stops to catch his balance.

"Oh my God! I'm so sorry—"

He kisses me back, though. Long, firm, and…

My hands find their way up, my fingers reaching for his ears. We really…go at it this time. He moves forward, and I walk backward, leading us to the corner of the building. Oh…we're already here at the dorm building. DAMN, we were either walking this whole time, not realizing the amount of time that has passed or we simply, we simply…

What was I saying?

"I should really..." I attempt to tell him in-between air. "Alex…" Oh, God…he's going for my neck now. Finally, I pull back. "I gotta go!"

"I don't want you to." He forces me to stay, nuzzling into me again. And yet, I'm still here, tempted to ask something (yes...that)…

I mean, it's been a while…a long time. But I'm willing to see where it goes or how he responds. But before I can even ask him if he wants to come in, he is handing over the booklet with band stickers on the cover.

"Here. Take this."

"Alex, I can't—"

"JUST go through it and see which ones you like. Besides, it'll give me an excuse to see you sooner than later." Fine…I have no choice; he's convincing.

He kisses the top of my forehead, as I hold the booklet closer to my chest—my acceptance of it.

---

I've been up all…well, all night to be honest.

My eyes are heavy and sore from following into the Team No Sleep category. I only recognize the time when the first stripes of sunlight reflect onto my back, warming it up like I'm some sort of frying omelet. But it feels nice though, *genuinely nice.*

I sit back and lean against my bed frame. Still finding myself…thinking of Alex. The way he looks at me, the way he tastes…

Oh, Jesus Christ! Now, I'm making this sound like some weird wannabe soft porno. It's not. It's just…It's been a while since a guy has treated me so right. And it's the first time I have been enjoying it.

Lowering the volume of my phone, tuning down Reed's voice, it all hits me; that lightbulb goes on. My workflow has to be put on pause as I momentarily stay seated to view my work. With the new Polaroids on the floor, my eyes scan the new side of the project. It's official…I'm merging the past and present-day…

The new Polaroids of myself, Bianca, and Alex. The last photo of us is Alex and I kissing on the Brooklyn Bridge.

Nearby is Alex's notebook with my post-its sticking out on certain passages—bookmarks to remind me which quotations and lyrics to use in the project.

---

A cab waits nearby, approximately ten or so feet behind Dad. He watches Mom and I exchange one long, and silent, awkward hug. Her perfume—Beautiful—tickles my nostrils as I take another breather. God, it's strong! And just then, we both hear, "I can't do this."

Mom and I disengage, immediately looking to Dad. He's all…fidgety and it says a lot that his eyes scroll from Mom to me. Not the other way around.

"Robert," Mom warns, taking a step towards him. "We should get going."

But the tension between them is sticking out like a sore thumb.

"What's going on…?" Really, no response—just the white part of your eyes growing smaller due to the dilated pupils. "Dad?"

"Nothing is going on," Mom snaps back. Yet, she refuses to look at me, either. I notice her knuckles are already whitened from gripping so tight onto the handle of her purse…

"Erica," Dad complains as soon as I whip around and storm off—fuckin' OVER this.

"Jesus! What does it *matter*? We'll be back soon anyway."

"Shit. Really, Cat…"

Uh, WHAT?!

By now, I'm at a stop; the ground is concaving my feet further in. My legs jerk which forces me to finally turn around and stare my parents back in the eyes. Dad is consumed with guilt like he is doing a walk-of-shame. Well, I guess he is sort of doing one as he tip-toes towards me.

"Honey, I was going to tell you—"

"The firm's opening a branch upstate," Mom interrupts, putting Dad at a complete halt where he now stands; like a foot or so from where I'm lingering at. Mom meets his level and never takes her eyes off me. "They're interested in me running it. I was at an interview the other day."

"You're moving *here*?"

"Nothing has been confirmed yet," Dad responds.

*Frown.*

Business my ass…I can't believe I fell for that one the other day…before we went to Katz. Oh, my God. I think Dad was using Katz as bait. Shit...

"Erica—?"

"And you knew about this?!" I silence Dad from the horrified and shocked tone that rises more. I'm…just so angry right now. Why, WHY.

He's acting like my mom.

"You know, most kids would be happy to be closer to their parents—"

"Mom, I didn't say anything!"

"Well, you didn't have to!" She composes herself, adjusting the buttons of her peacoat which has a few lint balls rolling around on it. "Your face says enough."

"Oh, so now my face bothers you, too!"

"Erica," Dad pleads, reaching for my wrist; but I yank back away from him, too. I think that leaves a stunned expression on him; I hurt his feelings.

"Is this about Alex?" I ask Mom and only her.

Mom breaks eye contact with me. Her sight goes to the floor and from what it seems like, she is staring at Dad's shined shoes.

"Well, we should get going," she tells Dad, "or we'll miss our flight."

Although, I'm quite sure that is also directed at me—she steals another, 'I'm so disappointed in you,' jab at me. Whatever.

"This is complete bullshit." And I'm telling them both; Dad's eyes enlarge; Mom's jaw parts open. "You're both full of SHIT!"

I flip them both off…it just sneaks right on out of me. "Have a safe flight back!" Oh, how the sarcasm just gets under Mom's skin as she squints and forces her eyes to appear beady.

I whip around and pace and pace and pick up speed, distancing the hell away from them.

"Erica! Come on!" Dad shouts, which is followed by what I think are Mom's high heels clicking away, too, like I am. "Everyone! Jesus fuckin' Christ! Why can't we all just be friends?!"

---

I pace across the floor, back and forth—back and forth. Dabbing at my forehead again, the tips of my fingers are doused with sweat.

"Erica," Dr. Mansell says from the other line, "you're not looking at the positives. Finally, out on your own. Around more of your peers. You do *realize* how big of a deal that is."

Again, she's being rhetorical.

"But why is she doing this now?!"

Ouch! I bit my thumbnail too hard, getting some skin—a papercut line is bleeding. It stings. I think my face is red.

"I think your mom misses you. The long-distance is just sinking with her. Besides, the community college was closer her way. Back home."

True, very true. I let out a sigh…

"Something is still on your mind," Mansell beats me to the punch.

"It's because…" Just tell her, Erica. "…Things are moving quite fast here."

Bianca. Alex...

God, I force myself to sit back down on my bed, dripping from nervousness.

On Mansell's line, I hear movement—I think she's sitting on the couch in her office. "What was that?"

"I just gotta stay focused, you know? The deadline is coming up next month and I..."

"Okay. So, the deadline is what, a few weeks away? Well, knowing you, you're making progress. Like always."

God, if I were not mistaken, I'd say she was trying to uplift me like one of those, 'Say YES,' spokesman. Or spokeswoman in this case. I eye Alex's journal that sits beside me on the comforter...

Running my fingers over the faded-out stickers, it sends this tingle up the rest of my hand and arm, consuming me with…

> I remember being back in my old room, reaching for one of the numbered Polaroids in front of me. I turn it over. Then, I repeat the same action with

> the others. The numbers are no longer facing my way, but the first signs of...of him in the Polaroids. All of them. All fifty-eight of them—the white backdrop behind him; his hand; his ear; and lips. My fingers work their magic, slowly piecing together the Polaroids...connecting...like a puzzle.

"Erica?" Mansell asks, yanking me back into. The NOW.

My fingers are trembling, which makes it difficult to hold up my phone. I lie back, but then immediately sit up. There's pressure tightening my forehead—you know, that space right above the nose. It doesn't hurt but it is unbearable. The reason for my vision spotting out to black dots—

*Shit.*

Closing my eyes, I answer her, "I just wish they knew sometimes." Even though I take a deep, deep, deep breath, I slowly take in oxygen...somehow.

"Erica, remember what I used to tell you: there are no prerequisites."

I know...I know that. But there's this tightness roaming around my chest. *Guilt.*

"You sound exhausted," Mansell responds to the unstoppable sigh that slips through my lips—shit, I was trying to do that away from the receiver. "Have you been getting rest—?"

"I'm fine." I snap sooner than expected. "Doctor said to continue with my routine, as long as the attacks aren't severe."

*Fuck!*

On her end, I hear the leather of the couch giving that familiar squeak—I'm assuming that she's sitting up, all alert from me not telling her that piece of information. "Doctor?"

"Uh, yeah," it's all that I can think of saying. "I had an attack—but that's it. They sent me home and said I just needed to take it easy."

Shit, now she's sighing. I'm stressing out my own fuckin' therapist. Great. Shit. FUCK.

"Erica, I want you to answer the first thing that comes to your mind. How are you doing mentally?"

And that question silences me. My palms are pressing further into the sheer fabric of the comforter—the itchy part. Only, I don't care at this moment. It's slowing down some of the tension that departs my throat. Unless I'm holding my breath—I've done that before during a…

My eyes lower to the floor, where the Polaroids and camera sit, next to my backpack.

"Erica?"

There are two replies—the yeses and nos.

"Erica?" Mansell's tone grows louder, interrupting that ringing that was making its way back to my ears.

I retreat.

"I gotta go!"

"Erica—"

I "hang-up" up on her, like a phone call, but in-person. Shut her out. I regret it, but it's my only option.

Reaching over, I lift the bottom of the comforter—some sort of curtain, making direct eye contact with the shoebox underneath the bed.

# Bianca

Erica has that *look* again…

She's already tense before class even starts. "You beat me again!" I tell her and take my usual seat next to her.

She brings her hands back onto the table—I hadn't noticed them being underneath it.

"So…" I try again. "How was the rest of your break?"

And we hear the footsteps, along with her roller backpack; Mrs. Newman trollin' in. "Alright, everyone! Let's check-in." Newman wakes up the projector screen by clicking the mouse button on the computer. From the podium, she references the computer and calls us off one-by-one. "Bianca and Erica. Progress?"

Oh, shit. Almost like magic, I rise and notice that I'm the only one doing so, especially since all eyes target me. I glance at Erica and give her a nudge. She stands, but her eyes divert away, remaining on her desk—or the van Gogh painting, I think.

"Great!" I finally respond to fill in the long, awkward silence that circles the room. Someone coughs, and it echoes off the walls. "Just working on another rewrite."

"Good. Thank you, Bianca." Newman must have a list in front of her on the podium. She uncaps a pen and jots something down and follows with a long scratch. "As for the Polaroids, I know it's been a debate with the theme." And that is for…

Erica snaps out of it and finally meets Newman's look. "Uh," she spits out. "Sort of."

Sort of? Jesus, something is off with her today.

"Oh-kay." Newman sets her pen down and leans forward, her elbows resting on top of the podium from what it appears to be at our distance. Damn, we're in the nosebleed seats in this big-ass classroom. "Would you please elaborate for us?"

All eyes on Erica. Poor thing, she is all tense; the back of her back stiffens. And then, I think I'm the only one who notices, as Newman calls for everyone to get ready for notes as she pulls up a PowerPoint—Erica's nervous/stressor tick; she's pressing her fingernails into her hand, which reddens her palms. It takes over around the hand like…blood.

I look at her, but she is too focused on staring down at the table. Shit.

---

Erica leads the way and I follow. Man, she is chatty—NOT: "Jesus! I kept rambling on and on. I looked stupid!"

Whoa—that dude almost ran into her. Only, Erica is not affected because she keeps walking and finding miraculous ways of dodging people who are not paying attention and staring down at their phones. That chick is making faces at her phone—social media selfies…Jesus.

"Don't sweat it, Erica. You're fine like white wine." Hoping for life, I see that her knuckles are turning white from squeezing her fingers into fists. Shoot.

"You know," she tells me and comes to a complete halt, almost giving a spin to face me. Luckily, I halt to a stop in time, missing her by an inch or so. "I think I'm just going to go back and sleep." Her tone is softer and lower, almost…like she wants to give up.

She sighs, and I catch a whiff of the cold air from her breath. I don't think she's eaten anything today.

"Do you work today?" I ask, which catches her off guard; a look of caution and confusion—she even has one of those eyebrow furrows across her forehead from the tension.

"No. I don't."

Oh, well then…

"Come on." I grab her hand and lead the way. She does not protest and half-ass follows me. "We're having some much-needed gal time then!"

Yep, still no attempt at an excuse to stop me. MUH-HA-HA-HA!

# Erica

It's slow right now. Yet, it is still the middle of the afternoon, people are still at work. Well, most anyhow…

A man in this blue velvet three-piece suit is swaying his hips as he belts out some slow, bittersweet melody. I think…he's crying, too. His eyes are closed so the music has him traveling down some form of memory lane. Damn, what a drama queen. He's straight, too, because—

"Melanie!" he cries out. "This one is not for you."

Clearly, it is for Melanie. I'm glad we are not seated close to the stage this time, considering that the guy must reek of booze, booze, and more hard liquor. His tie is unadjusted and loose—probably just came from the office, a.k.a. he's playing hooky.

Ricky sashays over to our table and does a perfect, 'bend and snap,' movement—hitting his ass on the floor, not even injuring himself. Somehow, in between his little routine—which gets Bianca all wild up—he sets down our two sour green apple Cosmo onto the black tabletop.

"Thank you, Ricky!" Bianca raises her glass to him, almost slipping off her chair. Luckily, I tug at her arm to bring her back up.

"Anytime, baby girl!" Ricky hisses at her; Bianca does one back, along with some air kisses.

God, they really are going at it with the whole back and forth of "I love you more, soul sistah!"

"And where's my sweet little prince?" His eyes troll to me and stay on me…

Yikes, this is a bit awkward. I grab my drink and sip and sip. Thankfully, Bianca assumes that the question was solely for her. "I don't know. Erica, where is our *third*-party member?"

Oh, I see what she's doing. I shake my head and remove the stray from my drink. I chug that sucker back which takes both Bianca and Ricky by surprise. By the time I look back up at them, they chuckle. Ricky sticks out his hip—damn, he does have a nice 'S' shape—and sets his hand on it. Whoa, he has some pretty, shiny, black and gold cat claws.

"Oh, I see," he says with some extra sass, clicking his tongue and wiggles it. "Wrestling in the sheets are we—"

Uh, NO.

Only, I can't find myself responding. Instead, I grab Bianca's drink and down it. She busts out laughing and she snorts. Ricky is not on her level at the moment. He's still watching me, frozen like a statue. If statues were frozen…

"I'll be back with a second-round," Ricky tells us and whips his head around, giving his short ponytail a good ol' showoff, and sashays back to the counter.

For whatever reason, I just stare at him, watching him this time.

"You know what we should do?" Bianca turns towards me, her knees are touching my thigh. "Never have I ever." She gasps and right on cue, Ricky sweeps in and drops off our two new Cosmo. Shit…I hope I don't have to pay for everything—

"It's on the house," Ricky then informs us.

"Well, in that case, Ricardo—" Bianca then gives her glass a tap, tap, tap. Yeah, she's wanting to go hard tonight. She returns to me and raises her glass. Oh, I guess it's my turn.

Okay…then.

"I don't know, Bianca, I'm not really—"

"Never have I ever took it up the ass!"

"Jesus."

Indeed, Jesus would be pissed off at us. Bianca drinks. I do not.

"Huh," she reacts with a hint of disappointment and shock. "Really? Hmm. Okay. Your turn."

Alrighty. I sit for a moment, going over what I could—or should—ask her. I pick up my glass and raise it higher. Now, she is all smiles, and licks off what appears to be drip-drops of sour green apple on her lip. She talks an awful lot while still being able to take a sip.

"Never have I ever..." Wow, I'm bad at this game *and* already LOSING.

Bianca gasps for real this time and gives the wooden tabletop a big ol' booty slap. "Threesome?!"

I can feel my eyes popping out of their sockets. *"Bianca..."*

"What? I haven't. I was just curious if you have."

Neither one of us drink. I can't…focus right now. I lower my arm and set my drink back down onto the table. "I forfeit," I say to her and take a baby sip.

I think she can sense that my mind is going elsewhere. The back of my neck is starting to burn like the sun has been shining there all day.

The irony is that the karaoke bar has blacked-out windows, therefore, the place only has its technicolor coming through the LED and other rainbow color lights. There's also a neon rainbow sign that is pointing to the men's and women's restroom in the corner. The sign reads, R A I N B O W. What an interesting tour guide to the bathrooms.

My posture is stiff, and my fingers tighten around my glass.

"Hey," Bianca interjects my trail of thoughts. I jump a bit, feeling the warmth of her hands cradling over mine. She loosens my fingers from my glass—shit, I don't remember doing that.

For a second or so, she's quiet. "I don't think I've ever asked you about high school. How was it like for you?"

"...I wouldn't know," I tell her and find my eyes lowering back down to the table. "I was homeschooled, except for my freshman year."

Whoa, I can't believe I finally shared that piece of me with her. My hands work their way to my jeans, rubbing over my thighs, leaving streaks of sweat that slip off my palms. I hear Bianca's chair give a few squirts—she's sitting closer to me, pressing her elbows onto the table. She studies me—what I see from the corner of my eye.

"Trust me, you weren't missing out on anything."

I can see her honesty; she's no longer smiling or looking happy right now. It's kind of intimidating and I find myself reaching back for my glass. Crap—the glass is empty. *Man, this liquor is getting me all*…this *fuzzy* feeling in my head and tickling my palms and the bottom of my feet. Oh, my God…I'm *buzzed.*

"You know," she taunts and sits up straighter, leaning her arm on the back of her chair, "we still haven't done a duet together..."

Uh, huh…

Yeah, that's not going to happen. Only, I find myself sticking my hand up and giving a snap.

"Yays!" Bianca cheers and pumps her fist up to give a few dog roots.

"Ricky," I call out, "make it a triple!"

Shoot, I'd meant a double.

# Erica & Bianca

Bianca sings her heart out, doing an electric slide over my way—

Man, Erica is sure not singing loud ENOUGH. I'll fix that.

*Standing on the corner/*
*Suitcase in my hand/*
*Jack is in his corset/*
*And Jane is in her vest/*
*And me/*
*I'm in a rock'n'roll band/*
*Huh/*
*Ridin' in a Stutz-Bearcat/*
*Jim/*
*Y'know/*
*Those were different times—*

Off Bianca's nudge, I find myself raising my voice.

*Oh/*
*All the poet/*
*They studied rules of verse/*
*And the ladies/*
*They rolled their eyes/*
*Sweet Jane/*
*Whoa/*
*Sweet Jane/*
*Oh-oh-a/*
*Sweet Jane!*

# Erica

"I do NOT sound like a man!" I bark at Bianca. My ass cheeks fall off the stool. Bianca and I lose our shit.

"*Sweet Jane/Oh-oh-a*!" she sings all deep and stern like a man.

Bitch, ha!

Ricky swoops in behind the counter. "Alright, you two," he warns, eyeing both of us like an annoying, disappointed parent. "Gonna have to cut you off..."

But he refills our glasses.

"Welcome to the rockstar club," he says to me with a wink. Awe…

I grab my chest, all touched, and…What was I saying?

"Awe," I cry out. "I'm part of the club. Wait, it's not like some weird cult, right?" That makes Bianca laugh, but I'm being serious—it better not be some weird sex thing, either.

"Go easy on the Cosmos," he says to me again but yet again, pours us two new glasses. I don't know what drink this is, but the liquid is this pretty, shiny blue. Whoa…

"Um," Ricky chimes back in, giving a fake cough. "Speaking of clubs..." I follow whatever his eye fuck—the dead giveaway—and Bianca and I both see—

"Alexander!" We shout/sing.

"Wow, someone's drunk!" He's still in his work uniform, all haggard but still cute as hell. I jump off my seat and find myself throwing my arms around his shoulders, kissing him…for a while. I hear Ricky and Bianca slapping hands which leads into one of their rituals of greeting one another. But I can't with Alex. He smells bomb as fuck still—some new cologne he's wearing—and tastes amazing, too. Whoa…maybe that's just the blue liquid talking; I still don't know what that is.

"Oh…kay." Alex can find freedom, but I'm not going anywhere. He brushes my hair behind my ears as I go to give him a peck on the top of his mouth and then the bottom. Then, I find myself mauling the rest of him which he does not mind. He's still thinking and tasting the liquid that I'd passed over during our exchange of spit. "Ah"—it hits him—"Raspberry." He licks his finger, enjoying the taste and then, looks to me and kisses me back, long…and hard.

*Faaaauuucccckkkk*…I'm giving him a—*what the hell*—I'm acting like a horny teenager and it's driving me insane. UGH.

"Uh, get a room, you whores!" Bianca tosses a handful of popcorn at us from the munchie bowl on the bar countertop.

It grabs our attention. Bianca sticks out her tongue and gives Alex and I a thumbs down, crackin' up. She chokes on her drink. Ricky pours her another shot, eyeing me—vodka, I think. Bianca could care less because she tosses back the shot, which miraculously stops her coughing/choking.

Now, Alex and I bust-up. So, does, Ricky.

"I gotta pee so bad right now!" Bianca squirms and does that weird, 'I gotta pee dance and everyone get the fuck outta my way,' walk-of-shame—more like sprinting—to the bathroom. She's lucky there isn't a line.

# Alex

The place is packed now! Body heat everywhere—wherever I turn, there's some dude; then I turn the other way and there's some chick.

When we see the first booth clear up, Erica ditches me at the bar and claims it, flagging Bianca and I over to join her. I follow. However, when I peek over my shoulder, Bianca is suddenly MIA. What the hell…

I approach the booth as Ricky slides in and drops off two sour-apple—the green one—Cosmos. He gives me a wink and I swear if I don't move now, he's going to pinch my ass or something. He doesn't. That's because I slide into the booth, moving as close as possible to Erica. But she grabs me anyway and starts kissing me—

"Get a room, you SLUTS!" Bianca yells at us. I catch her dancing with a group of guys dressed as the YMCA people. Man, they are all getting down and dancing the night away for sure. Bianca drops it low and slaps her hands on the black floor as the YMCA cop guy grinds behind her…and whips out his baton.

Jeez, I hope that's not real. *Ouch,* if it *is.*

"Here take it with me," Erica says and grabs our Cosmos, passing mine over. We drink, and I cough which makes me take a swig of water from the only glass we have—oh, Ricky; he always does that because low key, he's that waiter who wants his customers to get *turnt.* But at least, he doesn't charge us for the extra—thank God for Bianca and, now Erica, being regulars. "What? You don't like it."

Damn, Erica pounds her drink back—every last drop of it, too. She puckers her lips, and I'm not quite sure if she wants me to kiss her or not. Unless she's just savoring the last bits of sour apple that remain on her lips from the rim of the glass. Ricky added in a mix of sugar and salt along the rim because it tastes like tequila as if Christmas and a *Quinceañera* were merged. Oh, man, that sounds fuckin' racist on my end—but the drink is called, 'Hello, goodbye, and nighty night!'

Yep, with the '!' in it too.

"I'll never understand how you guys drink this crap," I tell her, washing it down with water—just kiddin'. Now it's a bottle of apple beer that Ricky swaps out of my hand. I swear…that dude must be a magician in his past life. OR his other job.

"It's not that bad, my dearest, Alexander!"

"Trust me, it is." I finally meet her gaze; God, she's really pretty. She always is but this time, there's this new glow to her. She seems happy—the genuine kind, too. We hear a thunder of LAUGHTER and glance over our shoulders to see—

Bianca and Ricky are in the middle of salsa dancing. Once she whips around—flailing her invisible skirt—Ricky scoops her up and they evolve into a swing dance. I swear those two are like lost soulmates—sisters, as they put it. I know it means a lot to Bianca, and him, too.

I appreciate it as well.

The group of YMCA men chant them on for their dance; some of them drop it low as well. The Native member and disco one start making out, one of them pressing the other into the nearby wooden pillar. The group of women and two dudes at that booth—behind the pillar—root them on. They're in the middle of their bachelorette party, sippin' drinks out of…penis straws. Hint the dick balloons around their booth like curtains to some underground lair.

I feel Erica leaning into me. She lets out a sigh of relief. It captures my attention and I give her my undivided attention. Resting my head against hers, we sit in silence for a few moments. Well, it's not completely silent; otherwise, the speakers would not be blasting out the Village People's—none other than—"Y.M.C.A." song.

*Young man, there's no need to feel down/*
*I said, young man, pick yourself off the ground/*
*I said, young man, 'cause you're in a new town/*

"Alex..." We both tilt our heads to see each other. I'm looking down and she's looking up at me. "Do you want to get out of here?" That look in her eyes...

*Holy shit...*

# Erica

The heater kicks in, coming in like a warm breeze through the ceiling vent. Bianca puts on a record. Velvet Underground & Nico's "Femme Fatale" starts to play.

"The banana cover album," Alex whispers into my ear. I can't help but smile at that, tilting my head against his shoulder. I feel his nose nuzzling into the right side of my hair as he kisses my cheek.

*Here she comes, you better watch your step/*
*She's going to break your heart in two,*

Bianca dances around, very shit-faced, like no one is watchin'. She sings aloud to the song, all bright and vibrant like a rockstar's solo on stage. Alex and I watch Bianca put on a show for us, dippin' and poppin' her hip to the left and right. She removes her scarf and sways it around like a color guard team—those girls in high school who are sort of like cheerleaders but are really not who swing and toss around poles with flags sometimes. Bianca can dance, stomping around the wooden floor panels, shouting out to Reed in the Holy Heavenly sky.

"I FUCKIN' LOVE YOU MOTHERFUCKIN' LOU REED!" she professes her love to him, a.k.a. the ceiling. Alex and I howl in agreement.

*...The things she does to please/*
*She's just a little tease!*

KLUMP! Bianca hits the table leg and tips over. Alex and I jump out and go to her—she's already bottom flat on the floor, crackin' up.

"Come on, drunkie," Alex says to her. He tosses one of her arms around his shoulders and waits for me to repeat the same move, but on her left side. Together, we help her to her feet on three…sort of. Bianca is dragging her feet along, muttering Reed, who continues to sing from the record player in the corner of the living room.

Rounding the corner, we walk down the hallway—

"Did I TELL YOU?!" Bianca pulls us in closer—poor Alex has to hunch down to meet Bianca and I's shorter stature. "I love you guys!"

"Uh, huh," Alex mumbles.

"Like…so MUCH." Bianca kisses his cheek, leaving a big red lipstick mark.

"We love you, too, Bianca," Alex gives a half-ass agreement as she pulls me closer and smacks a big ol' lipstick mark on my cheek—it feels sticky once she removes her puckered mouth from my skin.

I laugh. "Love ya girl."

"Muah! And MUAH!"

"Okay, drunkie," Alex announces as we reach the third door on the left. "Here we are."

"I'm not drunk, hun—"

"Bianca," I scream as soon as Alex goes to hand her off to me to open the door to her bedroom.

"And Paige from *Degrassi* is out to play."

---

"Oh, my *gawd*! And I totally forgot about Drake!" And now, Bianca is belting out one of the biggest throwbacks of Aubrey Graham, a.k.a. Drake.

*Man, she's more trashed by the second!*

Alex holds the door open and turns to us. He waves over to Bianca, who sticks up her hand and wiggles her fingers at him. Smiling, he points to the floor in front of him as a, "Come here, NOW."

Bianca frowns and shakes her head. Damn, we will be here all night if someone doesn't give her, well, that extra push. So, I do it—

"Hey!" she protests but I still win because my nudge against her back gets her to Alex. He mouths a big, THANK YOU. I chuckle. Just as Bianca steps past the doorway to her bedroom, she eyes Alex and then me, grinning. "Don't do anything that I wouldn't do..."

Oh-kay now…

"Come on," Alex reacts quickly, giving her a second encouraging nudge on her back before she can progress her further sexual gesture at his—hint: it looks familiar to eating a popsicle. She gives us a wink before slipping out of my sight, at least.

Alex is all embarrassed; his cheeks are turning redder by the second. It's kind of adorable and I giggle at it.

"I'll be downstairs in a minute," he informs me before he walks into the bedroom.

The doorframe in front of me cuts off anything beyond the doorway for me to potentially see. Unless I move of course. But

I don't, my feet remain planted on the floor. "Bianca—get down from there!"

---

My fingers run over the stacks and stacks of vinyl records that sit adjacent to the record player. My knees begin to throb, and I shift, sitting Indian style on the floor. That's much better; my legs are crossed now so I kick off my flats. Much better.

*See the way she walks/*
*Hear the way she talks/*

Okay, so I'm sort of a hypocrite and have ZERO idea on how to switch out a record. But this song is fitting for tonight as the nearby candle flickers in the shadows of the moonlight. I bring my knees back towards my chest and lean my head onto them. My head is tilted away from the hallway, where Alex, Bianca, and I were minutes ago...

Well, it's been twenty-eight minutes to be exact.

"She does that a lot," I hear Alex and turn to see him linger in the doorway. He's wearing a different shirt now; it's checkered, and I think his pajamas.

"What happened?"

Alex does a charade of throwing up. I cover my mouth, preventing a laugh but I completely fail.

"I'm sorry," I tell him.

"You sure about that?"

He joins me on the floor, sitting on his knees. He's gawking at me…and it's extremely intimidating. I chuckle for some reason and look away, back at the floor seems to be the safe…

Shit. I'm scared.

Tension starts throbbing in the back of my neck. I go to reach for it to get out the kink. Only, he's already scooting around me to massage the sore spot. OH…that feels good. Ouch—right there. My eyes close.

The song comes to an end a second later, leaving that scratchy sound as the blank part of the record circulates underneath the pin.

"I should…go," I whisper to him as his lips suck the side of my neck—FUCK.

"I'll walk you home," he whispers back, giving a nibble on that section of my neck, forcing me to lean my head back as he works his way around…

Yeah, neither one of us is going anywhere.

"Bianca and I…We're on a deadline, Alex." But I couldn't care any less at this particular moment, spinning around and crawling on top of him. I wrap my legs around his waist as we kiss longer, harder, and faster. My lips are becoming sore—

He winces. I stop and pull back to make sure that he's okay.

"You're good," he mutters, his breath smelling like mint—that little shit was preppin'; that explains why he was MIA for a while. I see that the top of his lip is pink—oops. "Hold on." He reaches over to restart the record player.

Ah…that's how one does it—you just move the pin on and off the record.

*'Cause everybody knows/*
*(She's a femme fatale)/*
*The things she does to please/*
*(She's a femme fatale)/*

"Come here." He pulls me in closer, giving my bottom lip a nibble. It tickles a bit and I giggle, drifting back and allowing myself to fall onto the floor.

He hovers over me and slowly dips onto me. Brushing the loose, fallen strands of hair from my mouth. He stares into my eyes, sort of studying every aspect of my face. He kisses my eye, nose, and cheek. It feels nice, his version of butterfly kisses. Our lips meet again…

And then, he pulls back…going slower again, removing himself from me. Now, he's lying next to me on his side. Oh…he's not going to push the envelope there.

"Hey," I say to him. He looks to me; something is *wrong*. I don't know *what* but it's bothering me. My fingers find their way to the side of his face. We both allow another moment or two to sit between us.

And then, every part of us needs the missing piece again. I throw myself at him, climbing on top of him. He pushes himself up to his elbows on the floor, holding me up a few inches forward. We never break focus, except when he helps me unbutton and remove my jacket. He kisses my neck again. My gaze drifts off to the burning green candle that sits on top of the old-fashioned TV set box. It's actually a table, a.k.a. just for looks.

Before he maneuvers around to meet my mouth, I stop him. "Your room?"

---

The door opens faster than expected, slamming into the wall. We laugh and move silently into the bedroom. I kick the door shut—damn, we're absolutely failing at the whole, "We need to be quiet," thing. Falling onto the bed, we go at it. He turns over so now I'm on top. I lift my arms as he helps me out of my long-sleeve shirt. Just me in a bra.

"You're so beautiful," he tells me and leans in, kissing my breasts. *Oh, shit…*

I turn over, making him get back up on top. I don't like being on top. Leaning up in his bed, I reach behind me and unhook my bra. I remove it. He inspects my face for a moment, taking a moment before his eyes go to my breasts. I pull him in, kissing him. He works his way down, kissing both of my breasts before he latches onto one of them. *Shit…*

My eyes shut as he sucks on my left breast long and hard, making me squirm a bit. He stops for a second. I realize that he's watching me, all wide-eyed and scared. Oh, my bad. "It's okay," I tell him. "Really."

Hesitant for a second, he moves back in, going for my right breast. I lie there, running my fingers through his wavy locks. Messy, if you catch my drift—*Oh, Jesus that was a lame attempt at being all sexy and cute.* Jeez, I can't believe I'm actually here with him…now.

I stare up at the ceiling, as he forms a kissing trail down from my breasts, stomach, and the edge of the button of my jeans. He goes to unbutton them and his fingers brush over my stomach. I immediately flinch, and it forces me to reopen my eyes—all I see are the brief shadows that reflect off the white ceiling from the cracked blinds of his only bedroom window. I think there's a brick wall behind it, the alleyway for the apartment buildings' dumpsters.

"Wait," I say as he unbuttons my jeans. "Alex...Stop. Stop!"

He does stop and moves off me. I scatter to the edge of the bed and swing my legs to the floor until my feet touch the carpet. Good, it's there. It's there…We're both out of breath—I can hear him catch up with his, just like I am. It stirs my curiosity, so I turn around and see his back; we've turned away from each other.

"Did I…hurt you?" he asks, making us both look at one another.

"No. No you didn't." Off his sigh, I move my legs back onto the bed, facing him; but his back is still to me. "Alex, it's not you. Really."

But he doesn't believe me…Fuck, FUCK. I *fucked up…*

Tightness bottles up from my stomach and I gasp.

He turns around, finally meeting my gaze. "Hey, Erica…" He scoots closer to me and reaches for my hands.

I don't squeeze his back…I can't…

"You don't want to, so what," he tells me. "It's fine, Erica. Really."

But that's not the case. It isn't…

We just sit there in silence; maybe catching a car honk or two that echoes through the alleyway and into his bedroom. Not to mention the shouts, screaming, and fun that everyone else seems to be having outdoors…Alex and I should be *there*, too. But we're not.

"Ah! You've never done this before," he says, coming to his realization. He turns to me. I can't bear to look at him anymore. I'm silent…huh, the irony now—silence. But I can feel his eyes on me; those things can burn a hole if they'd like to. He's patient. My breathing is steep now and my fingers tighten into fists…

> Mid-work, I recall the feel of his arms crossing over my shoulders. They wrap around my upper chest. I like how strong his arms are, as well as the tan he got over the summer break. I tilt my head back and look up and give my biggest smile. He leans down and kisses me—

"Erica?" Alex's worried tone draws me back in. "Hey, Erica?"

Fuck, my eyes had shut, and I know it wasn't out of a fuckin' trip down memory lane. It's because I'd almost fainted—Alex is pulling me up by the arms. Even in the dark, I can see that he's pale. As he touches my arm—it just sends another spin around the room. Oh, well I guess it's just me getting dizzy again.

"I, I should go." I ascend to my feet to catch my balance—my head…it's still feeling heavy, drooping to one side and not the other. My vision is fuzzy—the black and white dots start from the corner. Gasping for a deep breath, I squint and blink and repeat as I stumble to the door.

"ERICA?!"

Alex calls out for me some more, but I never look back. I just get the fuck outta there.

# Alex

"I don't know," I say aloud, pacing back and forth. "I don't get it! One minute, she's turned on and the next, she isn't!"

Bianca groans, all hunched over in bed underneath the bedsheets. Her hair is messy and could use a hairbrush to get the knots out. Shit, she's probably going to want me to help her cut some of them out—she fell asleep with her extensions again. They're the threaded ones, too.

"Bro, T.M.I.," she tells me and gags. It stops us in place. It's like a game of freeze tag until she realizes it's a false alarm. "Anyhoo, no, no! She didn't get turned off—I heard you guys a bit last night. *Lovaboi*."

She cracks up and snorts at the same time—uh, oh, she gags again. Not once but twice! Her hand remains over her mouth. I wait until she says something…

Say something, Bianca.

False alarm—oh fuck, she gags again and this time, it forces her to sit up. I rush over and take a seat at the edge of her bed, grabbing the trash bin and holding it for her to target. She shakes her head a minute or so later. False alarm for good.

Phew.

"Sorry. You were saying?"

Man, forget it! I scoot onto the bed and lie back, resting my head at the bottom of the pillow—I'm terrified she barfed on it last night. No offense, but I'm not taking a chance there. "Did I do something…wrong?"

That angers Bianca because she sits back up, glaring at me. It's kind of scary so I avoid eye contact. "Alex, are you fuckin' *kiddin'* me?!" It's rhetorical. She's going to make a point in five, four, three…"No. No, you didn't do anything wrong."

Yeah, yeah, I know that…But I must've fucked up somewhere at some point.

"I just wish she'd talk to me..." I take a deep breath and sit up. My fingers run through my hair—jeez, I'm acting like a crybaby, pathetic, sore, idiot LOSER.

It's upset Bianca. "Alex, don't overly self-identify, as Zimmer would put it."

"You just quoted your therapist." Yep, she *had*.

"Look, I just think she's going through some family stuff. I mean, fuckin' Cathy man..." Bianca hiccups and cackles like Sandy B's infamous laugh-snort in *Miss Congeniality*. But she gets me to smile for a second—

That's enough in Bianca's book. She gets all proud parent status and grabs and pinches my cheeks like I'm her infant. Shit, only *she* could get away with something like that. And then, her smile fades away fast as soon as she sees my hands gripping onto my pants, on top of my knees—nerves, nerves, NERVES. *Fuck, they will never go away…*

I sigh but end up gasping for an inhale. Bianca scoots closer and sits with me, holding my hand as I exhale and inhale…and then, exhale.

"You're really falling for her," is all she says without a second look. Plus, the doubt is not in her tone either. She has *always* known the answer, way before I did. I swear, she should be a medium for picking up on others' instincts. Typically, she decides for them, a.k.a. she CONFRONTS the situation. Prime example…this moment with her.

"I'm kind of freakin' out," it slips right out of my mouth. Bianca reaches and holds onto my hand. The warmth of her hand stops the shaking of mine…traditional, ever since we've been kids.

She waits until I meet her sight. Oh, man…she's crying. Well, at least the tears are there. Immediately, she leans into me. My arms find their way around her. She squeezes onto me tight, tilting her head into my shoulder. Piece of her hair—the ones that did not make their way into the hair tie. I don't have to ask or see, but the standup mirror across from me, adjacent to her bed, is my proof. Her mirrored reflection rises slightly as she sighs. I notice how the veins in my arms are poppin' up from the tension that builds…replaying everything from last night. Erica…

My eyes avert to the top portion of the standup mirror—the sky; the clouds drifting about, calm, and relaxed; the opposite of Bianca and I…as well as Erica.

I take a deep inhale and exhale, too.

# Bianca

I knock on the door. "Erica?" Followed by another knock. I'm pretty sure that she's here. I mean where else would she be. Alex said she didn't have to work today.

I knock again.

"Erica? Jesus Christ," I mutter the last part to myself. Really, she's not going to answer?

*Fuck,* I pull up the three text messages that she has *yet* to respond to. I could call again, but she didn't pick up ALL four of my incoming. I stand there in place. My body is turning one way, pressuring me to leave, while my eyes stay on the door and those suckers refuse to blink.

*Goddammit…*

I bang my fist on the door again and again. Off the third knock, I hear footsteps trudging closer from behind her door, followed by the rattling of the doorknob—her unlocking it. Finally!

The door squeaks open, but remains ajar…Okay then…

A group of girls laugh, and I glance off to my right side and see them making their way down the hallway—seven of them. I take a step forward, toward Erica's dorm, as they pass. They are dressed in workout attire—most in yoga pants and jogging tennis shoes. I bring my attention back to the door—

"JESUS FUCKIN' CHRIST," it rolls off my tongue.

Erica plants herself right in front of me. Fuck, my pulse is still speeding. I clasp hold of my chest, exhaling like a maniac from this little shit scaring the bejesus outta me.

"Why didn't you say anything?" I say, not expecting an answer from her to be honest. "I was gonna call but you didn't pick up any of the times."

"What are you doing here?"

Really…?

Before I can press any further, I notice in the background: the bedsheets are on the floor, all tangled up with the comforter that is half on the bed and half not next to the project along with her pillowcase. She slept on the floor; at least, it looks that way…

"Making progress, I see." I take a step forward, and then another one, squeezing my way into her dorm. Erica does not oblige. She remains by the door, her back to me as I scan the place.

"I didn't get much sleep," Erica breaks the silence and closes the door, locking us in. She keeps her back to me, standing, too…still. It's eerie, especially with the room being so dark—it's two o'clock in the afternoon, too. She just has her curtains drawn shut. Now, I get a whiff of the room—all lukewarm, dusty, and grey like a warehouse.

"I'm just going to…" But I make my way over to the window anyhow. I can feel Erica watching me the entire time, except when I pull back the curtains and the sunlight strikes in instantly. I almost have to put on my sunglasses for it takes me off guard. Ugh, it sucks—now the room heats up. So, I go to crack open the window. Can't believe she was in this stuffiness.

"Dude, it was like a sauna in here," I say. "How the hell did you…sleep?" Man, she was not kiddin' about getting no sleep.

Erica's eyes divert away from me, but that still does not hide the fact of how pale, frail, and just exhausted she looks. "What?" she asks, shifting in place and cradling one hand over her wrist.

I bite my lip, trying to prevent myself from saying more; but a cry escapes my mouth. "Ugh, I made these." I forgot I was holding them, too—the small box I put on the bed before opening the window. It's a small purple wooden box that Alex's dad had once carved for me as a kid. I hand it over.

She just stands there and stares at it.

"Well, open it," I semi-order her. My tone rises an octave or so and is stern.

# Erica

It's all there: pages of typed-out music lyrics and quotes in beautiful, bold fonts and styles. There are even a few handwritten ones in cursive, matching what you would see in a Word document.

"I had some rough drafts," Bianca says to me, "but last night sort of got me in the mood."

Yeah, yeah, I wouldn't know the feeling right now. Oh, GOD! My palms are already sweating again. As I go to wipe them across my jeans, I hear—

"Erica..."

"I have some homework to do," I snap, rejecting her reaching out to me—literally—and find myself taking a stumble backward, all tense. Ugh, the room tilts a bit.

I close my eyes, taking a breather…

> My hands reach for the side of his face. I can't forget his facial hair: even though it's a five o'clock shadow, it's prickly. I run my fingers over and over it as he scoops me up and carries me to the bed.

"Newman's the only class of yours, isn't it? Or the only in-class..." Bianca is now in front of my desk. She studies the 'yes' and 'no' Polaroid stacks on the floor, along with the camera and unfinished project. "So, the rest of your classes are online?"

It's rhetorical, coming from her because there's this look on her—the kind where someone has finally pieced everything together like a gigantic puzzle.

I feel my pulse quickening and my fingertips find their way curling into fists...all tight and whoa, that's starting to hurt. Fingernails being pressed into my palm—

Bianca has been watching this entire time, horrified and shocked. And I see her watching my every move. It's unsettling...making me fidget, almost like I have Parkinson's disease, as fucked up as that sounds. There's just no other way of explaining it.

I take a step back, as she takes one towards me. She respects it, the whole invasion of privacy, and decides to stand in place. She even crosses her hand together, looping her fingers together to secure them tightly. I think she's trying to avoid any confrontational reach outs to me. She probably needs to avoid me with whatever has her mind racing at the moment, her eyes staying leveled at the floor.

"Distractions are good," she then speaks and finally returns her worried eyes to me, "as Zimmer tells me. Writing is mine, and I know photography is yours—your distraction. I just don't know from what, though."

Okay. So, I'm only working on something that I love and, mind if I say, BEEN FUCKIN' WORKING ON FOR YEARS AS A SO-CALLED 'DISTRACTION.'

*What the fuck...?*

"Well, don't overly self-identify, Bianca, as Mansell my therapist would put it."

I can tell that hurt her feelings; a slight scoff fights its way out of her lips. Yet, she's doing a great job at composing herself, staying silent but thinking and then, rethinking what she's going to say NEXT. "This project has been hard for me, too, Erica. I don't ask for much because I don't ever want to press. Erica, I want you to know whatever is going on, we care—"

"DON'T...do that! I already feel bad enough." And I...Really, I do. My eyes shut because the tips of my fingers start pressing and pressing, and then hold my fingernails into my palm. I can feel a singe of shock shooting throughout my body. My hand is burning...bleeding from the new fingernail stabs.

"Erica..." I hear Bianca, but her voice is distancing away as well as my vision from the here and now. Instead, as Bianca approaches me—she immediately vanishes out of my sight because behind her...I see *us*...

> It's almost dreamlike...We're going at it. He drops me onto the bed and climbs on top of me. I pull him back in, kissing him as his lips, move around to my neck. This is not Alex by the way...

"Erica, your hand!" She grabs a hold of my hand and it forces my fingers to uncurl. She gasps and stumbles a few steps back as soon as she sees...the bloody cuts on my palm, along with the scars from previous...

I, I need to get out of here!

"I need to work, Bianca!" But I go against my word and instead find myself headed to the door until she tugs at my arm. "Let GO OF ME—"

"Let me help you!" Bianca pleads. "It's okay...Everything will be okay—"

"Really?! And how do you know that—did Dr. Zimmer tell you that?"

Her jaw drops. "That's uncalled for—"

"Riiiight! Because you're just *so* capable of helping others. I need to focus here, Bianca. Not all of us are fuckin' perfect and can finish something in a short amount of time!"

"*Perfect*? What the fuck! Erica, where's this even coming from?"

I balk at her reaching out. It makes her sob, but she's good at holding back the tears, a.k.a. the waterfall kind that will just stream and stream down your face. I take a step back, closer to the door, but find myself backing into it, panting and panting. But it's not for air this time. It's from holding it all in…it's just too much that builds and builds.

"You guys have been nothing but kindhearted. I just fuck it all up! Like every friendship, love…all of it."

"Erica, that's not true…"

Her tone falls short which makes me look at her, studying the stages of her expression from sadness to tiredness, and now…her lips slightly part because it hits her—a lightbulb goes off in her head. "This is about last night? Alex is so upset—"

> Now, he's pressin' down into me, reaching down to unzip my pants as his other hand lifts one of my arms back…and holds it there. I break my lips from him for a second. This doesn't feel right. But I don't move…until I tell him to stop-stop-stop-hey-what the fuck-STOP-STOP.

"Erica?"

"I think you should go," I tell Bianca who tears up again. "I said GO!"

"Don't do this—" Off her touch, I scream, and it jars both of us. Bianca just bawls at this point. Fuck…FUCK. I ruin everything…

I find it harder to breathe now, my belly going in-and-out rapidly as my back slams into the door. The room is tilting. The floor feels…heavier just like my body, which slides down on its own. It makes me slam into the door again, this time it's my elbow. It builds and builds from my chest up…

I run out of there—

"Erica—wait!"

But I pick up speed without looking over back. My feet are kicking back higher off the carpet as my eyes target the end of the hallway, the opposite direction from my fellow dorm peers who head back into their dorms. A group of them linger in front of the elevator, waiting to head to the main lobby, a.k.a. the first floor where everyone is probably all happy, cheerful…and just fuckin' happy!

"Erica!" Bianca calls me by my name again. Her voice echoes off the walls and tunnels down to me as I distance myself from her. I know that she has stopped because her voice becomes lower and lower…

FINALLY! I make it to the end of the hallway, speeding by a fellow female dorm peer here and there—one of them presses up against her male companion, otherwise, I'm going to ram into her. They're all turning their heads to me, and I try to avoid eye contact—

*Shit! It's Alex.*

Fuck—we collide into each other as he rounds the same fuckin' corner that I'm aiming to circle. Or was, by the looks of it now.

He has a loose hold of my forearms. I'm panting, slowly catching up with my breath. But a raspy gasp comes out instead. "Shit…" I find my hands already reaching for the nearby wall. He helps me, having us go to the wall together to let the ongoing traffic of people go by—that's right, there was some Greek-themed mixer.

Luckily, ninety-nine percent of them are intoxicated as fuck. Otherwise, they'd do a double-take on me…

"Hey, hey," Alex consoles me, still holding me…

"Stop. Don't." I release myself and take a few steps backward.

Alex just looks at me. Great, now he's similar to Bianca—I'm just disappointing them.

"I'm," he tumbles over his words, "…Sorry."

"It's not your fault."

And just like Bianca, he reaches out, but I flinch away, peeling his hands off my hands. "Stop, Alex!" I demand, and it makes me…sob.

He's paralyzed in place. At this point, I don't know if we've drawn a crowd or not. I hear footsteps scattering and trudging by and smell the scent of people—a mix of flowers, cologne, someone has too much peppermint on.

"I don't know what you want me to do," he says. "If I stand here and do nothing, I'm just going to feel guilty—"

"Well, don't! No one's forcing you to help me—"

"I want to!" He grabs a hold of my arms, moving closer to me. He won't let me go; his fingers going from my forearms to my hands. I'm not telling him to do so, either. I let him…hold me for a brief moment.

"Alex..." I say, but the cat got my tongue. This brutal tension throbs at the back of my throat. *Shit.*

He pulls me into his arms. I hear her approaching…

"Erica?"

Great, it's Bianca. She lingers at the corner, the one where Alex and I had almost died at by running into each other like bulls. Thank God, it was just our shoulders since he had better reflexes than I and dodged it first.

My cheeks are burning red, enflamed from them just not leaving me the hell ALONE. I go to pull back, but he won't let me.

"Talk to me. If not her, then me. Please." By now, he is lower for direct eye contact with me. I can see the agony and overall frustration in there. "Please…"

"I…I can't—"

"*Why?*"

"Because I'm a liar, living a double life! You don't get it! There's so much you don't know about me!" Jeez, my voice is cracking and the back of my throat is throbbing like it has its own pulse. It eats me up bad.

"Erica," his tone is softer now, "we care about you—"

"Yeah, we do," Bianca chimes in, hiccupping back a sob.

She peers away, dabbing at her eyes as a dorm peer in workout attire circles around the corner and passes by us. But she has on her headphones—some R&B song is blasting through them, she is in mid-text convo.

"Well, don't!"

"Don't what—care about you?" Alex retorts, struggling and trying to fight something off. But he fails, once he draws in closer, looking me in the eye. "I'm in love with you!"

No, no, NO…

"Fuck," it slips out of my mouth because I can hear it in his voice and see it in the eyes. He's telling the truth, never was or is lying to me. It's…killin' me and hurtin' me on the inside. It has me hunching forward to catch my breath trying not to lose it completely and have a full-on cry fest.

"Say something," he whispers, pressing his forehead with mine. The back of his palm is behind my head, while the other caresses my chin.

"Well…I don't." We meet eyes. "…I don't feel the same."

What, why would I say that…?

"Okay," he sobs out. "That's fine. It won't change how I feel about you. But just let me help you."

But…I can't. It's too late. I want to tell him, though—that it's not him nor her. But they stand there, waiting for me to speak. They're patient, although they are utterly heartbroken when I'm the first to break focus and refuse to return my attention to them from here on.

"Just don't do anything." I give my arms a shake and it forces his hands to slip off mine.

"Erica," he begs, giving it one last shot.

It does stop me dead in my tracks. With my back to him, it's already a sign; but I still glance over my shoulder at him. He moved about a foot or so ahead, broken free from Bianca who's still in her spot. She's full-on crying. I am completely lost for words…

I did that. I did this to them. I'm such an asshole.

An aching pressure concaves my chest, making it difficult to breathe again. Alex's thick breathing fades in and out because that weird ringing in my ears is back.

"I can't..." is the last thing I say to him and her before I whirl back around and hurry out of there—

The sweat is dripping down from my forehead. The tears are streaming down my face—

"Oh, my God—Alex!" Bianca's scream bounces off the walls, traveling down to me. I turn back, but a swarm of people run over and circle by as he grabs a hold of the wall, clasping hold of his chest—

Fuck. I go to him, only my feet force me out the other way—the exit.

Everything just drains from my ears, including the shouts, Bianca begging for someone to go get a doctor while another nearby voice insists on calling 9-1-1 as I step out into the stairwell. I stumble to the railing, and for whatever reason, I look down at a bottomless pit. I'm on the second floor. Only, hearing the beat of my heart battling and battling against my chest. But it won't burst out of my skin.

"Shit," I slur—the bottom of my lip is sliding, like I'm drunk or something—my legs turn to jelly, sending one of my feet sideways. I cry out, hearing a voice asking if I'm okay. As I go to look at whoever is ascending the staircase—the dots are back. Everything goes black through my eyes...

Wincing, I only catch the glimpses of blood from a reopened fingernail wound on my left palm. It drips down my hand and onto my wrist, a red stream, once I bring my hands up. It's so gross...I can't...I can't breathe...

The ring grows louder in one ear, sending me forward until I next see the ceiling above me, distancing away as I lie on something hard and cold—the tiles. Someone grabs me, but I can't see who...the tension crawling' on the back of my neck refuses me to turn. It hurts too much if I do—physically.

I stare over at the center window across from me, radiating from the sunlight...

And then, I just allow myself to go to sleep—the black-spotted dots conquer the white ones through my eyesight, making everything go dark...

Darkness.

# Bianca

The darkness forms into sunlight and streaks through the window of the glass doors of the emergency room entrance. I've been sitting here by myself for the past...God, no it's evening time so. A few hours must've passed by now. I don't...remember...

> One minute, I'm running with the paramedic team with Alex, squeezing firmly onto his hand. But they tell me to calm down—Alex even says to chill—because it was only triggering more anxiety for him.
>
> And then, I was told to stay back as the paramedics rushed him through the 'Employees Only' double doors. I can't believe it...

My knees won't stop shaking. I gasp and force myself to sit up, leaning my head back against the white wall. I close my eyes, and I allow myself to breathe, but my bottom lip continues to quiver. Come on man...don't fuckin' cry right now. It's just that...I haven't been able to see Alex or Erica since they've admitted them. Alex's nurse came out like twenty-minutes or so ago to inform me that he was stable...He was only having a panic attack. *Only*...

So now, they have him resting up in the backroom, sticking him with IV tubes filled with drugs and other vitamin supplements.

I'd expected Erica's nurse to come out and do the same and update me. But...no one still.

It's why I'd screamed at the nurse at the counter that I wanted to see my sister. The nurse declined, threatening to call security if I didn't hush down. OR, shut the fuck up in her book. I mean, she *is*. Blood doesn't mean shit at all.

Fuck, *blood.*

It's all about love when it comes to Erica and Alex.

# Erica

I've been staring at the floor since we've got into some sort of office. I'm assuming it's Mr. Doc's right over here. He's been jabbering away. When I was looking at him, he kept making a lot of hand motions and whatever. But I could care less…

My parents have been with me this entire time. The nurse had allowed them into the other room, where I woke up with IV tubes being poked out and poked back into my skin—

> "Sorry," said the nurse; huh, it's funny how she thought that would change my mood or something. "Get some rest."
>
> Yeah, right. Like I'll be able to get some so-called rest at this point—I couldn't fall asleep once I woke up and found myself being wheeled down. A million things were just happening—
>
> The rush of cold air brushed against my face, as the lights on the ceiling zoomed by. This and that paramedic and nurse and then, Mr. Doc, were all advising me that I was going to be okay. What I was having earlier was a—
>
> "Panic attack," I'd muttered through the oxygen mask over my face. Yeah, I'd know that for sure by now.

The bottoms of my feet press further into the metal part of the bed, as my spine weaves in and makes me, well, arch even more. I can feel my mother's eyes of disappointment and the itch for her to lecture me on sitting up straighter…but no, more tension. Especially since Dad struggles to hold in his weeps. Oh, right, the doctor is breaking some sort of news…

I decided to tune back in. "…Stress is common for college students," Mr. Doc. goes on. "Often, we get more than twenty or so admitted teenagers and young adults each month due to an anxiety attack."

Ugh, those two-words again. They make me shake—freaking out Dad because he joins me, dragging his chair next to the bed. He takes a hold of my hand. It's a nice gesture, the warmth and security of a father's love for his daughter.

"…So, what are the options," Mom chimes in.

It finally makes me look up at her and her only. She's still standing across the room, next to the door to the office, which is shut. When she finally takes a seat on the chair that was beside Dad's, Mr. Doc stutters. He probably didn't realize that it was his turn to speak.

I thought Mom was going to say something further as well.

But the room sort of leaves me. My body is here but my mind flies off. It's familiar to being…well, what had happened. That feeling of your inner body looking down at the physical part of your body from above. At this moment, I'm a fly on the wall, watchin' it all play out. Doc. speaks and uses some more hand gestures until he reaches for my chart and clicks out a pen to jot something down.

He hands over a slip to me from what I can see from my out-of-body experience. Dad is the one who takes it since my eyes are back to the floor. I guess they can tell that I'm in shock. And…sad.

It's a prescription for anxiety and depression meds.

Now, I really won't look anywhere else but at the small teal and black polka dots of the tile floor...

"...Honey," Dad says one-minute or maybe minutes later. "Bianca and Alex want to see you...*Erica?*"

The teal dots shine bright; probably from not blinking still.

"...You're coming home," Mom tells me. "That's final."

And then, the black polka dots spot out on their own—taking over and consuming the teal ones. It's not coming from my eyes this time either, but my mind just wanting to spot out everyone in general. To escape...

Because this time, I'm the one who's in control of shutting my eyes first. *Not* the anxiety.

---

It's all really a blur...

I see Bianca and Alex standing at the curb, watching me as I approach the backseat—the door behind the passenger seat of the cab. Dad is with me. Mom isn't. I steal a glance at them over my shoulder—Bianca is visibly upset and walks away, disappearing behind the small mover's truck that is behind the cab. Dad was able to rent one last minute.

I can't hear anything...not even the birds who fly by or the chatter and updated lives of the student body; well, at least those who pass us by. I can't even hear the tire screeches or car honks as they speed by and zigzagging of cabs and cars...

Oh, my God...I'm going...*numb.*

I feel Dad's finger tapping' onto my shoulder, and finally, I catch up with him as he circles around the cab to load in the last box—the 'Projects' one. It's impossible to stifle it all back and I refuse for Alex to see me this way. From the corner of my eye, I see his silhouette waiting in the same spot as before. He's...waiting to say goodbye. Only, I get into the cab and shut the door right away, all without looking at him—

"Just go," I tell the cabbie and he obeys, and puts the car back into drive mode, and soon...

I turn around, watching as Alex distances further away from us once the cab pulls out into traffic and drives off. He sticks his hand up at me—

"Alex," I let out a soft cry, reaching and touching the backseat window as if I can turn back time and just be with him...and her.

I should've stayed in their hug just moments ago—

> "We love you, stupid," Bianca said to me, directly into my ear. "But fuck...Erica, if you truly feel this is the...right thing to do, then I'm not going to beg you to stay."

It's still in my ears, their voices.

"Yeah," he'd even agreed. "I echo what she says."

# DECEMBER 1st…

# DECEMBER 2nd...

# DECEMBER 3rd…

# DECEMBER 4th…

# DECEMBER 5th...

# SEVEN DAYS LATER...

*Spent my days with a woman unkind/Smoked my stuff and drank all my wine.*

...I've been in bed.

The last thing I remember is coming home and tossing back day one's pill of my new prescription. I climbed into bed...

Only to stay here.

At least Zeppelin has been keepin' me company through my earbuds—

*Going to California with an aching in my heart/*

I've been watching the sun and moonlight comin' and goin' as my head rests on the pillow. My back is to the bedroom door...I guess Mom and Dad come in and out. Probably, sitting or lying with me. Last night...

*Someone told me there's a girl out there/*

Cold fingers grab onto my own. I'm asleep, or at least halfway because all I see is darkness, but I hear...Mom weeping, even with my earbuds on. The left earbud stopped working—probably from overuse...these have been rammed into my ear pretty much since getting back...well, as Robert Plant puts it in this song, "Going to California". Those are her hands—I can tell because they're softer and smooth from the cocoa butter lotion she lathers them in day and night. Almost like baby skin, fresh out of the bath or sink water, cooing and all happy.

But Mom isn't happy. She's crying now…

Only tonight, she's with me.

*Standing on a hill in my mountain of dreams/*
*Telling myself it's not as hard, hard, hard as it seems/*

The chirping of the birds awakens me the next day and I find myself staring out the window across from me in bed. I don't need to get up because I can already tell that today is going to be a good one…

I see the first sign of sunshine breaking through the fluttery clouds. It's bold and radiant, a perfect circle of…a sign. I think…it's time for me to get out of bed.

Slowly, I push myself up and land on my elbows. God that even hurt. The prescription has me sleepy still—the room still blurring fully into focus. The back of my neck and head is throbbin' along to the beat of my heart. It's not fast, thanks to the medicine, but it's enough to keep me…alert.

The digital alarm goes off—shit, it's still a habit from going to school—I reach for it.

Oh, I guess Dad or maybe even Mom must've moved it to the end table, next to the cell phone, a.k.a. the other clock, and lamp. But I realize that it's not my alarm…No, I think I turned those all off as soon as I woke up the next day, realizing that I was back in California. No…

It's a calendar reminder…for today. My heart is SINKING and so is my body as this heaviness just takes over and pushes me back down onto my mattress. The back of my head hits the pillow like it is a pile of goose feathers.

It's December 14th…

The day that the project is due.

Sitting up to my elbow, struggling from the great amount of strength it takes. I *don't* see the 'Projects' box, Polaroids, and the shoebox on the floor in front of my untouched desk…So, my sight trails off to the right, following the fluffy carpet that leads up to the closet door. It's closed. I don't have to see it, but in the core of my small intestines, I feel my instinct give a small KICK. Darkness has already consumed the items in there…on the floor…where they sit…and where they will forever remain…

Out of everyone's sight.

# Bianca

It's louder today than usual. Yet, I still find myself tuning it out. Walking up the staircase to the back row—a.k.a. my usual spot—I stare at the steps. They're dark, some gray and blue color mixed to give off the impression that the art department, indeed, looks like one. I mean for God's sake; they're adding in another half-armed naked statue; like we need *another* Greek goddess at the entrance—

Fucker made me scream because it's literally being positioned and rooted into the cement around the corner of the main entrance leading up to this place. I'm counting on multiple run-ins with that thing. Someone has probably already broken their nose from colliding with that thing. We all know everyone just prefers to stare down at their phone, rather than attempt to look up, and God FORBID...be smiled at or greeted by a proper stranger. Well, I hate when people do that, too, sometimes. They ask how your day was and you're just awkwardly answering with a lie, *'Oh, fine/great/good'* and my favorite hypocritical response, *'How was/is your day?'*

The sound rings back into my ears as I take my seat, automatically gazing out to the millions of people who roam the pavement below me. I feel like a queen who sits at the top of her throne, expecting everyone else to fetch me...whatever they drank and ate back then. Besides, wine and grapes. Yeah, I could never do either—grapes and wine fuckin' suck, no sugary or a good taste. Ugh! Wine burns my throat even by taking a sip of it, almost like I'd just downed a few shots of Fireball.

And Fireball isn't my thing either.

My hands are already pulling out the golden folder from my bag that rests on top of my thighs. While everyone else does some sort of last-minute prep with their...partner, I find myself bowing down my head. So, I could avoid and prevent myself from seeing what they are all doing. Although, there is one group already at the podium. One of them gives the top of the microphone a tap—sending that eerie static around the room.

"Sorry," they announce and resume back to whispering whatever to their partner.

They both turn around, especially when the taller one and, well, cuter boy partner does a double—no, now a triple—take on me. What an ass; he even initiates it, too, by placing his palm on the back of his partner's neck to guide them to give their backs to everyone else. Especially me. Oh…you little shit.

Slowly, I find myself dreading the inevitable though. Trust me, my mind will play tricks on me but subconsciously, I am still aware of the…well, the project.

I fumble as my fingertips flip, peel back the cover of the folder. There it is, staring right back at me in its cover page, label protector: a hard copy of The Extraordinary Ordinary.

Yeah, I wasn't planning on coming empty-handed…It was still due. Regardless of her not being here anymore; *her* as in the empty seat next to me. The blue chair that I refuse to let anyone else sit. Just in case, I set my binder on top of the chair with the cover facing up—the van Gogh replica painting.

She would've liked that.

# Erica

"...We're disqualified, even if one of us turns it in today," I tell her.

The sound of the clock ticking by makes me straighten up. I tug at my sleeves, and I find myself looking back up at Dr. Mansell. She is in the usual position of her back pressed up against the beige, sofa-like chair in the corner of the room. It's not fair how I, as well as her other clients, have to get the leather couch—fuck, it squeaked again, sounding like a fart.

But I stop moving, feeling drained and just…defeated. It must show because as I open my mouth to speak, nothing but this softness and weakness comes on out. Great. "I'm nowhere close to being finished…"

Mansell makes a sound of, 'Oh that makes sense' and 'Ah, I see.' "You're disappointed with yourself."

And that's not rhetorical…ever coming from here. I just stare right back at Mansell, lost for words; unsure how to…answer that. Until I give a nod and then, another one.

It cues Mansell to jot something down onto the wireless pad of lined pieces of paper—she even has the yellow kind, too.

"I still can't open that box," I spill. "You know, the one with him...pictures of..." Oh, boy, here it goes. "The pictures of Josh."

"Your collage from high school."

"Yeah…that one." I take a deep breath, but it still forces up my shoulders. Mansell sees the tension that consumes me, so I lean forward and press my elbows into my thighs, bringing my rolled-up hands close to my mouth.

"Erica, you know...you took your first step when you had picked up your camera again. That's huge. You know that, right?"

Oh, she's actually asking me on that last part. Her pen is tilted to its side as her attention remains on, well, me only. I should probably mock the whole, 'You have my undivided attention,' body language, too. *Here it goes...*

"Yeah, but I broke the one before that." Wow, I'm barkin' at her, not talking in my 'grownup' tone. "After what he did to me..."

"You still feel obligated to pay them back—your parents, for the camera."

My head turns away, forcing me to gaze down at the floor. Huh, I'd never noticed the boxes of puzzles and board games in the opposite corner of the room, across from Mansell's chair.

"Yes," I finally answer, but the tension of my neck keeps me positioned as I am; not giving her my undivided attention anymore...

"Why?"

"I've already hurt them enough. And to be back on meds..."

God, this fuckin' SUCKS. I don't or ever will...get it. Get *this*.

"Erica," she assesses, and it still amazes me how...calm she sounds. I look at her and she is still watchin' me, not the studying kind but...giving me advice as though any friend or loved one would. "Neither your past nor your present makes you less of a photographer, an artist, or human. If it throws you off of your schedule and you're unable to work, just see it as an off day."

"Yeah, one long-ass off day. It's just, I don't want to be..."

"Please, go ahead."

"Look, I'm not in love with Josh or anything." Okay…Erica, where are you going with this? I keep talking, "But, I feel this...this *need* to include him in my project."

"Because he was your muse." She doesn't have to rethink or reanalyzed any of this now…

It does…make sense. I guess that is the 'establishing the problem' part. Damn, she's good.

"A muse who took everything from me."

"It's not your fault," she reassures me with a hint of weariness rising in her tone. "You know that it isn't your fault."

"Yeah…but I *didn't ask* to be...*raped*. Besides, everyone believed *him*—still do—including my friends."

"They're not real friends then, are they? Real friends support you, not leave you during a time of crisis."

True, so true.

"You're right," I agree.

Mansell's chest rises for a second and then, descends—I guess she is on edge a bit, too; or, just relieved that I'm on the same page as her, too. "Why is it that we care so much about our pain?"

"That's a good question," she says, and adjusts in her seat and then re-crosses her leg over the other. It does get this smile out of her, not the happy one but the kind where she could just relate. "I suppose a lot has to do with saying goodbye to that piece of yourself."

"Is that why I've been ignoring them since I've left—Bianca and Alex?"

I can see her now, fully, next to Dr. Mansell. She's on her stomach with her feet kicked up in the air, jotting down into that composition book of hers. She's humming a tune, bobbing her head along to the music—ah, Lou Reed.

*Sometimes I feel so happy/*
*Sometimes I feel so sad/*

"I don't know where to even begin," I choke back on a sob. Finally, I loosen the scarf around my neck and unbutton my jacket to let the room temperature air hit my skin…Ah, thank God. No wonder why it got hot again with being bundled up and all…

Shit, I think it was triggering a panic attack for me, but I'm not so sure…because my hands aren't as clammed up and they're not shaking either. Maybe a mini one?

"It's okay to be scared, Erica."

"Why though? Why's it okay to…"

"Not be okay," she finishes on my behalf, and sits taller in her chair. "Because you care too much about them. You think who you are now, because of what had happened to you back then, makes you toxic."

And then here comes Alex vanishing into thin air, adjacent to Bianca. She doesn't see him…or at least, not acknowledging him. He doesn't either. His profile faces me—the left side of him, as he leans over the sink, taking a deep, hefty breath, consumed with thoughts. I think…he's having a panic attack, but one that is not so taunting or really chaotic. It's the kind where one can mentally focus and mentally talk their way out of—

Oh, no, his fingers are tightening around the edges of the sink. Alex, come on…

And Bianca stops jotting down in her journal and instead, she's in a daze, her focus aims towards the floor by my feet. She's no longer humming or smiling. My opinion…she's sadder than before.

"I failed, Dr. Mansell…I failed."

"Well, I've always seen something entirely different." Dr. Mansell sets aside the notes onto the floor, almost on top of Bianca—until her and Alex both disperse into thin air. No longer in my sight. "Failure is when one simply stops, never giving something a shot or a second chance. Now, why do I see that and not yourself?"

"I…I don't know."

"You're looking at this through a hopeless lens. There's always a conclusion, Erica. Both life and art have their ups and downs; and when both meet up, it's just a moment to surrender."

Oh…kay…

And then it hits me like a pile of bricks. "The anxiety and depression."

It gets a smirk from Mansell; she's…proud of me, I guess. "It's a battle. Physical effects also come with emotional. The storm is never prolonged, Erica. It, ultimately, surpasses when you just allow yourself to embrace the thunder and lightning."

I still listen but have no desire to speak. I allow it to simmer, sinking in...

"What if I'm not strong enough?"

"But you ARE, Erica. Just part of the healing process is sometimes helping others. But don't you forget to help yourself first." And she might as well add in the, 'never,' considering the seriousness of her tone.

In my mind, I can see them again—YES! Alex looks up at his mirror reflection, while Bianca sits up and shuts her composition book, and removes her earbuds. They are both on a mission and leave, zapping out of my mental sight. I think…they'll be okay. And it makes me cry…not for them, because I'm happy as long as they are, but for…

"I want to get better," I tell her, my tone diminishing with each word.

"You already are. You're here." She smiles at me, leaning back into her chair. Her work has only begun but she appears…content. The work being done still needs improvement. I'm the work-in-progress…and I'm okay with that.

At least, for now.

For the first time, I believe her because I feel the knots unraveling from the back of my shoulders as they lower down to their normal position. My fingers unwrap themselves, too, freeing out my fingers to their long length. I'm okay…

I'll be okay.

And I just allow myself to breathe and breathe, catching the first sign of the sun rotating to this side of the family practices building, shining bright and mighty through the curtain-less and blind-less window. It's…going to be a perfect day…

*Just a perfect day/*
*Drink Sangria in the park/*
*And then later/*
*When it gets dark, we go home/*

I hear ya' Mr. Reed. I hear ya'. Only, I'm not going home to just wallow in the dark. I have further work to do myself.

---

As soon as I drive home, I find myself pondering for a few minutes in the car. I turn off the ignition, but my fingers remain wrapped around the steering wheel as though I am about to take off for good. Forever.

Dr. Mansell…everything we just spoke about rushes back like a lightning strike. So, it gets me thinking some more. Making direct eye contact with the rearview mirror, I catch glimpses of children and teenagers passing by. So young, maybe even naïve—for some of them—but filled with laughter and…
Oh, well that one is just texting. Seriously, she's not going to look up—what if I were to back up?

Whatever.

I unbuckle myself and open the door.

# THE FOLLOWING DAY ...

It's still early. Only a few minutes have passed since I made it back up to my room. I didn't see Mom or Dad downstairs...I did hear the blow dryer go off and the spinning of the elliptical machine in the spare bedroom. Mom is still getting ready in the bedroom and Dad is squeezing in one of his half-ass workouts; he calls them that, somewhat jogging and then running.

The sunlight spills through the window that takes up the entire wall across my bed. Thankfully, we got shudders for those—for some reason, just having the curtains pulled back and together wasn't enough...privacy. I accidentally left it open a few times during high school...especially when *they*...

> Some of the bad kids threw rocks and then...he, well his *new* girlfriend tossed a brick through my window. To be honest, Mom had a fit and wanted to move. Well, she demanded but Dad asked what *I* wanted. That was when the court had ordered Josh to move far, far away from me; otherwise, the court would've thrown him in jail. The judge was a woman too...
>
> "It happened to me, too," she once said to me before the first court hearing. I didn't know what that meant until I saw the rage and disgust that filled the room as soon as Josh had walked in with his asshole of an attorney and his parents. They kept eyeing me throughout. Ironically, his mom called me everything in the book—
>
> "Little harlot."
>
> OR:
>
> "Whore."

OR:

"Why didn't you speak up sooner?"

That one enraged Mom. Dad and I had to pull her back from lunging at Josh's mom and gouging her eyes out. I don't know, but I would have liked to see Mom do that. But Dad was terrified that she would go to jail; "Goddamnit, CATHY!" he'd yelled.

I think that was the last time when Mom had really…stuck up for me. She wasn't happy at all when the judge turned to me that one evening, asking me what I felt was in my best interest—Josh moving away from me, which put an indefinite restraining order on him, or throw him into prison with a restraining order of five-thousand feet or more.

I just…wanted it to be over—the court trial and just those looks and name-calling. I didn't want to run away…but that was also the last time when we—Mom, Dad, and I—spoke of the incident. I'd asked them to. Only, Mom started making her typical jabs…never quite agreeing with me. It got so bad one night. She called me something and I then returned the 'favor'—I'd called her a…I'm not too proud of it…but a *hypocritical* bitter woman.

I screamed it at her, shaking up the entire house. Anyone can probably piece together the rest. Our relationship has never been the same since.

As I stand in the doorway to the closest, pressing the side of my head into the doorframe, I let out a sigh. It's all there in front of me…away from the sunlight that floods the rest of the room: the 'Projects' box, Polaroids, and shoebox.

I lower to my knees, just taking it all in. It's still in the same condition as before…luckily, nothing was precisely ruined, just a few crinkles here and there. Ironically, it's on the older Polaroids—the ones that have to do with him.

---

A few minutes later—fifteen minutes and eight seconds to be precise—I find myself sitting in the middle of the floor, surrounded by nothingness. Everything sits in front of me. Here it goes—I turn over the last numbered Polaroid on the floor. The shoebox remains next to me but is empty. Scooting myself back a few inches, I drag my legs to my chest, hugging them tighter…

It's all there. He's there, and so are they: the Polaroids have a story forming one big puzzle piece…all forty-seven pieces tell a story. It's my story, or was—a younger me in high school, and I'm makeup-free. To me, I look the same but at the time…when he was giving me notes, he thought I was so beautiful and amazing….

In the Polaroid, my high school self is smiling at Josh—*not the asshole* from NYU, but the *real one*. Him, as in the one who took…

I breathe, realizing that is sort of going against what Mansell and I had agreed on—Josh DIDN'T take everything away from me. He never nor ever will. Right…

I can't believe how much love there is in the Polaroid of me with my head tilting into his shoulder with this look of lust and love…And wouldn't you know, the asshole is not even batting one eyelash at me but staring off to the side, only giving the camera his profile, slightly out of focus.

Prick.

At least, I've...Holy shit...It's done. All of it.

I recoil back—all fast and holding most of my weight on the back of my hands. What the fuck...Holy fuckin' shit. It's done. I need to call—

The creak at the doorway gives me a startle—Mom is doing her best attempt of passing by, but I already see her giving me one too many double-takes. She lingers just outside of the bedroom doorway, all dressed up with her prim and pressed plaid skirt and matching jacket for work. Although, she appears the complete opposite of waking up and kicking today's ass!

I know she was about to leave and probably, still is. "I heard you getting up..." is all she gets to before I follow her eye trail...Oh, right—the project. It's a habit, hiding things from her; or I used to.

Mom is silent but not the cold type that I'm used to seeing. She's stifling...holding back tears. Oh my, God...

She's triggered by the project.

"They're just pictures, Mom. They're just pictures." That last part was more for me, wanting to reassure myself that I believed what I said earlier (if that makes any sense).

I hope so.

Silence stands still between Mom and I. It's the first time where we don't know what to say to just each other. Is this a moment for a celebration or a time to grieve? I'd say both, in my opinion.

"Erica?" Dad pops in the doorway from the opposite end of Mom. He looks from me to her. Mom breaks focus. She is already lost in thoughts, heavy ones by the look on her face. I notice it too…her hand is caressing over her wrist. She remains silent. Dad is also dressed for work. It's Friday so he's rockin' the jeans with the button-down and blazer coat. Weird…how time flies by; yesterday, I thought it was Sunday.

"This was on the porch," he says, aware of the dynamic shift in the room but I think the gold envelope in his hand has him too preoccupied. "It must've arrived last night."

He passes it over. By the time it slips into my hands, I can see who the sender is—

**NYU, Tisch School of the Arts/Office of Dr. Lansing**

I open it right away, turning around as soon as I see the stanzas of writing. It's a letter, addressed to me…

The heaviness consumes my chest, closing up my throat—no, no, Erica, it's not closing up. *That's just the anxiety. It's all in your head. You're here and safe; I'm even holding the back of the desk chair—it's a chair, that is a desk in front of it, and I'm standing on the carpet…*Alex's method…It's *working.*

"What is it?" Dad asks me.

But the words are forcing me to reread them over and over again like lines to a theatrical play—a one-woman show. "She…turned it in."

I hear Dad taking a few steps closer because his breathing is closer, as well as the presence of someone being behind me. But it's the tiptoeing that is proof—he's not surprised, but he already knew. As I face him, Dad smiles and gives me a nod, 'Yeah, she'd texted me.'

Oh…those little shits.

"Mum's the word"—My eyes return to Dr. Lansing's letter to me as Dad takes a hold of one end of the hard copy, reading it aloud to all of us—"Bianca wanted to personally mail a copy of *The Extraordinary Ordinary* to you herself. But as policy stands, we are unable to release anyone's home address, whether they are a former or a current student, to third parties. Although, I highly regret to inform you that your project does not qualify for this year, we certainly look forward to it for next year's showcase. Blessings, Dr. Lansing."

"Director of Tisch School of Arts," I say, making eye contact with Mom.

Mom stares down at the floor with her arms crossed. She does not shift nor is there a hint of remorse or anger in her tone as she asks, "That's the piece?"

Oh, she's acknowledging it. She's…I suppose coming to terms with it.

"Yeah. This is it." I find myself rising taller, fuck inhaling, and just hold my breath. It makes me hunch forward, slipping my hands to my thighs. Dad and Mom don't run over to me. I just feel Dad giving me a pat on the back…an encouragement and the only support he's going to give me. He tells me to take a deeper breath and rise as I'm doing so…

So, I do. Then he tells me to exhale and lower my shoulders, but slowly. I do…

Free—the tension in my chest is no longer aching my heart. My fingers curl up into fists, but not tightly.

"Read it," Dad says to me. "I want to hear it." He takes a hold of the poem, THE EXTRAORDINARY ORDINARY and pulls out the desk chair and turns it so I can sit down.

I don't ask but I just sit and wait until he hands back Bianca's piece. He kneels next to me, waiting. Mom watches the both of us. As I go to read, I see her pacing into the room, listening to it as well…

# Bianca

God, that light is really bright, but I know it's expected when you're not used to addressing a room full of people. Only the spotlight on the ceiling across the room, leveled at an angle to point down at the small stage which I stand in is keeping the people in the shadows. I can see their silhouettes. There is no sign of Alex just Mrs. Newman, who stands on the sidelines of the stage, the first of the line where some of my classmates await their turn to speak.

My hands smooth out the bottom tutu material of my cocktail dress as I take a step closer to the microphone and speak. The shaking of my fingers starts and ends up in the center of my chest—shit, it's my heart that's racing faster and faster. But I know Erica would want me to do this,

The poem, THE EXTRAORDINARY ORDINARY, has the lines: *"The best years of one's life/Not for all of us/It takes more than putting on that smile/And act like everything is okay/To pretend we're okay/That we love others/Life/Ourselves".*

# Erica

*"We think we deserve the worst to happen/Including death*
*Far beyond it*
*We hate ourselves for what we've become*
*For the path we have chosen*
*Only*
*We are so naïve*
*Like the cry from a newborn*
*Innocence/Once pure*
*People like us*
*We've never deserved the bad*
*Ever*
*We are worth it*
*Worth every moment*
*Every second of other's*
*And our lives as well*
*We have to know this*
*We made it out*
*We are alive for a reason*
*We just have to learn to keep living*
*Know that these best years of our lives are sometimes cold*
*Like winter's snow*
*Coldness*
*That will soon be warmed up*
*Like a twinkle of a starry night."*

*– THE EXTRAORDINARY ORDINARY*

Starry Night. van Gogh...

She does care…

She wrote for this for me.

She cares.

# Erica & Bianca

**BIANCA** wrote:
This is where we must be/
Amongst the ocean colored sky/
Where the sunshine swoons in/
And parts through the clouds/
That is where we have all come from/
Like a caterpillar that transforms into the thinnest layer/
Of something extraordinary/
The Extraordinary Ordinary/
Life is a fragile of beauty/
So live/
For the sake of yourself/
We see it in different ways/
But it doesn't make us bad people/
We struggle/
But fight/
To make it right/
We have believers/
While others/
Seek inspiration from those who inspire us.

**ERICA** reads:
One thing to always remember/
Destroy the negativity/
Forever.

**BIANCA:**
Things aren't supposed to be easy/
As they say/
Sometimes/
It even seems impossible/
The truth is/
Neither of us will know/

Until the end of time.

**ERICA:**
We all have a specific purpose to be here/
But in order to be successful/
Content/
Happy/
We cannot dwell so much on what will become...

**BIANCA:**
Our destiny.

# Erica

The pages of THE EXTRAORDINARY ORDINARY slip out of my hands. Dad catches it before it hits the floor. The weird thing is my hands are not sweating or shaking. They're...fine...

But I'm not. I can't stand up. I just sit there.

# Bianca

Slowly, my eyes rise. The crowd roars with a round of applause. For me…what the hell? I don't know what to do, especially when hands hitting together drown out my ears—

It raises my panic.

I step away from the microphone, as Mrs. Newman approaches me. She sets her hand on my back, and guides us to center stage. "Ladies and gentlemen," she announces, beaming brighter than the light above us, "our special recognition honoree, Bianca..."

I see the shadows of hands clapping and clapping and more people jumping up and cheering—I see a few fists pumpin' up and up. *What…*

It all drains out of me for me, as I receive a certificate from Mrs. Newman. She practically rams it into my hands which won't let go of the Extraordinary. The lights seem brighter, almost like it's spinning and spinning, including the stained glass windows…

Only, I don't think anyone else notices because they're all getting ready to leave as Newman is, oh...she's speaking at the microphone now. I scope the crowd and immediately see Alex as the men, women, and children (some of my classmates are parents themselves) get up to leave or move around to mingle. Most go to the art pieces on the walls to sip their wine and nibble the finger foods of cheese, olives, grapes, and whatever else can make this night one big cliché…

"Are you okay?" Alex mouths out as he walks over to the stage; he has a way to go, considering he was standing in the back to watch.

I nod, only I'm not matching the sad, small smile that appears on him.

# Erica

The Polaroids are displayed in an arch on the floor faces…Bianca and Alex, as well as myself, are in all of them. One by one…

Shit, my heart is beating a bit faster now. I scoot up to sit on my knees to reach for the pill bottle on my desk. It rattles lightly—maybe…like four to five capsules are left—as I bring it in front of me. When I open it, I find my fingers going numb and not from the anxiety…

Wait, actually my fingers aren't shaking anymore. They're…stable. Instead, they chuck the pill bottle across the room. I fumble for a hold of my earphones that are in the big zipper of the backpack in front of my desk. By the time I slip them over my head, I can already hear Reed's voice blastin'—

*Sweet Jane!*

The room goes still as my hands work their magic, piecing together the Polaroids…or, unlike the Polaroids that make up that photo of Josh and I, they stop here and there. I grow flustered, unsure if this Polaroid of Alex and Bianca should go first or the one where Alex and I are rockin' a selfie…

But I just work. I just DO IT. I get it done.

You could say that my bedroom is rotating around me because the shadows casting down on the carpet—there's an orange, yellow hue and then, pink, and purple; and then, it's dark like a purple and blue. The next thing I notice, my hands start slowing down from shuffling around the Polaroids in different directions. Now, they're only sliding one Polaroid to the center of the…new puzzle piece…

I crawl back on my knees, almost tipping over, even though the walls have stopped spinning around me like I'm the sun. Oh, the irony at this moment—the sun is that metaphor aspect to the afterlife of going through…well, trauma and how to…move on. Without it running my life because now, I choose if it will or not. It's not…It's NOT.

Balancing one of my hands on the floor, I push myself up to sit taller as I gaze from left to right and right to left of the Polaroid project…it's completed. *For good.* Smiling, I let out a cheer of victory and toss my hands up into the air. I guess you could call this my *Breakfast Club* moment. It's all there…

If I'm counting accurately right now, there's only one…five…fifteen…TWENTY?! There are only twenty Polaroids from the high school version that have remained in the updated version of…The Extraordinary Ordinary. Whoa, that's all there is because the rest of it are Polaroids of Bianca, Alex, and myself in a few of them. But mainly, this is them—their story, too. With Polaroids of them being on the right side, it's truly their candid moments of laughs, smiles, laugh-tears, and faces that are helping my high school self-complete the project. *Literally,* because the puzzle piece that makes up my teenage moment is no longer staring at Josh, who has been replaced. I'm smiling at them, both in the then and now.

The song ends and the next one shuffles, giving my headphones a crackling sound—I lower the volume, fuck these are already breaking—

*Oh, it's such a perfect day/*
*I'm glad I spent it with you/*

Oh, Reed…it is a perfect day. The start to a perfect life.

---

Dad is on his feet, standing next to the chair at the countertop where he has his morning coffee, oatmeal, and catches up on the paper. I can't believe we are one of the few who still keep up with the current events in hard copy. Well, only he does.

"Well…" Cathy finally breaks the silence, setting down the—irony moment—knife from slicing up fresh strawberries into pieces. It usually goes with a protein shake with her and Dad; Mom has this new thing since I've been back with meal prepping. God, my parents do look good…but I know we've all lost a few pounds from the…stress. Of everything. "I don't want to be the bad guy here…"

She has more to say but is biting her tongue. Her attention diverts away from me and even Dad. I'm still lingering in the archway to the kitchen and conjoined dining room. My fingers grip onto the handle of my roller suitcase; not out of anxiety *per se,* but it's more of something to make me feel…support. I guess it's a new comfort method—I've been noticing since getting back from New York—where I sort of stop the anxiety from happening. I don't know if it's the sturdiness of an item that makes me feel mentally…grounded. The walls of the room don't spin nor do the items feel like they're about to outgrow me in size.

I'm here in the now; *in the now.*

Mom is still not too…*happy.* I wouldn't say she's disappointed but more of a self-reflection moment that she's having as she stares out the window with her profile only being visible to me and Dad. She has our attention.

"Cathy, we don't think that," Dad says, removing his hand from his hip and bringing both of his hands to the countertop. He rests them on the white and gray marble, watching her, even leaning forward to get a better look at her.

Only, Mom doesn't flinch. I can't even hear her breathing like she usually would by scoffing or giving an over-the-top sigh. No, she's silent. We only hear the chirps of the birds, nearby lawnmowers, and the beeping sound of—from what it sounds like—a mover's truck or some sort of work truck hauling closer. The loud *vroom* doesn't even get any of us to look over our shoulders at the front door. It's even red on the interior…

God, maybe we are the *American Beauty* family. Minus the Dad lusting-over-the-teenage-friend part. No, we are just the family who has gone on too long by fakin' it with their, 'Nothin is wrong,' attitude.

Especially me.

"And let me guess who bought her the ticket..." Mom brings her eyes to Dad, still and monotone as hell.

"I paid half"—that gets her looking at me now—"with money from the music shop."

"That's not my concern, Erica. Far from it." A smile—a.k.a. her scoff—breaks out across her face. "What about school? You didn't look once for something here..."

I know…I already know that. Dad does, too, considering that he is the one to avoid any eye contact now with Mom and me.

But I also…I also don't belong here. And I tell her that, too. It's a weight off my chest, but just by the shift of her body, bending her neck to look down at the counter, I know it's not for her. It never was. But this is for me…for me…

My fingers loosen from the handle of my suitcase.

"I'm just…" Setting her hand on her hip, she sighs and scans around, almost like she isn't sure where to gaze off to now. Oh, my God…She's nervous. All fidgety, she's taking another glance there and here…

And then, my hand breaks completely free from the suitcase handle, as it gives a knock against the white doorframe after it leans over. I…I find this benevolent force drawing me closer to her, toward her as it sort of creates this clear pathway to…to be there with her. To soothe her.

"It was my choice to not report him. The same choice you also didn't make thirty years ago, when it happened to you. It didn't stop you from living. You met Dad. We're okay, Mom. I'm okay. We've survived."

Mom can barely stifle back the tears. Tears are already streaming down her cheeks. She is still trying to hide them, turning her head away to wipe them away. From the corner of my eye, I see Dad shaking his head…disappointed in her. He knows where this is headed.

"Guess I'll never understand. Any of this," she says but not to me. Her tone diminishes, almost like it's a thought that was not supposed to leave her mind. It was meant for herself.

Yet, she doesn't look disappointed. Well, at least she doesn't sound like it—I can't say if she's carrying it physically.

"Maybe," I cautiously approach this, "one day you will." And I find myself smirking at her once she whips her head back to me. My hand is lying atop hers, but my fingers won't wrap around. Neither do hers.

I'm not mad. I get it—she's struggling to accept this. I don't care though because, for the first time in MY life, I'm doing what is best for me. Not her or Dad. For ME.

---

Dad could say differently though. He has that stature of looking in the opposite direction in a time of confrontation—a moment of truth.

You could say this would be a more awkward moment but the engines of the airplanes starting up and taking off into the sky fills up the air space. Also, it's busy bullshit as usual—people saying goodbye or hello to their loved ones or J-walking to the opposite sidewalk to make it to one of the garages. The rolling of their wheeled suitcases also sends vibration throughout our parked car—imagine, twenty or so going by every five seconds. Yeah, shit would've made me think that I was having a panic attack.

But now, I'm immediately going straight to that it's *not* me, but *the world*.

I unbuckle my seatbelt off Dad's silence as he sits there with his head resting onto his fist. But as I go to reach for the passenger door handle, he speaks: "I love your Mom."

My hand nor the rest of my body has moved at all. Remaining the way that I'm currently in, I continue to listen to him: "And I can understand her side of things...because there's not a day that goes by where I wouldn't switch spots with you in a heartbeat."

"Dad…"

"But," he says and sniffles at the same time. He's already dabbing at his eyes, but he's still full-on crying, "When I think about everything you've accomplished so far, I'm just so proud of you. And I wish...I wish I'd tell you this more often."

We hug right away—I reach for him, knowing that he needs me at this moment. He needs to know that it's OKAY. I'm not mad nor ever have been. It wasn't Mom's fault; it's not Dad's fault, either…

And it's not my fault either…It's not my fault…

It never was.

---

As I press the side of my face against the window, I can already spot it out as we fly above…

New York City. The towers. The millions of ant-sized cars that are either speeding by or hitting something. Home…

This is home. The clouds parting ways in the sunny day sky is perfect, 'Welcome home, Erica.' Oh, man…I feel a tingle creepin' through my fingers. Not like a pulse of its own, but enough to make me shift around until I find myself sitting up straighter. Wait, I feel myself archin' now—

Fuck, this is going to be tough. I hope it is…worth it. The flight, the rush through T.S.A. to make it to my flight on time—passengers were boarding by the time I got there. I nearly collided with every person that passed me like a speeding light…

*Breathe…Just breathe, Erica. You'll be fine. You got this.*

I hope so. And now, t-minus…three hours or so until I see her—Bianca.

# Bianca

The clicking of my heels is the only thing that holds my attention as I walk down the lower east side…Oh, wait that sounds like I'm like a hooker or something. Shit! No wonder there are a few cabbies who whistle at me, along with their passengers in the backseat.

Dumbasses. This is why I can't wait to move…

Only, first thing's first—find a job.

I think the interview went well—EWW, a dead rat! *Gross.*

God, they say once you start dressin' like a BOSS BITCH, you'll change your perspective on everything from the way you speak, move, and the world around you in general. Oh, wait a minute—I'd meant BOSS, comma, BITCH. HA! I told Alex that one time…

Man, I hope I'd landed this job! Otherwise…at least, I looked cute today with this beige button-up blouse and blue pencil skirt—FUCK YES! I'm a BOSS, BITCH.

And then the strutting of my high heels comes to a stop because I stop dead in my tracks. Not literally, but like I can't move…

Erica is sitting at the bottom of the staircase to the main entrance of our apartment building. She's off to the side so my fellow neighbors can walk up the steps without asking or awkwardly demanding her to move out of their way.

Once, someone told me to go fuck my hand when I'd fallen on our way home on karaoke night with her and Alex…

She has her suitcase with her.

"I saw your name in the *New York Times,*" she says to me, standing up and brushing off lint or whatever is on her thighs—oh, wait a second…it's not that. "Congratulations."

She means it, too, but there's a hint of guilt and…shame because her tone rises at each letter of C-ON-G-R-A-T-U-L-A-T-I-O-N-S and cracks at the end.

"Thanks…" is all I can think of saying back. To be honest…I'm not sure what to do.

"So, Crystal got an agent, huh? Zane's...five-page magazine interview is cool, too…"

Damn, this is awkward as hell. It is a touchy subject for both of us.

A jogger coughs as he passes by us, which startles us, but we soon realize that he was oblivious to our conversation because of the big-ass headphones on top of his head. Still hella awkward…

Erica is even diggin' her hands into her pockets, not searching for anything but to place them somewhere like it's the only body part she can hide until she can do so herself. "Bianca…I rang the bell, but looks like you were at work?"

Oh, right—my outfit which she has never seen me in. It's brand new. "Interview. I'm not sure if I got it."

"Well, I'm sure you will. Otherwise, they're fuckin' idiots." She smiles at me. It's difficult to return one at the moment…for now.

"It was for the school paper. It's not a big deal, really…"

And I see it in her hands—how the fuck could I miss it. She'd picked it up I guess during our conversation. Otherwise, I'm just blind as a bat. Her fingers cradle around the edges of a Converse shoe box. It looks like a size…six or seven. Not sure, but it seems like the size I'd wear. Written on the top, in bold Sharpie is **The Extraordinary Ordinary**.

Whoa.

"Duane Reade Pharmacy is making your copies of the Polaroids," she tells me, not having to do a double-take or whatever on me or the shoebox.

She knows that I have taken notice way before she said something—obviously because I must look like one of those creepers who stare with their mouth wide open when something…just extraordinary itself comes their way; or bypasses them. Man, I'm weird as fuck…

I LIKE it.

"They said it'll be ready in an hour unless you want the originals." And she says it so nonchalant because it truly doesn't matter. All that matters, based on the vibe that is roaming my way, is for us to be in the same place at the same time. To be with me, and I with her.

"Uh…" I find myself letting out a laugh, glancing around, and only seeing that no one else gives two-shits to watch us. Well, except for the creepy cabbies. What is it with them today?

"I don't know what to say," I speak like a normal person, now. I even shrug and mock her hand movements of burying mine into the fronts of my pockets—*Jesus Christ!* I forgot; this damn tight, hip-hugging pencil skirt doesn't come with pockets! Screw it, I need to return it—PRONTO, TOO.

"Did I tell you that I'm back in therapy?" Finally, her eyes rise to mine. We hold eye contact. There's a new vibe of sadness and, well, reality. "To help me wean off of the medicine..."

She lets out a chuckle, but an embarrassed one because now…she's all fidgety, swaying like she has to use the bathroom, but everything is occupied.

"Erica…" I take a step forward; she refuses to make any eye contact with me as she wipes her arm over her eyes.

"I should've called. But I just needed time...to think."

Yeah, I get it. I do.

"Gotta put yourself first sometimes."

I allow the silence to sit between us briefly, as the cars speed by some more, tires scrapping around the corner at the signal ahead. Children laughing as their older siblings—teenagers or preteens—walk them home.

"Well, I was going to email you, but…technology is Photoshop for me. I hate it. I prefer hard copies. It's real. Natural, unlike a housewife's tits."

That gets a smile out of her; one of those accidental ones since she snorts and attempts to recover. But it gets us both chuckling. This is good. I stick out my hand. For a moment, she just looks at me, in the process of transitioning one thought to the other. Then, she takes a hold of it. We hug.

"I've missed you, dingus." My arms tightening around her as I tell her. I do miss her…

"I know," she agrees. "I've missed you, too. Always have and always will."

# Erica

The Polaroid Project is displayed on the small coffee table. It's all there—pieced together as one giant puzzle piece. Bianca tries to process all of this. She's quiet for a moment, as I do my best to watch the movement of her eyes following each Polaroid…giving each her time. She cares about them—about us. It's both moving and heart-wrenching for her. She removes herself from the seat next to me on the couch and goes to the floor. On her knees, she only gets a closer look at the Polaroids…

"And Josh," she starts and takes a deep breath, but she doesn't look at me, "where is he now?"

My turn to speak—to go further into, well, the news that I broke to her just minutes ago. "Northern California. He ran off after his scholarship was revoked. It's weird—he was the one who'd encouraged me with the photography, until..."

"He'd raped you." And now, her eyes crawl over to me. There's this agony look on her, a mixture of wanting to burst out into tears and punch something. I mean, she is probably in some sort of mind battle from booking it and running the streets of Northern California until she tracks down Josh. And get an eye-for-an-eye.

I don't blame her, but I also wouldn't want her to do that. Josh is going and rotting in hell anyhow—he chose his eternity, ever after, that day he did it. Fuckin' asshole.

"He was my first." It still amuses me—the irony and cliché of my story. Maybe I'm just being hard on myself. Mansell told me I have been numerous times. "I haven't been with anyone since...that night. Nobody believed me. They still don't."

That kills Bianca to hear, as she painfully turns her head away. I notice her fingers are curled up in firsts, pressing down onto the chestnut table. "Real friends don't second guess you. Ever."

Rising, she takes a few paces across the wooden floor in thought, just trying to process.

"But I went into the room with him…" I did…I did…

"Making it your fault," she adds on. Now, I find myself staring at the edge of the table, where one of the Polaroids is dangling off. It's not going to fall.

"Meaning that I was asking for it…?"

"It's no surprise. Most abusers won't ever take responsibility for their actions. Fuckers." I hear her footsteps coming to a stop. By the time my sight returns to her, she's already staring my way…in tears.

"Innocent until proven guilty, right...It's bullshit."

"Complete utter bullshit," she agrees and shakes her head.

Pacing over to the nearby window, it only gives me her backside. She stretches out her arms to lean her hands against the ledge in front of the window. The white curtains—some type of fringe—keeps out most of the daylight. "But it's no surprise. No, it never has been or will be. It's just another stigma…another stigma that we survivors gotta fight through."

# Bianca

It has Erica in shock. I know this because of the silence that fills up the room. When I decide to turn around—she's sitting taller with her hands coming closer to her mouth. I nod, and then, she covers her mouth, stifling back a gasp and a sob. Yeah…the irony of us finding each other in this world. We are not nor never alone. Ever.

"You're not alone here, Erica." I go to her and take my seat again. Before I can do so, she's the one who grabs a hold of my hand—

They are sweating; not hers but my own. I'm a bit embarrassed, wanting every desire to break focus with her. But she deserves all the attention that is needed from me. I…I have to know that she's okay. Her fingers give my own a firm squeeze. And then, the door shuts and it startles us. It's Alex.

He comes to a stop in the doorway. Removing his earbuds, he keeps his head down like a guilty child who had taken the cookie and ate it before dinner. Even when his mother told him NO. Oh, my God…He heard *everything.*

He's in his work uniform, coming home from a long day at work so, it's difficult to tell if that's where the haggardness and pale face is evolving from—Erica and her…her past. I glance back to Erica, who is giving Alex her undivided attention—

Only, his eyes remain on the floor. I see it too—his arms tighten around his binder, hugging it closer to his chest; there's a sticker of the Velvet Underground & Nico's banana cover album on the backside.

"Well, I'll let you two..." God, it's all I can think of at the moment because of that tension of lust, maybe even love, and frustration that is vibing off their presence in the room.

I'm an odd man out. They need some time to hash it out. "Duane's," I turn and tell Erica. "I'm going to get ready for that. Be back in a bit."

And I turn on my heel and walk out, squeezing both Erica and Alex's arm as a boost of encouragement. They deserved it—and NEED IT. Jesus Christ do they need someone such as my fuckin' awesome self to tell them both that a.) They LIKE EACH OTHER b.) They are both so FUCKIN' STUBBORN and c.) THEY NEED TO ACT UPON THAT ATTRACTION.

Man, this tires me out. But I get it…I had a difficult time getting intimate with anyone…after it had happened to me growing up. I round the corner of the doorway…

But you know that my nosy ass is going to eavesdrop. I lean against the wall, pressing my back into it, and I listen for what awaits next.

# Erica

Shit…this is awkward.

"How much did you hear?" I finally ask. Neither of us makes a move. We just stand there in place.

He's silent for a moment; I see that his eyes are shut. "All of it."

Now, he looks up, eyeing me and then the coffee table/project. His heart breaks for me. I just know that…

"You know," he says, his tone has become soothing…calmer than it should be in a situation like this. "I had this all planned out in my head. Wanting to tell you..."

"No, go ahead. Please."

I mean it, too; it has me on the balls of my feet, eager to just retain an answer.

He hesitates, but the anger and pain are still there—the heaviness of his breathing and the fact that his face is turning a lighter shade of red…or, how about the obvious of his fingers locking into fists over his binder. It covers the banana album cover from me.

"It's just…"—Come on, Alex, spit it out. He does—"You don't see me or Bianca flee to the opposite side of the country. But, after overhearing..."

Oh, no! Alex, please don't use that as an excuse. I go to him, circling the footrest of the nearby La-Z-Boy chair that is adjacent to the couch. "Hey—*I* fucked up. There's no excuse for leaving and hurting you guys." Oh, now…he's not looking at me, even standing a few inches away from him. "Look…I just don't know how this works."

Now, he can't hold back either; thanks to the desperation that raises in my voice. "Neither do I. Erica…I miss you."

He's touching me—his hands brush against mine before they move to the bottom of my mouth. He just holds this look with me. We're nervous—but the good kind; *the good kind.*

"We're a mess," I tell him, but that doesn't stop him from setting his hand on the back of my neck, while the other grazes the side of my face—AH! His fingers are fuckin' cold, but I don't find myself flinching to be quite honest.

"That's even better."

And it is me who leans in, kissing him first. He pulls back, engaging our hands together—it stops the shaking of mine. I find myself taking a deep breath. I can feel his eyes burning a hole in me, as he presses our foreheads together, quickening his own inhale-exhale-inhale-exhale.

Just breathe…God, what the fuck is WRONG with us.

"You're not running?"

I feel his head shake, which gets me to look at him as well does he. "Was never planning to."

And I can see it again…this honesty and sincerity in the eyes. It's all in the eyes. He never breaks focus with mine nor lets me go. He keeps himself close, but not holding me tight to prevent me from, well, escaping.

But I trust him…

Because I allow myself to trust him, we intertwine our fingers and I press my lips against his. I lean forward, forcing him to back up into the wall—and the small bump makes us laugh…as well as Bianca, "Jade/Alexander!" she sings…like she is standing behind the opposite side of this red wallpaper wall…

Oh, she's been listening. *Figures,* that girl.

# Bianca & Alex

**ALEX**

*...Barefoot on a summer night/*
*Never could be sweeter than with you/*

**BIANCA**

*And in the streets, you run a-free/*
*Like it's only you and me/*
*Geez/*
*You're something to see/*

# Erica

Man, oh, MAN! It is GOOD to see them back on stage together to belt out Edward Sharpe & The Magnetic Zeros' "Home."

He: Alexander part.

She: Jade part.

I watch them from the center table that is in front of the stage. If they were to take a misstep, they'd fall directly onto the black circular table, a.k.a. directly in front of ME. The lounge isn't too crowded…I mean, it is only 2:35…2:26 pm. So, people and the regulars are probably still at work or on their way over. Whatever the case may be, I'm just glad we sort of have the place to ourselves…counting the two-four-six other people who are here, too. Two of them—a man with another man—have drinks at the bar. The others are scattered about, sitting alone like me at a table, watching Bianca and Alex, too.

"Baby girl," Ricky says with sass, and as he claims—*ASS*, as he drops his booty to the floor to collect two empty shot glasses from our table. He glimpses at me to the stage and gives a wink. "You should be up there, too."

**BIANCA & ALEX**

*La/*
*La/*
*La/*
*La/*
*Take me home/*
*Mama/*
*I'm coming home.*

"Uh, yeah," I tell him, already rising to my feet with my camera. "That's NOT going to happen."

"Mhmm." He poses with the tray with his hip popped out to the side for some of the Ass plus Class equals Beyoncé; or, in a mathematical talk: ass + class = Beyoncé.

"I'm going to get to work," I reassure him, waving the Polaroid camera as a gesture. But Ricky doesn't need to say more because of—

"ERICA!" Bianca screams in the microphone, which sends that loud ring pulse throughout the speakers around the karaoke bar. OUCH.

By the time I can fully remove my fingers from ramming into my ears from the noise, Bianca is already pointing to me like a Disco song has just come on. Oh, she's wanting me to join them on stage, too…Ha, yeah. That's a FUCK NO.

I decline Bianca's invite, now awkwardly standing there, shaking my head. One of the six attendees at the tables hollers out, "JUST FUCKIN' SING!" When I turn my head around to find the culprit, I feel two arms wrap around my waist—

"Ricky!" I cry out, but as tiny as he is…Man, he's strong because next thing I notice, Alex and Bianca each take a hold of one of my arms and pull me up on stage during a brief instrument solo.

"Just have fun, honey bunny!" Ricky tells me and whips back around, doing an in-between of an Elle Woods', 'Bend and Snap,' and dropping it low like he's a part of a hip-hop music video. "Oh! Almost forgot." He sashays over to me, removing one of the four shots off the tray. Handing it over to me, I down that fucker like it's the cure to cancer or something.

I feel the weight of Bianca's arm looping around my shoulder, which draws me in closer to the side of her body. I bring my head down, and finish the shot of…I think that was a Fireball with a twist of lime? Alex is now passing over the third mic. He moonwalks backward as the Alexander part of the song takes over…

# Erica, Bianca, & Alex

**ALEX**
*Jades?*

**ERICA & BIANCA**
*Alexander?*

**ALEX**
*Do you remember that day you fell outta my window?*

**ERICA & BIANCA**
*I sure do/*
*You came jumping out after me/*

**ALEX**
*Well/*
*You fell on the concrete/*
*Nearly broke your ass/*
*And you were bleeding all over the place/*
*And I rushed you out to the hospital/*
*You remember that?*

**ERICA & BIANCA**
*Yes/*
*We do.*

**ALEX**
*Well/*
*There's something I never told you about that night.*

# Erica

And...Bianca takes a step back, toward stage right, and then another step—

But Alex keeps singing and circling to the opposite side of me. *I can't leave him hanging.*

**ERICA**

*What didn't you tell me?*

**ALEX**

*Well/*
*While you were sitting in the back seat/*
*Smoking a cigarette/*
*You thought was gonna be your last/*
*I was falling deep/*
*Deeply in love with you/*
*And I never told you/'til just now!*

And it hits me like a pile of bricks. I lower my microphone, almost dropping it as my arm goes limp. It stays by my side, pressed against my upper thigh. I hold his gaze. He also moves his microphone a few inches or so from his mouth, smiling at me.

*Holy shit...Holy FUCK.*

Luckily, my silence doesn't affect the dynamic and fast-paced, upbeat anthem of this song. Bianca takes over and in perfect drunk tune.

**BIANCA**

*Home/*
*Let me come home...*

Speechless, I am paralyzed in place. But Alex is the braver one and walks over to me. Then, he takes a hold of my hand. Shit.

SHIT. I don't know why I'm tongue-tied or even glancing out to the crowd…what the fuck, now a few people are walking in—FUCKIN' SHIT FUCK. I can't see details of their faces, just the silhouettes of their bodies. I can tell that their bodies are facing the stage, a.k.a. US.

**BIANCA**

*Our home/*
*Yes/*
*I am home/*
*Home is when I'm alone with you…*

And then, I can't hold back anymore. I lunge at him and kiss him long and hard. I feel his hands slip to the small of my back to balance our weight, otherwise, we would have fallen over. Again. I can feel his teeth and open my eyes to see that he is smiling. So, I pull back to double-check—he cups my face, his hands sliding onto the sides aligned with my chin, to bring me back in.

"Get a room!" I hear Ricky shouting nearby, followed by a 'woot!' and probably a fist pump. It gets a few people to mock him, but it's not over-the-top or anything. It's funny as fuck because now, I know that Alex can feel my teeth as I break out into a smile and a chuckle.

Bianca owns this last verse and is already receiving a few claps from the nearby woman who shouts, "Yays girl! Fuckin' ROCK IT." The man—I think he's sitting at a table on the left side of the room since his voice appears to be echoing from there—gives a few whistles. The energy is extraordinary now, filled with this attitude that things will be more than okay.

**BIANCA**

*Alabama/*
*Arkansas/*

*I do love my Ma and Pa/*
*Moats and boats/*
*And waterfall/*
*Alleyways/*
*And payphone calls/*
*Home is when I'm alone with you/*

Coming up for air, I keep my hand steady on the back of Alex's neck. We stay close. I tilt my head back to get a better look at him.

**BIANCA**

*Home is when I'm alone with you!*

Home…

He makes me feel that. I reach for his chest—his heart is beating fast, but not racing. It's more of a tempo that matches this song…our song if it's official.

But I think…I KNOW it is because he places his hand on top of mine, caressing it. He's okay that it's there. He…approves. And so, do I. Alex beams at me. My cheeks are hurting from the beam I return to him.

**BIANCA**

*We are the Extraordinary Ordinary!*

We can already sense her eyes coming toward us, so Alex and I both look over at Bianca who raises her glass—someone bought her drink. Ricky most likely bringing the tray to her. "To the motherfuckin' extraordinary! To the EXTRAORDINARY!"

And before she goes for a mic drop, we all shout at the top of our lungs—

# Erica, Bianca & Alex

"TO THE EXTRARDINARY!"

# SONG CREDITS



Allard, Peter and Ellen. "Here We Go Zudio". 2006.

Bee Gees. "Stayin' Alive". RSO. France and Miami. 1977, December 13.

Bennington, Chester and Shinoda, Mike. "Bleed It Out". Warner Bros. Los Angeles. 2007, August 17.

Burdon, Eric and War. "Spill The Wine". MGM. 1970, May.

Castrinos, Jade and Ebert, Alex. Edward Sharpe & the Magnetic Zeros. "Home". Rough Trade. 2010, January.

Cobain, Kurt. Nirvana. "Heart-Shaped Box". DGC. Minnesota. 1993, August 30.

Clapton, Eric. "Cocaine". Shelter. 1977.

Ginuwine. "Pony". 550 and Epic. 1996, August 20.

Lazzarus, Q. "Goodbye Horses". 1988 (U.S.). All Nations Records. 1991 (U.K.).

Misch, Tom. "Memory". 2014.

Plant, Robert. Led Zeppelin. "Going To California". Atlantic. England. 1971, November 8.

Radelet, Ruth. Chromatics. "Kill for Love". Italians Do It Better. 2012, March 26.

Reed, Lou. The Velvet Underground & Nico. "Femme Fatale". New York City. Scepter. 1966, December.

Reed, Lou. The Velvet Underground. "Heroin". Hollywood. Scepter. 1967, March 12.

Reed, Lou. The Velvet Underground. "Oh! Sweet Nuthin'". Cotillion. New York City. 1970, November 15.

Reed, Lou. The Velvet Underground. "Pale Blue Eyes". Hollywood. MGM. 1969, March.

Reed, Lou. "Perfect Day". London. Trident. 1972, November 17.

Reed, Lou. The Velvet Underground. "Sweet Jane". Atlantic. New York City. 1973, August.

Reed, Lou. The Velvet Underground. "Sunday Morning". Verve. New York City. 1966, December.

Rocha, Zack de la. Rage Against the Machine. "Killing In The Name". Epic. 1992, November 2.

Rodgers, Paul. Bad Company. "Bad Company". Swang Song and Island. 1974.

Samberg, Andy; Schaffer, Akiva and Taccone, Jorma. The Lonley Island. "Jizzed in My Pants". Universal Republic Records. 2008, December 6.

Stefani, Gwen. "Hollaback Girl". Interscope. New York City. 2005, March 22.

Sarandon, Susan and Bostwic, Barry. Rocky Horror Picture Show "Dammit, Janet!" Ode. London. 1975.

Tankian, Serj. System of a Down. "Chop Suey!." Hollywood. Columbia Records, 2001, August 13.

Tankian, Serj. System of a Down. "Aerials". Hollywood. 2002. June 11.

Turner, Tina. "What's Love Got To Do With It". Capitol. 1984, May 1.

Various Artis. "Where's My Shoe". Broadway play, "She Loves Me". 1963.

Warfield, Justin. She Wants Revenge. "Tear You Apart". Geffen and Perfect Kiss. 2006, January 10.

Willis, Victor. Village People. "YMCA". Casablanca. New York City. 1978, October 17.

# QUOTES



**Dean, James:** "Dream as if you'll live forever, live as if you'll die today."

**Hepburn, Audrey:** "Remember, if you ever need a helping hand, it's at the end of your arm, as you get older, remember you have another hand: The first is to help yourself, the second is to help others."

# ACKNOWLEDGEMENTS

**The Extraordinary Ordinary** has a history of its own. All of the songs mentioned in the book were created during earlier writing and editing days; it became Erica's playlist. This project started out as a screenplay and like most movies, it took a few years to see it on screen. From rejections to submitting the story to various screenplay contests, as well as rewriting and editing, this project kept me up day and night. The journeys of the main characters, Erica, Bianca, and Alex had to be told. I just knew it in my gut. Particularly, Erica's story had me on edge for quite some time due to my own personal experience with mental health and trauma recovery.

Remember, it is POSSIBLE to have a life after tragedy. And there are no prerequisites when it comes to recovering and overall, healing. Like my first two novels, *Elephant* and *Skeletons,* this story is also for the voices that go and feel unheard. You MATTER. There are people out there who are waiting to listen. If you or a loved one are in crisis, you can reach out to the National Suicide Hotline 1-800-273-8255, or text HOME to 74174.

I am fortunate to have such a supportive team in bringing *The Extraordinary Ordinary* to life.

First off, thank you to my team of editors, Katherine Walsh, and Ben Parris, for their patience and guidance in turning this story into its best shape.

Thank you, Shari Ryan, for a haunting, yet beautiful cover that took my breath away at the cover reveal.

Also, a shout out to Wendy Garfinkle for being those last pair of eyes and getting a book into its proper format prior to publication.

A very special thanks to Sarah Fader for her guidance and overall, support in putting your art out there.

I also need to give a shout out to other projects that served as both, an inspiration and guide in writing *The Extraordinary Ordinary*. I highly recommend checking out the movies (and books, if it is an adaptation): *Short Term 12*, directed by Destin Daniel Cretton; *Ordinary People* by Judith Guest and directed by Robert Redford; *Good Will Hunting*, directed by Gus Van Sant; and *The Spectacular Now* by Tim Tharp and directed by James Ponsoldt.

Last but not least, an extra shout out to my beloved Matty Cat, who has been an amazing fur baby. Animals are truly amazing. Over these past few years, Matty has become a top-notch support pet!

CPSIA information can be obtained
at www.ICGtesting.com
Printed in the USA
BVHW031413300422
635809BV00009B/168

9 780578 398204